A HOUSE CALLED SHIRLEY

A HOUSE CALLED SHIRLEY

Thelma Stone

ATHENA PRESS
LONDON

A HOUSE CALLED SHIRLEY
Copyright © Thelma Stone 2005

All Rights Reserved

No part of this book may be reproduced in any form
by photocopying or by any electronic or mechanical means,
including information storage or retrieval systems,
without permission in writing from both the copyright
owner and the publisher of this book.

Paperback:
ISBN 1 84401 476 2
Hardback:
ISBN 1 84401 477 0

First Published 2005 by
ATHENA PRESS
Queen's House, 2 Holly Road
Twickenham, TW1 4EG
United Kingdom

Printed for Athena Press

To John, who gave me confidence and encouragement along the way.

Contents

The House	11
The Booth Family	13
Chapter One	15
Chapter Two	19
Chapter Three	23
Chapter Four	41
Chapter Five	45
Chapter Six	56
The House	62
The Hornby Family	65
Chapter One	67
Chapter Two	73
Chapter Three	79
Chapter Four	85
Chapter Five	91
The House	104
The Farnham Family	107
Chapter One	109
Chapter Two	113
Chapter Three	122

Chapter Four	130
Chapter Five	146
Chapter Six	158
Chapter Seven	164
The House	177

The Baxter Family	179
Chapter One	181
Chapter Two	190
Chapter Three	196
Chapter Four	205
Chapter Five	216
Chapter six	224
The House	233

The Last Family	235
The Booths' Grandson, Mark	237

The House

It is a very exciting day for me; my roof is complete and the work on my chimneys is being finished. The builder, my owner, could have built a castle with turrets and a tower, or a church with stained glass windows and a spire, but instead he built a grand house – *me*.

He has done a wonderful job with his trusty craftsmen, working long hours and days through the cold winter months, but now it is late spring and he is coming with his wife, my mistress, to view the work.

The builder and his wife arrive, walking slowly up my gravel drive. It is her first visit to me. She is a slight, delicate creature, dressed in a dove grey-crepe dress with a cream lace collar. A small hat perches on her fair hair and cream leather gloves cover her hands.

My mistress looks up at me and I can see love in her eyes. I feel a surge of love for her and I am immediately very protective of her. Her complexion is very pale against the builder's ruddy colour. She clings to him and he supports her. She whispers to him, her face upturned to his, and they immediately turn and go.

I am alone again, but not for long. A few weeks later, they return. This time, the builder, my owner, helps her through my porch, up the steps and guides her straight into my heart, the hall.

She stands still, then removes a glove and starts to caress my panelled walls with her slim fingers. Her skin is as white as milk and like a feather to the touch. The builder, my owner, carries a small stool and places it in the middle of my drawing room. She sits and surveys the sunlight dancing through my new windows. Then, for the first time, I hear my mistress speak. A lovely soft voice. Oh, I am so in love with her. She starts to list colours, fabrics, furnishings, and he quickly takes notes. I am surprised she is so demanding, but he just looks at her softly and smiles. This continues through all my rooms. As she goes upstairs, she touches me all the time. Her eyes darting around as though trying desperately to remember every detail.

When they have finished, they leave me. My owner holds her gently under the arm and guides her down the gravel drive.

At that moment, she glances back. It is a wonderful moment as I am caught and held in her vision. Oh, how I love her and will protect her, my strong arms surrounding her for ever.

When they have gone I feel sad, but there is no time to waste; the summer is coming and my finishing touches are needed. Fleets of men and women come bearing fabrics, carpets and furniture. My mistress's choice is perfection and all my rooms come alive with colour. Some rich, some muted, the furniture gleams, we are like a stage waiting for the players. My owner and my mistress.

A week goes by and I am all alone. How long will I have to wait? Then one beautiful summer day, the builder, my owner, comes back. He looks smaller, his shoulders are sagging and his head is bowed. He walks slowly up the gravel drive, hardly able to put one foot in front of another. He raises his eyes to me and stares blankly at me. I have a feeling of foreboding rising inside me. As he enters my hall, I see my owner has tears streaming down his cheeks.

What has happened to this man? What sadness has engulfed this man, for my darling mistress has died and her name was Shirley.

The Booth Family

Chapter One

William Booth surveyed his new home with pride. 'What a fine house this is, Mother, we will be very happy here.' He addressed a small woman at his side. He towered above her in stature and demeanour. Gladys looked up to him and smiled, and replied, 'I hope so, Father.'

'We will, you will love it here, the house is well built and, of course, the finest timbers were used,' he boasted.

This was true as Shirley's timber was all provided by 'William Booth's Timber Yard' at Widnes, so he knew the quality of the timber was good. There were timbers from Scandinavia and Africa, nothing but the best for the builder of Shirley.

William Booth thought back to the day when the builder had come to him and told him of his wife's death. He had wanted to comfort the man but only spoke a few stilled words, embarrassed at his own emotion. After a few awkward moments he said, 'What are you going to do with Shirley?' The builder hesitated, then said sadly, 'Sell it, what else can I do, I cannot and will not live in that house.' William had waited a few moments, then said, 'Well, if that is the case, I will buy it from you, just state your price and I will buy the house and contents.' William Booth was a good businessman; he had a sharp brain and good intellect. In his way, he was helping the builder to remove a painful memory from his mind, but in another way he was realising a dream.

He had always wanted to get his family away from his business area and thought the leafy area that surrounded Shirley would be ideal for Mother and the children. So the Booths moved into Shirley. William Booth, timber merchant, and Gladys Booth, his wife, and their two children, William Junior aged five (and called Billy) and little Alice aged two.

The two children loved Shirley and the garden, and settled in right away, but for Gladys it was different. Although her previous home was much smaller, to her it was the home where the children had been born. She had close neighbours in the street and was never lonely. Here it was going to be different. The house stood on its own, surrounded by large gardens and a field at the back. Along the road stood equally large houses. To Gladys, the place looked intimidating. It was no use voicing an opinion, as William would just override her. She knew her place in life, the little woman bringing up her children and looking after her husband. She had no say in the buying of the house or the family finances, only the looking after of her children, Billy and Alice. The rest was taken out of her hands by her dominant husband.

So life began at Shirley for the Booths. William soon organised help from the village. He employed Mr and Mrs Yarwood, a good honest young couple, who he thought would be reliable. William was a good judge of character, but he never, for one moment, thought of asking his wife Gladys if she liked the couple. So the next day, Mr Yarwood started on Shirley's garden and orchard and Mrs Yarwood started at Shirley as the cook and general housekeeper. She brought with her a younger girl, Maisie, who would also do a lot of housework and live-in in the small bedroom at the front of the house.

Billy loved living at Shirley, the garden was so big to him. There were lots of trees to climb and Mr Yarwood made him a catapult out of a twig and a piece of rubber. He spent hours hiding up the trees trying to aim at birds or cats but his aim, thankfully, was not good enough. Alice, on the other hand, played with her dollies on the grass at the back of the house where Mrs Yarwood or Mother could watch her. Billy was to start school in September and Mother would walk him there with Alice, in the big Silver Cross pram.

Little Maisie worked hard all day under Mrs Yarwood's eagle eye, but she enjoyed her work and slept well at night. On Saturday at noon, she went home to the village and spent the time with her family, returning at 8 a.m. on Monday. All she wanted to do was get married and have babies. Her education had been poor, so housework was the best she could expect. She had a pretty face and neat figure, so it wouldn't be long before she would be 'snapped up' as Mrs Yarwood would say. Her life had been similar to Maisie's but she and Mr Yarwood had remained childless. A sadness that they had coped with, both being practical people. 'It's our lot in life,' she would say to her husband, and that was that.

When William Booth went to his work, Gladys surveyed the house. She could not help liking it, as she walked through the large green front door. The whole hall was panelled and to the left was a small cloakroom with a toilet. It was pink, which was very unusual for those times. Gladys christened it 'the Pink Lady'.

To the right of the front door was the dining room, again panelled, and a wooden and tiled fireplace stood high on one wall. The dining room table and chairs stood central in the room on a lovely large rug. The colours of the furnishings were very rich and reflected in the panels. When the fire was lit, this was a very impressive room. All of Mother's silver and china was kept in the long sideboard, and the tall oak chest housed all of William's household papers and bills.

Gladys cut roses from the garden and arranged them in a bowl in the centre of the long table. This room was used every mealtime, and a bell was fixed near the door to ring for Maisie to clear the table.

Gladys walked out of the dining room and into the sitting room at the back of the house. Here the atmosphere was different. Pastel floral furnishings – a sweet pea design – covered the chairs and the curtains hung full either side of the window, with French doors leading out to the back garden. The rug here was of shades of blue, which matched the tiled fireplace. It was very pretty. With Gladys's ornaments around the room, though large, it was a cosy room. The furniture was walnut, and in the corner Gladys had a small ladies' desk where she would write letters to all her friends. She did miss them so much.

In the kitchen, a big black range dominated the room and by the side were two rocking chairs. The big square kitchen table stood in the middle, where many a meal would be prepared. Through the kitchen was the stone-floored washhouse, and opposite, the pantry with a large number of shelves, which eventually would be filled with jams and bottled fruits from the orchard. Mr Yarwood brought in the vegetables fresh from the garden, ready for Mrs Yarwood to prepare for the meals.

As Gladys wandered through the house, she thought of the builder's wife and how she had put her heart and soul into furnishing this house. She had been so excited while the house was being built, choosing all the furniture, and it all came to nothing for her. She never experienced life in Shirley, caring for the house and her family. Gladys took a deep breath and looked around. How could she be so selfish as not to enjoy Shirley, not to nurture her family here? She would pull herself together and get on with her life here in Shirley. Her husband, William, had worked long and hard for this house and she would not let him down. Now she was mistress of Shirley, and she would do a good job and show him she could. She had to be stronger and more assertive. The cachet of the house would help, Shirley would help her.

Chapter Two

Next morning, Gladys waved William off to work, changed into a nice smart outfit and, with her shopping basket and list, walked purposely to the village. The shopkeepers greeted her warmly – they liked her immediately.

She moved from shop to shop. First the butcher, Mr Jones, who insisted that Sidney, his delivery boy, would bring all the meat, eggs, etc. to the house. She would have an account at his shop, which would be paid monthly by Mr Booth. This was all new to Gladys. She had always had housekeeping money from her husband and she paid the bills, but this was now the way the gentry lived, and she was classed as one by the shopkeepers.

Her next call was in the greengrocer's and Mr Brown treated her exactly the same. 'Just send Mrs Yarwood in with your order at the end of the day and we will deliver the next morning, Mrs Booth,' he said, doffing his cap to her.

The bakery next door was wonderful, smelt glorious, and Gladys enquired about bread and cakes. Mr and Mrs Sewell, the bakers, showed Gladys their wares and said if Mrs Yarwood called in at 7.30 a.m. they could take the order to the house that day. They worked long hours, up at 3 a.m. to get the bread ready for the next day, so opening up for Mrs Yarwood was no problem.

On down the street Gladys walked, looking in the wool shop window and the chemist's window. She made a note of the Post Office and then went into the newsagent to enquire what time they could get a paper to the house for Mr Booth to take to the office. 'Too late,' was the reply. So her husband would have to read the paper in the evening.

At the lower end of the village, she found the coal merchants, Scragg and Sons. The large range in the kitchen had to be kept lit all year as it heated the water and they cooked on it. So she ordered her delivery from Mr Scragg. As soon as she walked into their office in the yard, Gladys felt intimidated. Mr Scragg stared and his two sons leered at her. They moved closer to her and she didn't like the atmosphere in the office. Quickly she said, 'I want coal delivered on a regular basis to Shirley through the summer, then double the number of sacks for the winter. Is that clear, Mr Scragg?'

Mr Scragg looked her up and down and muttered, 'How will you be paying, Mrs Booth?'

'I shall pay on each delivery. You come to the back of the house and Mr Yarwood will meet you and show you.'

'*Mr* Yarwood is it?' He emphasised the 'Mister' and the two sons grinned. They stood close to her all the time, making her feel very uncomfortable. She certainly would not come into the office again and would keep herself in the house when they delivered. Their grinning and leering completely unnerved her, and when Mr Scragg stood up and put out his grimy hand to shake hers, she grabbed her basket and pushed past the two sons, her head held high, and out into the yard. She turned back and said, 'Good day to you, Mr Scragg, start delivering tomorrow,' and out she shot into the fresh air. She found her legs were shaking.

Across the road she saw the church. Gladys walked swiftly up the path and into the church. What a different atmosphere there was here. Peace and tranquillity. Flowers adorned the altar and the windowsills, so she sat down in one of the pews to recover from her ordeal.

'Excuse my asking, but can I be of help?' said a kind voice from the back of the church. Gladys spun round and gasped. 'Oh, I am sorry to startle you,' said the young man. The light was streaming in from the altar window and cast the man into the shadows 'Let me introduce myself. I am the vicar here, the Reverend Baines, and you might be?'

'Oh, I am Gladys Booth, and I have come with my family to live in Shirley,' she said.

'Ah, that is interesting, I am so pleased the house is at last occupied, Mrs Booth, but may I ask why you are so distressed?'

'Well, I have just been to Scragg's to order coal and I got quite frightened there,' whispered Gladys.

'Oh, my dear, you should not go there, it is no place for a lady, those sons are very uncouth and intimidating. Please do not go there again, keep out of their way. It's a pity they are the only coal merchants in our area. The women and girls keep well away from Scragg and Sons.'

'I didn't know,' said Gladys trembling.

'No, you wouldn't know, but my advice is to stay well clear of the family,' said the Rev. Baines in a smooth tone. 'Anyway, you are looking better now, so perhaps I can accompany you home?'

'Oh, there is no need for that, Reverend, I am well recovered now and can walk back myself. I have done everything I needed to do in the village and I shall soon be home,' she said cheerfully.

'Well then, perhaps we shall have the pleasure of your family at church on Sunday?' he asked tentatively.

'I am afraid not. Mr Booth is a strict Methodist and will be going to the chapel, our children, Billy and Alice, to their Sunday school. My husband will go morning and evening.'

'And what about you?' he asked.

'I shall be too busy with meals and running the house on Sundays.' This was an excuse Gladys used to William, her husband. In all truth, Gladys was not very religious and had no time for the pious Methodists, but she did rather like the atmosphere in this church and especially liked the young vicar.

As she walked home, she giggled to herself. 'Behave yourself, Gladys,' she said, 'You're a married woman,' but she knew one day soon she would visit the church again.

When she got home, she related her experience to Mr and Mrs Yarwood. They were horrified. They had no idea she was thinking of ordering coal or they would have warned her. None of the women ventured into the Scraggs' coal yard, as the reputation of the two sons had spread around the village after the eldest had tried to molest a girl at the May Fair last year. Mrs Yarwood made Gladys a strong cup of tea and apologised again.

'You weren't to know I was going there,' protested Mrs Booth to Mrs Yarwood. 'Anyway, I shall not go near that place again, and when he delivers the coal we shall stay inside, Mrs Yarwood.' They both agreed and Gladys went to find Billy and Alice, who were with Maisie in the garden.

The little ones ran over to her and hugged her legs. Gladys leaned down and kissed both their heads.

'What have you been doing?' she asked.

'Playing in our house that Maisie has made,' said Billy. Maisie had constructed a house out of an old clothes maiden and a big sheet. The children had taken toys inside and when Gladys looked into the house, there was Maisie sitting on a rug with Alice serving her make-believe tea out of her little china tea set.

'Oh, thank you, Maisie, for entertaining the children while I was away,' said Mrs Booth.

'That's all right, madam, I like playing with them, they are such funny and happy children,' said Maisie. 'Life would be dull without children, wouldn't it madam?'

'You are right there, Maisie,' said Mrs Booth, whilst wondering how lucky she was to have Mr and Mrs Yarwood and Maisie to help her through the day. She made a mental note to thank William when he got home for choosing them. He was a good husband, a solid and totally reliable husband. But was that all she wanted out of life? She wondered.

Chapter Three

May Day was a glorious day. The park was full of people, the brass band played loud and strong in the bandstand, and girls in pretty dresses started to dance round the maypoles. These poles were garlanded with flowers and colourful ribbons that hung down from the top. The girls danced round each other holding a ribbon, and weaved the ribbons round the maypole. The villagers manned stalls around the park, selling cakes, sweets, fruit and craft wares. The villagers brought picnics and rested on the grass, listening to the band playing.

The Booths arrived at 2 p.m. and spread out their rug on the grass. The children were so excited and little Alice kept running around. Father had to keep shouting to her to stay close. They ate a delicious picnic, which Mother had prepared, and then moved to the chairs near the bandstand.

Suddenly, the cart and horses carrying the May Queen entered the park and everybody cheered. It stopped close and they could see the May Queen, a pretty fair girl, sitting on a throne on the cart, which was decked with flowers. She made her way to the bandstand, where she was crowned. Everybody cheered and the band struck up again. What a lovely day it was! Mr and Mrs Booth at last felt part of village life.

Through the crowd a young man made his way over to them, and Gladys saw it was the vicar – the Reverend Baines. She blushed slightly.

'Hello again, Mrs Booth,' he said to her. She quickly introduced her husband and the children.

'This is Reverend Baines, the vicar from the village church,' she told her husband.

A puzzled look came on his face. 'Have you both met before?' asked William.

'Oh yes, I met Mr Baines in the village the other day,' she said quickly.

'Well, it was a pleasure meeting you, Reverend Baines. Come along dear, we must be going,' said William quickly, and walked off with Gladys and the children in tow.

'Why didn't you want to speak to him dear?' enquired Gladys.

'We have nothing in common with that church, we are Methodists,' William boomed.

'Nothing in common?' asked Gladys 'But don't we worship the same God?'

'You don't understand, Gladys, they are different like the Catholics, their worship, their churches, their beliefs are different to ours,' said William.

'You mean yours,' Gladys muttered under her breath.

'What did you say Gladys?' snapped William.

'Nothing, dear,' said Gladys smoothly. But the whole episode soured the day for her. How intolerant her husband was, what a complex person she was married to. He was trying to mould her to his ways, his beliefs; would she be strong enough to resist?

★

As the weeks and months drew on, Gladys settled into her role of the lady who lived in the 'big house' called Shirley. Shopkeepers, workmen and neighbours liked Gladys; she was easy to talk to and a caring person, always enquiring about their families and their health. In turn, this helped Gladys to become one of the community, although not quite in the centre of it as she had been in her last home. She did miss the talk, the gossip and the 'tickle tackle' as she called it. The people in the village were aware of her position in relation to them, and she felt this and knew that she could not become one of them. They weren't jealous of her, they weren't stand-offish; just faintly cautious in their approach to her.

True to their word though, the shopkeepers delivered their provisions to Shirley, and the butcher's boy, Sidney, cycled up to the house every day with Mrs Yarwood's order. He would come into the kitchen and have a mug of tea with Mr and Mrs Yarwood and Maisie before returning to the village. Maisie looked forward to seeing him and made sure she was in the kitchen area. He started ringing his cycle bell as he came up the drive to make sure he would see her. They were a similar age and Sidney had been working in Mr Jones's shop since leaving school. He was learning the butchery trade and hoped to make a living working for Mr Jones.

'How are you getting on, Sidney?' asked Mr Yarwood. 'Not chopped off any fingers yet?'

'Not yet, have to be careful though, those cleavers of Mr Jones ain't half sharp,' said Sidney. He was a pleasant lad, a bit cocky, but that was a good attitude in the shop, as he gave as good as he got from the women he served. Mr Jones liked a happy atmosphere in the shop; then the women would spend more.

Maisie watched him, her eyes shining over the hot mug of strong tea. Sidney tended to show off a little in the kitchen, as he had an attentive audience in Maisie. Then, after ten minutes, he would thank Mrs Yarwood (always politely), doff his cap, jump on his bicycle and race down the big house drive and off down the lane. Maisie would run upstairs and watch him from the front bedroom window as he waved to her, cycling 'no hands' along the lane. Mr and Mrs Yarwood would nod to each other and Mr Yarwood would wink knowingly. Then back to work for all of them.

With both children at school now, Mrs Booth would read or embroider to pass the time till Mr Booth came home. He was always in a good mood when he came home and looked forward to dinner with the family.

Prayers were always said at the table, and then Mrs Booth would serve the meal, which had been prepared by Mrs Yarwood before she left for the village.

Mr Booth's timber business was doing well. It had grown in size and was now employing a lot of local men. In charge of the men was Danny Ross, a strong, stocky man who managed well. He was firm but fair, smoked a pipe and enjoyed a pint at his local inn. He was in total contrast to his boss who was tall and thin, didn't smoke and loathed anything to do with the demon drink. He thought that most men drank their wages away on Friday nights, returned home, and beat their wives who were left with little money for the rest of the week. He was convinced alcohol was the devil's invention, as were gambling and womanising. He was extremely bigoted in his views, but did not air them at work, only at home and at the chapel.

At work he was a good boss, very fair and considerate. He paid good wages and never took advantage of his fellow human beings, so Danny Ross and Mr Booth worked well together. He thought Mr Booth 'a good gaffer'; the more money the timber importer made, the more money was around for the workers.

The timber company was in Widnes, at the West Bank Docks Estates. The timber came from all over the world, brought by ship to Liverpool and by rail to the yards. Scandinavian red pine, white pine, African mahogany, Brazilian mahogany, afromosia and iroko – weird and wonderful names to conjure with.

The wagons were full of mixed widths and lengths, which then had to be tallied and measured by the tallymen. The different timber and lengths were then stacked in the yard by gangs of men awaiting delivery. Danny Ross was in charge of all this. He was worth his weight in gold to Mr Booth, who was up in his office ploughing through the shipping forms, order forms and delivery forms. He had two young clerks in the office with him and insisted they dress correctly in stiff collar and tie and suits.

The office was a hive of industry, but Mr Booth loved every minute; from up in his office he could survey his kingdom. And what a kingdom; a lucrative business, and soon even more lucrative with his plan for a joinery shop, where window frames, doors and staircases could be made out of the finest timber. He had it all planned out in his head and was waiting for the machinery to be delivered into the shed at the bottom of the yard. The shed was large and it had been cleaned out and benches had already been made and installed. He had appointed a head foreman who, in turn, had found good joiners and a few lads from the local school who would become apprentices. An older man would sweep up, bag the sawdust and brew the tea. Mr Booth was hoping that all this would be up and running by the next month. He was very ambitious and wanted to produce a fine business, which, in turn, would provide work for a lot of men and boys in the area. This is what Mr Booth worked for, not for personal gain.

He had a good car and a fine house – now in a good area – but he still thought of his business first and foremost as a provider for his workforce, his men.

When he came home, he changed. He never discussed his day with Gladys in fact she had never visited the timber company. She had been driven past, but had never gone through the big gates which bore her husband's name. Women had no place in the workforce there; it was a male-orientated world. When he arrived home, she would say, 'Had a good day, William?' He would always answer, 'Yes dear,' even if he had had a swine of a day, and that was that.

He never asked about the running of the house, the children's day at school, Mrs Yarwood's or Maisie's day. Only Mr Yarwood would enter his thoughts, and he would wander out on a Saturday morning to check on the garden.

Gladys and William, although married, lived very separate lives, just sharing the house, the marital bed and meals together. At weekends, William would go out walking in the park and on Sundays he spent nearly all day at the chapel.

Gladys just busied herself with the household and the children, nothing else. She never involved herself with chapel; secretly she thought them bigoted and too strait-laced. She only accompanied William on Easter Sunday, at Harvest Festival and at Christmas. The other Sundays in the year she made the excuse of preparing meals – anything rather than go and sing dull hymns and listen to long, boring sermons from the minister, who seemed to think they were all doomed to hell and damnation. When the minister visited their home during the week, she would hide behind William's respectability and generosity to the chapel, and the minister would not dare enquire about her non-appearances. She made him tea and offered him homemade scones and listened to his droning voice on subjects such as the wayward working class and their drinking and womanising. She rather thought he enjoyed the discussions about these topics, as they were the sole excitement in his life. When he had gone, Gladys would go immediately into the kitchen and have a good mug of tea with Mrs Yarwood and Maisie, and a good chinwag.

One day, Gladys sensed an atmosphere in the kitchen. 'What's the matter, Mrs Yarwood?' she asked.

'Nothing to worry yourself about, Mrs Booth,' replied Mrs Yarwood quickly.

'Yes there is, I know there is; what is it? Is Mr Yarwood all right? What's happened?'

'Nothing to worry about, Mrs Booth,' replied Mrs Yarwood again.

'You have just said that!' Mrs Booth sharpened her voice a little. 'Now come on, you two, you know you can tell me and it won't go any further. What is it? What has happened? Please tell me.' Mrs Booth was so sincere and caring in her enquiry of them that Maisie burst into tears. Mrs Yarwood immediately put her arm round the girl and pulled her to her ample bosom.

'Quiet now, Maisie, don't you go on so,' she said.

'Well, are you two going to tell me now?' said Mrs Booth quietly. Her voice softened as she spoke. 'My dear Maisie, are you ill, can I help you?' she said.

'No, she ain't ill, Mrs Booth. Shall I tell Mrs Booth, Maisie?' whispered Mrs Yarwood. Maisie pulled her face away from Mrs Yarwood, her face swollen with tears. She nodded and then quickly buried her face again. 'Well, Mrs Booth,' said Mrs Yarwood slowly; she took a deep breath and said, 'Maisie is 'in the family way'.'

'Oh no!' cried Mrs Booth, and then regretted her outburst as it made Maisie howl even more. 'There, there, Maisie, it's not the end of the world.'

'Yes it is, it is, it is, what am I to do?' cried Maisie.

Mrs Booth took a deep breath and took command of the terrible situation. 'First, let's all have another mug of hot tea, put a little brandy in Maisie's, it will do her no harm. I keep a small bottle at the back of that cupboard, Mrs Yarwood, for the white sauce on the Christmas pudding. It is Mr Booth's favourite sauce at Christmas, but he has no idea there is alcohol in it.' Mrs Booth prattled on, trying to lighten the atmosphere in the kitchen. So at last Maisie sat down round the table and stopped crying. 'Now then, what are we going to do with you?' said Mrs Booth kindly. 'Do you want to keep the baby, Maisie? Have you thought about it yet?'

'No Ma'am, I haven't,' said Maisie.

'What does your mother say?'

'Oh, I haven't told her yet,' Maisie's voice started to go higher.

'Now then, calm yourself,' said Mrs Booth.

All this time, Mrs Yarwood sat quietly, quite relieved that Mrs Booth was taking command of this difficult situation.

'Now Maisie, I am going to have to ask you a difficult question, but as we all know, the fairies at the bottom of the garden didn't put you in the family way, did they?'

'No Mrs Booth, but do I have to say?'

'Yes, I'm afraid you do, Maisie,' said Mrs Booth. 'It bears on to a lot of the decisions we will have to make,' she added kindly. 'Maisie,' she spoke slowly, picking her words carefully, 'you weren't attacked, were you?'

'Oh no, Mrs Booth!' Maisie's face coloured deep red.

'Well then, who was it then?' she asked slowly.

'Do I have to say?' she looked pleadingly at Mrs Yarwood.

'Yes, you do, my girl, and quick. Mrs Booth cannot waste any more time on you.'

'Oh no, Mrs Yarwood, let Maisie tell me in her own time,' said Mrs Booth quickly. She looked at Maisie and took her hands in hers. 'Now then, Maisie, just tell me,' said Mrs Booth.

'It was Sidney, it was him; Sidney and me love each other, Mrs Booth.'

'Do you, Maisie? And how long have you been walking out with Sidney?' she enquired.

'All year, Mrs Booth. He loves me too and has been kind to me. But at the summer fair we got carried away...'

'I should say you did,' retorted Mrs Yarwood. 'You should have had more sense, my girl.'

'Now then Mrs Yarwood, be quiet please,' said Mrs Booth. 'So you are about three months, Maisie? Is that right?'

'Yes Mrs Booth, I think so,' mumbled Maisie.

'So we have established that the father is Sidney. In a way, I am glad it is him and not one of the boys from the coal yard. Sidney is a nice young man with good prospects at the butcher's, so we must think about what is to be done,' said Mrs Booth.

'Shall I have a word with his mum and dad?' asked Mrs Yarwood.

'Yes, I think so,' said Mrs Booth, 'but tonight you must pluck up courage and tell your parents.'

'Oh no I couldn't, Dad would kill me!' wailed Maisie.

'Well then, I shall come with you tomorrow and speak for you,' said Mrs Booth.

'Oh would you, Ma'am? They respect you. Please tell them that me and Sidney love each other and want to get married,' said Maisie.

'Well, in that case, if Sidney is in agreement, I could have a word with that nice young vicar in the village and see if he will marry you, in your condition. No likelihood of that happening at the chapel,' she sighed. 'But enough said. Also ask Sidney to see if Mr Jones will rent out that flat above his shop on the corner. If Sidney's future is to be with Mr Jones's butchery business, then it may work out well for everybody concerned.' Mrs Booth paused and watched Maisie's reaction.

Maisie's eyes lit up for the first time and she looked relieved and happy. 'Oh that would be wonderful! Me, Sidney and the baby, oh, Ma'am, do you think that Mr Jones will let us live there?'

'Yes I do, but there is a lot to do. First, you must speak to your parents.'

'You said you would come,' bleated Maisie.

'Yes, I will accompany you, but you will tell them yourself, Maisie.'

'Yes Ma'am,' whispered Maisie.

'Then I shall speak to Sidney and Mr Jones before I broach the subject with the vicar,' said Mrs Booth.

For a long time Mrs Yarwood had been silent, then she said 'Thank you, Mrs Booth, for being so kind and caring to Maisie. She is a good girl, though she is in trouble now, but not the first to fall and she wouldn't be the last. Thank you again. Mr Yarwood and myself think of Maisie as our own, she is the daughter we would have liked to have.' Mrs Yarwood paused. 'Is there anything we can do?' she asked.

'Not at the moment,' replied Mrs Booth. 'Let's get over today and tomorrow and then see how the land lies.'

At that Mrs Booth started to leave the kitchen. 'Speak to Sidney tonight, Maisie, and tell him our plan then. Stay at home tomorrow and when Mr Booth has left for work, I shall take the children to school and then come down to the village to speak to your mother first. Do you understand, Maisie?' Mrs Booth said.

'Yes Ma'am, I will wait for you in the morning. I shall not sleep a wink though,' said Maisie.

'Nor will I,' muttered Mrs Booth under her breath.

She dared not speak to William about this situation until it had all been worked out. She knew what his reaction would be and Maisie would not stand a chance of keeping the baby. He would arrange a place in a home for her, then adoption would follow straight after the birth. That's how it was usually arranged for unmarried girls who had fallen. But Mrs Booth didn't want that to happen to Maisie; she was a good girl and would make an excellent mother, and Sidney would be a good provider for mother and baby. Perhaps they were starting married life the wrong way round, but in her eyes, if they loved each other, what the hell! But she would have to pitch her words carefully when she told William.

Next morning, she couldn't wait for William to go to work. Then she bustled the children off to school so she was free to go visiting in the village. First call was at Maisie's family home. She knocked on the door of the tiny house and, to her surprise, Maisie's father came to the door.

'Good morning, Mrs Booth; come to see where Maisie is? Lazy girl, said she wasn't feeling well, not like me with me bad back, something chronic it hurts...'

'No, I haven't come to see Maisie,' spoke Mrs Booth calmly, 'I have come to speak to you and your wife. Can I come in for a moment?'

As she walked into the parlour, Maisie's mother rose up to greet her. The house was spotless, although sparse. It was obvious money was short here. At that moment, Maisie came down the stairs looking washed out. Her eyes fixed on Mrs Booth and she looked terrified. 'Well, shall we all sit down now?' she said, taking command although it wasn't her home.

So Mrs Booth started. 'It has come to my knowledge that Maisie needs my help. That is why I am here.'

'What do you mean?' snapped her father.

'Well, it seems that…' she paused for a few seconds and started again, 'Well, it seems that Maisie is in the family way and…'

But before she could finish, the father had jumped up and roared at Maisie. 'What's this, a daughter of mine, been messing about with boys, you dirty girl,' he bellowed.

'Now then, she has not been with boys, only with one whom she loves and he loves her,' said Mrs Booth, trying to stay calm.

'Rubbish, she's been attacked wait till I find out and I'll break every bone in his body, I will that!' shouted her father. Her mother looked terrified as he ranted on and on, not daring to say a word.

'Please, please be quiet until I have finished,' Mrs Booth shouted at him. He had never had a woman shout at him before and it stopped him in his tracks.

'Now,' said Mrs Booth calmly, 'the way I see it, is that Maisie wants to keep the baby and…'

'What I want to know is who's the father?' he bellowed again.

'I am just coming round to that,' said Mrs Booth. This was worse than dealing with William when he got on his high horse, but she ploughed on. 'Maisie wants to keep the baby and the baby's father wants to marry Maisie. This is your grandchild we are talking about – your own flesh and blood. Just think what joy this will bring you both. If Maisie gets married, this will be forgotten and you can look forward to perhaps a grandson.' This touched a nerve with Maisie's father, as he had always wanted a son and his wife was unable to give him any more children.

'So, what are we to do?' he said to Mrs Booth.

'Well, I will speak to the vicar today and also Mr Jones, the butcher,' she slipped this in quickly.

'Mr Jones, did you say?' Maisie's mother spoke at last. 'What's it got to do with him?'

'Well, the father is Sidney, who works for him, and I think there is a good chance of him letting Sidney and Maisie live over the shop.'

They both looked dumbfounded at this knowledge about Sidney. At last Maisie's father spoke slowly and said, 'Well, lass, he's not so bad as some, he's a good lad and a good worker, I'll say that.' The relief on Maisie's face was so noticeable that Mrs Booth thought she was going to faint. She put an arm round Maisie to support her.

'There, young lady, another step forward. Now we must go and see Mr Jones and Sidney and find out his decision about the rooms. Of course Maisie can work for me as long as she is able and after the birth she can bring the baby to work,' added Mrs Booth. 'Thank you, to both of you; it must have been a great shock for you to hear this news about your only child. But with help all around we should come through this, and I am sure you will look forward to your grandson's birth.'

At that, Mrs Booth shook both the father' and mother's hands and left their house with Maisie in tow, as quickly as possible. She didn't give the father a chance to argue, but she could see he was quite happy for her to deal with the situation. 'Let's hope and pray it's a boy, young Maisie,' said Mrs Booth. She was quite sure that her handling of the situation was the right one for Maisie and Sidney's future. Next stop, the butcher's. As they entered, Mrs Booth was relieved to see the shop empty of customers. Maisie stood behind Mrs Booth.

'Good day, Mr Jones,' said Mrs Booth.

'Good day to you,' replied Mr Brown. 'Well, I know what you have come about, Mrs Booth, and I am more than happy to help out in this difficult predicament.'

Mrs Booth sighed with relief. 'That is good, Mr Jones. I am sure Sidney will work hard for you in the future with a new wife and baby to support, so I think the arrangement will be good for one and all,' said Mrs Booth, smiling.

'Yes,' replied Mr Jones, 'I have discussed finances with young

Sidney, as he will have a family to support, and also rent for the rooms. They are sparsely furnished but will have to do for the present. As long as they have a roof over their heads, that will do.'

'I do indeed. Thank you, Mr Jones, and I am sure Sidney and Maisie will not let you down,' said Mrs Booth gravely. Sidney and Maisie stood holding hands, listening to their future being mapped out by Mrs Booth and Mr Jones. But they didn't care, all that mattered was that they were going to be together with their baby, and that they loved each other.

'Off you go to Shirley now, Maisie,' said Mrs Booth. 'That's all you can do for now.'

Maisie turned to Mr Jones and said, 'Thank you so much. We will both work hard and we won't let you down.' At that, she gave Mr Jones a kiss on his cheek and darted out of the shop. Sidney shook Mr Jones's hand and thanked Mrs Booth profusely.

'Off with you, young man, don't let me down,' said Mrs Booth, and she turned and walked out of the shop into the sunshine. What a morning it had been, but she was pleased with the outcome. In fact, she felt quite exhilarated and, with a spring in her step, she set off to the church. She kept to the right side of the village, away from the coal yard and the vile Scragg family. Nothing must spoil the day. It had been a success, and Gladys was proud of her negotiation skills. She walked down the narrow path, through the neat graveyard, to the church. But the church door was closed and locked. Her spirits dropped immediately. She had been on a high since her success and she realised she was looking forward to meeting the Reverend Baines again. To the left of the church was a small house with pretty borders around it. Wondering if this was the vicarage, she walked over the grass to its front door.

Just as she raised her hand to knock on the door, it swung open. This startled her but at once she saw the Rev. Baines, smiling at her. 'Do come in, Mrs Booth,' he said.

'Oh, thank you, I came to the church to see you.'

'Yes I know, I saw you come down the path, but do come in and make yourself comfortable.'

The room was small and cosy. There seemed to be chintz

material everywhere; curtains, cushions, covers on the chairs – the whole room was a riot of colour. She looked around in amazement. Not the type of decoration for a young vicar. He caught her eyes wandering round the room. 'My predecessor's wife, I'm afraid, not my choice,' he said apologetically.

'Oh, I am sorry, I shouldn't have looked around, it was very rude of me,' said Gladys. He laughed at her confusion. Then she started to laugh.

'Would you like tea, Mrs Booth?'

'Oh, I would. I have had a difficult morning.'

'Not at the coal yard again?' said the Rev.

'Oh, no, but if I could have a cup of tea, I will tell you all about it,' she said. The Rev. Baines left the room but was soon back with a tray of cups and saucers and a pot of tea. 'Shall I pour?' said Mrs Booth.

'Yes, if you would,' he said, and he watched her closely. She was a lovely lady. He could see she was a caring soul, not demanding like some ladies he knew, but a really lovely person, and he wondered what she could possibly want with him. He knew her husband was a staunch Methodist, so he had never included Shirley in his pastoral visits. He knew he would be made unwelcome by Mr Booth. So what could she want of him? No doubt she would tell him in due course, but at the moment he was enjoying her company.

'There you are, Mr Baines. Now, do I address you as the Reverend Baines or Mr Baines?' she asked.

'You can call me Robert if you like as I think we are friends now,' he said quite naturally.

'So well then, you must call me Gladys,' she said.

'Now, Gladys, can I help you in any way or do you want to discuss something with me?' he asked carefully.

'Yes I do,' said Gladys. She took a deep breath and started the tale of Sidney and Maisie. When she had finished, she paused and waited for the reaction of Robert. She was not disappointed. He smiled at her and said, 'You are a very kind lady. Indeed Sidney and Maisie are fortunate to know you. My answer is yes. I will help, and marry them as soon as possible,' replied Robert.

'Oh, wonderful! I was so worried about approaching you,' said Gladys, smiling.

'Absolutely no need, my friend, if I may call you 'my friend'?'

Gladys's heart leapt. 'Oh, of course Robert, you may.' She had never felt so at ease in male company as she did with Robert. He treated her as his equal, not as the little woman. Their eyes met and they smiled at each other.

'Now then, let's decide on dates etc.,' Robert said quickly.

'Well, the sooner the better, under the circumstances,' Gladys said, a little embarrassed.

'How about next Saturday at 2 p.m.?' enquired Robert.

'Excellent, I shall pay for your services, the organist and the bells,' said Gladys.

'That is most generous,' Robert replied. She stood up and put her hand out to Robert. As he shook her hand, a great warmth engulfed her body. Her whole being seemed to be on fire. She pulled her hand away quickly and made for the door. 'Well, we have a week to discuss the service. Perhaps Sidney and Maisie will call and see me and I can arrange the service to their liking,' said Robert, holding the door open.

'But of course,' said Gladys, moving quickly onto the path. 'Thank you again Robert. Thank you so much for your help,' called Gladys over her shoulder as she walked swiftly down the path.

Gladys walked back to Shirley slowly. She needed to calm down. Her cheeks were flushed and her heart was pounding. What a silly goose I was with Robert, she thought. But she knew no man had affected her like Robert. There she was, a married woman with two children, and she was behaving like a giggly schoolgirl. She must stop this behaviour at once. So she quickened her pace to Shirley.

On her return, Maisie and Mr and Mrs Yarwood were in the kitchen, preparing the evening meal. As she walked in, they looked up at her in eager anticipation. 'Well, that's done. The Rev. Baines has agreed to the marriage and it will be next Saturday at 2 p.m.' She was quite triumphant in her statement.

'Oh, Mrs Booth, thank you, thank you,' cried Maisie.

'Now, Maisie, as a gift to you and Sidney I shall pay for the service, the organist and the bells. We can't have a wedding without bells, can we?' She was as excited as Maisie now. Mrs Yarwood said, 'And Maisie, you can borrow my wedding dress and veil. I was the same size as you when I was a girl, would you believe!' She and Mr Yarwood laughed together. They were a very happy couple, and perhaps the dress would be a good omen for Maisie and Sidney.

'Well, that's settled. In the meantime you will have to tell your Sidney to get his skates on and set up the rooms above the shop. Come next Saturday, my girl, you will be a married woman,' said Mrs Booth. Maisie's face was a picture. She was so excited. Her father and mother had calmed down with the prospect of a grandchild, and her life with Sidney was soon to begin. Sidney loved her so, and, with the baby, life would be complete.

'It's like a dream come true, Mrs Booth,' said Maisie.

'Well, I don't know about dream, you wait till you are up with the little one through the night, then tell me about your wonderful dream,' Mrs Booth laughed at Maisie. But this didn't stop them all enjoying the moment. 'A toast,' said Mrs Booth, 'to Maisie and Sidney,' and they all clinked their mugs together over the kitchen table. 'Well, come on, all back to work now,' said Mrs Booth quickly.

When Gladys was left on her own in the sitting room, she pondered over what she had done. She had single-handedly taken on the whole situation and, out of chaos, she had created a calm and loving future for the two youngsters. But, and it was a big but, what was Mr Booth going to say on his return from work? Gladys pondered the best way to tackle this problem, and in the end decided a direct approach was the best. After dinner, when the children were safely tucked up in their beds, Gladys and William always retired to the sitting room. In the summer the French doors were open and sometimes they sat in the garden. That night Gladys said, 'Let us sit outside for a while, William.'

'If you please,' said William, and they both walked into the garden.

Mr Yarwood did a wonderful job in the garden. He bought bedding plants in the late spring and planted them out in rows along the edges of the borders. The grass was beautifully cut, and he made stripes with his mower the length of the lawn. The whole garden was immaculate. Even the orchard and vegetable garden to the right of the house was well maintained. He truly was an excellent gardener. He loved his work and looked forward to every season, knowing every job that had to be done for the preparation and cultivation of a garden.

'You were very quiet during dinner, my dear. Is there anything troubling you?' William asked.

'Well, dear, I have something to tell you,' Gladys paused, then with a deep breath she started. 'Maisie is pregnant, William. And before you say anything, I myself have sorted out this problem.'

'Have you, my lady?' replied William pompously.

'Yes I have, William,' and she went on to tell him what she had accomplished.

'You have done what?' shouted William.

'Don't shout, William,' cried Gladys. 'It is all arranged; these two people love each other, so that is that,' she retorted, amazed at how strong she was against him.

'What will people say, knowing she worked for us, knowing she lives with us? Gladys, she must go away,' shouted William.

'No, she and Sidney want to marry and have the baby, and that's what is important to them. We have to show our compassion as good Christians, William, and not turn them away. The people in the village will respect our decision, not condemn us,' cried Gladys. But she knew he was not thinking of the villagers, he was thinking of the people at the chapel. Their strict, unbending rules. Their bigoted, narrow views on life.

For once, William listened to his wife. He had never known her be so passionate about a subject and he looked at her in another light. Gladys had grown up, she had matured into a person in her own right. Someone to respect, a good mother and a good wife. All these thoughts tumbled through his mind. Perhaps, just perhaps, she was right and his chapel ways were too strict for today's youngsters. The chapel was full of older people imposing their views on the young, who were made to come to the Sunday School and take the pledge – no alcohol for the rest of their lives. Times were changing, but the chapel congregation was not. 'All right Gladys, let me hear what you have arranged for this unfortunate pair,' he said begrudgingly. Gladys told him of her day, starting with Maisie's parents, Mr Jones's offer of the rooms above his shop and the Rev. Baines's offering to marry them.

'You went to see a vicar?' William said in great shock.

'Yes, I did, and a very pleasant man he was,' said Gladys. 'I also have offered to pay for the marriage service, organist and bells.' She rushed this statement out quickly.

'Have you indeed?' said William slowly.

'I can pay for it out of my own monies, dear,' replied Gladys.

'Indeed you will not, I have decided to give a sum of money to the couple as a wedding present, from Shirley.' Gladys could not believe her ears.

'Oh, thank you, my dear, you have made me very happy,' cried Gladys.

'Not that I approve of their, well, their goings on before marriage, but I will not have anybody saying that we are not a Christian family here at Shirley.' He could be quite pompous, but Gladys knew he had a soft side to him, and she knew she had reached out to that side. 'Well, when is the wedding?' he asked.

'Next Saturday, dear,' she said.

'You know we will not be going to the church service?' he replied.

'Yes, I realise that, dear. I knew you would not want to go to a Church of England service.'

'Yes, too much pomp and ceremony for my liking, all those responds and the church full of gold and images. No, not to my liking at all,' he stated.

'No, I know, we will not be going, but as long as Maisie and Sidney have their families there to witness their wedding, all will be well, dear. Do not worry, we will hear the bells ring out and know that they are man and wife,' said Gladys. She hugged William and kissed him lightly on the cheek. He was a good man deep down, although he showed little affection to her and the children. But she knew he loved them and now he respected her even more. 'But we could go to the village hall after for the wedding breakfast, couldn't we dear?' pleaded Gladys.

'Yes, I suppose we could. The children would enjoy that, but we will not be joining in the dancing. Do not forget that, Gladys,' said William sternly.

'No, dear,' said Gladys, resigning herself to some simple pleasure like the wedding breakfast. But no alcohol would pass their lips, as they had taken the pledge when young and, to William, this was the devil's water.

To soften all this restriction on the wedding, William had a little plan of his own. Though he was a strict father to Billy and Alice, he still had a soft side where they were concerned. Throughout the week he had been constructing a wooden shed at the bottom of the orchard near the vegetables. The family thought it was for storage, but Mr Yarwood and Mr Booth knew better. This was a fine henhouse, and as the Booth children had never seen one before, they had no idea what was to happen on Saturday morning.

Chapter Four

Billy and Alice rose early on Saturday, excited about the wedding breakfast later that day; but, unknown to them, Mr Yarwood and Mr Booth had been out to the local farm and purchased two hens and a cockerel. They arrived home just in time for breakfast. 'Come quickly, Billy and Alice, quickly!' called Father.

'What is it, Father?' they called out from the kitchen.

'Come and see, you two, leave your breakfast and come and see who is going to live in the wooden shed,' Father said, teasing them both. Billy, who was a young, strong boy, now ran out ahead of Alice. Down they went to the wooden shed.

'What's in the baskets?' called out Billy to his father.

'Well, look inside yourselves and see.'

The children peered in and saw the hens. One was white with a black ruff of feathers and black tail feathers. The other was all shades of brown. Then, in the larger basket, was the fine specimen of a cockerel with a fierce-looking beak. 'Oh, I don't like him,' squealed Alice. 'But can I have the black and white one for my own, and you, Billy, can have the brown one?' She was getting quite bossy with her brother these days. She was growing up fast, but Billy didn't mind as he was older than her and one day when he was a man like his father he would go to work. He often went into the yard with his father and loved the smells and sounds of the timber yard and factory. The freshly-cut pine logs smelt wonderful to Billy. This was where he would work alongside the men to learn the trade and then move into the office alongside his father. He never questioned his future, as it was an unspoken progression in his life. So Billy did not mind Alice bossing him about at home, as he loved his sister very much.

'Yes all right, Alice, you have the pretty black and white one and I'll have the plain brown,' sighed Billy.

'Lacy and Elizabeth, the bestest hens in the world,' shouted Alice.

'Shush Alice, you will frighten them,' said Mr Yarwood. 'Now I am going to put them in the henhouse and let them get used to their new home. If you visit them you must come quietly in case they are laying, and do not forget to fasten the gate to their run as you come in. I do not want them wandering into my vegetable plot,' said Mr Yarwood. 'Now, what shall we call the cockerel, Mr Booth?' he said.

'I think we shall christen him Napoleon, Mr Yarwood. That would be most fitting for him I think,' said Mr Booth.

'Napoleon it is then.' Mr Yarwood carried him into the hen run and Napoleon strutted round the patch like the Lord of the Manor. He was a big fine bird with a wonderful brown shiny coat of feathers.

'Well you two, let's leave them to settle into their new house. It's time for Mr Yarwood to go home for the wedding, so we will see you later at the village hall. Thank you for all your help Mr Yarwood.'

'Oh, thank you, Mr Yarwood,' chimed the children and then they ran inside to Mother to tell her all about the latest additions to the Booth household.

Around 3 p.m. that afternoon they heard the church bells ring out. 'That's it, they are wed now, man and wife, may they be happy in their marriage,' said Gladys.

'Yes, I hope so, not a good start to the marriage, but let's hope they make up for it as a devoted couple,' pondered William.

The family left the house and walked down to the village hall. Billy and Alice were excited as this was the first grown-up 'do' they had ever been allowed to go to. Alice looked very pretty in a pale yellow summer dress and her hair tied up with yellow ribbons. Billy had his Sunday best on with a yellow rose in his buttonhole like his father's. Gladys looked charming in a plain floral dress and straw hat trimmed with blue ribbon. She was a very attractive woman, slender and dainty, with naturally curly hair peeping out from under the straw hat.

The Booths arrived at the village hall and around the door an arch of flowers had been fastened. 'Welcome, do come in,' said Mr Jones, the butcher. He seemed to have adopted the role of Master of Ceremonies to the bride and bridegroom's families. Both Maisie and Sidney's families were simple folk. Good solid people who worked hard, but who were not used to organising an event like this. So when Mr Jones stepped in they were pleased and relieved. There was lots of good food spread out on trestle tables and ale and soft drinks at one end.

First Mr Booth took his family over to the newlyweds and congratulated them both. Maisie looked a picture in Mrs Yarwood's wedding dress. She had flowers in her hair and carried a small posy as well. Sidney was attired in a suit, collar and tie and looked uncomfortable but extremely happy and proud of his new bride. 'Thank you Sir and Madam for all your help to Maisie and me, we are so pleased you have come today,' said Sidney, and Maisie was nodding and clinging on to her new husband.

'You must thank my wife, for she arranged this for you, not me,' said Mr Booth gallantly. 'We are pleased for you both, are we not dear?' said Mr Booth.

'Certainly we are, we hope you will be very happy,' said Mrs Booth.

The afternoon passed on with plenty of eating and chatting and Mr Booth was quietly amazed how he was enjoying himself. The village people were extremely happy to see them there enjoying themselves. By 6 p.m. the Booths excused themselves and started to leave the hall. The dancing was commencing and people were getting quite merry now. Billy and Alice thought it was getting exciting now and wanted to stay and listen to the musicians and watch the dancing. But Mr Booth said, 'Home,' and so home they must go. How Billy would have liked to dance with the girls and twirl them around the floor! But it was not to be. Home they must go.

Gladys also would have liked to have stayed, and she had seen the Rev. Baines across the room surrounded by ladies from the church and their daughters. Gladys wondered which lady was his wife. But she didn't like to ask. Occasionally he would look over to her and smile but he didn't come over to her. She was surprised how disappointed she was and, as she left the hall, she quickly looked over her shoulder and saw that he was looking at her. This pleased her, and out she trotted after her husband. On the way home he said that he would give her the monies for the wedding service, organist and bells and a little something for the hire of the hall and food. He had enjoyed the wedding breakfast and was surprised how friendly the people of the church had been to him and his family. They never forced them to have an alcoholic drink, just provided a soft drink for them, and never queried their departure when the music started up. It had been a successful day all round. Gladys was glad of the opportunity to go to the vicarage with the monies. She would go on Monday when the children were at school.

Chapter Five

Early next morning, while the Booths were sound asleep, the noise started.

'What on earth is that, Mother?' shouted William.

'What is it, Father?' shouted Gladys.

'It's that cockerel crowing! What a noise, we can't have that, it will wake up all the neighbours,' said William.

'What are you going to do?'

'I don't know, woman. What can I do?' shouted William. He grabbed his dressing gown and slippers and made his way downstairs.

The crowing got worse, louder and louder, as he reached the back door. Out he went in such a temper – what a noise – and on a Sunday too! What would the neighbours say? Then he had a bright idea. He got his car keys and reversed the car out of the garage. Thank goodness there was nobody about to see him in his dressing gown.

Then he found the big basket the cockerel had come in, and off across the garden he went. Catching Napoleon was a problem, as he kept tripping over his slippers. But he persevered and eventually grabbed Napoleon. 'Come here, you devil, come here,' shouted William. He was so worked up, the words slipped out. 'Sorry Lord,' he said up to the sky. 'Got you Napoleon, in with you and no more noise.' He fastened the lid of the basket and carried him across the lawn. Then in the garage he lowered Napoleon, basket and all, into the inspection pit and closed the lid. Napoleon would think it was still night down there. 'That will fool the old bird,' said William triumphantly, and went back into the house.

From then on, when Mr Yarwood put the car out for Mr Booth, he would haul up Napoleon out of the pit and carry him home to his two wives in the henhouse. But at night time back he went into the pit. This did fool the cockerel and peace reigned at Shirley every dawn.

Monday came and Gladys was up early. She had a mission today – to take the money to the vicarage. Before she set out, she had brought the subject round to the Rev. Baines with Mrs Yarwood, who talked about the wedding service and what a lovely one at that it was. What a dear the Rev. Baines was and what an asset to the village, she had said.

'The Rev. was lovely and understanding of Maisie's predicament, wasn't he?' Mrs Booth asked Mrs Yarwood.

'You're right there Ma'am, he was.'

'He handled the service grandly, didn't he? And with his trouble to boot,' said Mrs Yarwood.

'What do you mean Mrs Yarwood, what troubles?' she asked.

'Well, didn't you know, his wife died in childbirth; also the baby, it was a girl, fair broke his heart. It all happened last Easter and since then he has been quieter than usual,' said Mrs Yarwood. 'But he has carried on with his parish work, services, christenings, weddings and funerals, yes he has soldiered on, God bless him.'

'Well, I never knew,' said Gladys quietly, 'I never knew.' Thinking back to their conversation over Maisie's pregnancy, it must have been extremely difficult for him. But he never faltered in his duty to them. What a wonderful, sincere man Robert was. 'I shall be back at lunchtime, Mrs Yarwood, I have some errands to do. Can you manage without me?' she asked.

'Yes, Ma'am, I can manage, and tomorrow Maisie will be back, all starry-eyed no doubt and I won't get much work out of her. But Saturday was well worth it to see those two so happy,' replied Mrs Yarwood.

So Gladys set out to the village. She took the money from William but also some cakes and scones for Robert. It was a lovely warm morning and Gladys felt young and carefree for once. She arrived at the vicarage and walked down the path to the front door. At the same moment Robert opened the door and said, 'I have been waiting for you; come in, my dear.' He drew Gladys quickly into the hall and took the basket and put it on the floor. He held her hands and leaned forward and kissed her lightly on the lips.

Gladys moved back slightly and looked into his deep brown eyes. Excitement welled up inside her as never before and she returned his kiss, long and deep. His arms encircled her waist and they stood kissing and swaying slowly in the hall. When they moved slightly apart, both looked shocked. 'Come into the sitting room Gladys, come quickly,' spoke Robert in a deep voice. They moved together and literally fell through the door into the room. 'Oh, my dear, I have waited all weekend for you,' whispered Robert.

'Yes, my dear Robert, since seeing you across the village hall, I have been anxious to be with you,' replied Gladys breathlessly.

'Seeing you for the first time a few weeks ago made me realise how lonely I have become,' stated Robert.

'Not any more, my dear, I am here for you,' replied Gladys. She snuggled closer to Robert on the large sofa.

He clasped her more strongly now that he was sure she felt the same attraction to him as he did for her. Their lovemaking was magical. Gladys had never experienced such passion in all her married life. Robert was tender one minute to her, then all-consuming. She responded to him as never before and he became more ardent and adventurous with her. Seconds turned to minutes and the moments became more and more magical.

They broke apart and lay on the sofa, exhausted but content. 'That was wonderful,' Gladys whispered to Robert.

'Was it Gladys, was it really?' asked Robert anxiously.

'You know it was, you wicked man,' laughed Gladys. They both smiled at each other, knowing this would be their secret, their secret world. Nobody would intrude; it was theirs alone. Robert helped Gladys dress, then held her close and kissed her tenderly.

'You know I love you, I did from the first time I saw you in the church,' he said quietly to her.

'Yes, I know,' and she put her finger on his lips, as nothing else needed to be said between them.

Their love had been sealed that morning and how they would cope with this revelation would have to be decided later. But, for now, nothing could break the spell between them.

Gladys left the vicarage and walked home, happier and content, a woman in her prime. She was loved by a wonderful man, what more could she ask for? There would be many more visits to Robert, she was sure of that.

Her love for Robert was paramount. She enjoyed her life at Shirley and as the children were growing up, she had more time to herself. William's business was extremely consuming. He worked long hours, but did enjoy every working hour. Even on Saturdays and Sundays, he spent most of the day at the chapel. Even though they lived together in Shirley, Gladys and William had little in common with each other's lives. In fact, Mr and Mrs Yarwood, though childless, spent more time together and were closer and more supportive of each other. But Gladys and William did not notice the pattern of their lives. Secretly Gladys was pleased with William's involvement with the timber yard, as this would give her more time to visit Robert.

As her husband left the house early every morning, Gladys could watch for the postman coming up the drive. As the letters dropped on to the mat, Gladys would gather them up quickly and look through the envelopes for Robert's handwriting. Every time she found a letter from him she would disappear upstairs to her bedroom and read his letter of love slowly to herself. Once read, she would place the letter in a tin box which she kept at the back of her wardrobe. This was her secret, hers and Robert's secret world, which nobody entered.

The villagers presumed Gladys went there for guidance in the Church of England faith, knowing that she never went to chapel or had anything to do with the Minister. Not a word was said due to Mr Booth's views on the church, so Gladys had a good alibi.

The evenings were drawing in. Some nights sleep eluded Gladys and she would slip out of the big double bed so as not to disturb her husband. She tiptoed downstairs and sat in the rocking chair in the kitchen. She was restless and her thoughts turned to Robert. Suddenly, in the middle of the night Gladys heard an unearthly sound, like an animal in distress.

'Father,' she called out from the kitchen. 'Come quickly, I think something's in the hen run!'

William came into the kitchen and said, 'I didn't hear anything.'

'There it is again,' said Gladys. A high-pitched screech filled the sky. 'What on earth is that?' cried Gladys. She grabbed her husband's arm.

'I don't know,' he said quickly. 'I'll go out and check on the hens.'

Out went William across the lawn whilst Gladys stood by the kitchen door in the shaft of light. 'What is it, William?' she shouted.

'I can't see anything and the two hens are safe,' he shouted back.

'Come in then, you'll catch your death!'

When William came into the kitchen he said that perhaps it was a field mouse caught by an owl. 'It must have been a big mouse,' said Gladys, and they both laughed.

'Well it's eleven o'clock and time to retire, dear,' said William. 'Can't do any more till morning. I'll leave a note for Mr Yarwood to look around the field in case it's an animal in distress.' At that they both climbed the stairs of Shirley to their bedroom.

Come morning, William left for work and the children for school as usual. Mrs Yarwood was busy in the kitchen and Maisie was starting to clean out the grates in the dining and sitting room. Gladys was making lists for the shopkeepers, stocking up on provisions, vegetables, meat and bread for the coming week. Gladys was extremely efficient at running the household; they never ran out of anything.

This made life for Mr and Mrs Yarwood much easier, as the house ticked along like a well-oiled machine. Maisie was a happy little soul now, wife and soon to be mother. Her little body was swelling up slowly but she still worked well. Mrs Booth made sure she had adequate rests through the day and the work was not too heavy for her.

Suddenly the kitchen door burst open, making Mrs Yarwood drop the pan she was taking off the range.

'Oh my God, woman, it's awful,' cried out Mr Yarwood.

'What on earth has happened? Have you hurt yourself?' she asked him.

'No, woman,' he shouted at her. 'There's a body in the field!'

'A body! An animal, do you mean, a dog or cat?' she looked shocked.

'No, it's a *body!*' he was getting agitated. 'A body of a girl,' he shouted at her.

Mrs Yarwood could see he was very upset and shocked. 'Sit down here and tell me,' Mrs Yarwood tried to calm him.

At that, Mrs Booth and Maisie came running in. 'What's all the commotion? What's happened?' demanded Mrs Booth.

'There's a body of a girl in the back field,' shouted Mr Yarwood.

'Oh, my goodness, what are we to do?' cried out Mrs Booth. 'Are you sure she is dead?' she asked.

'Of course I am, with her head in that state, she be dead,' he said.

'Shush, think of Maisie, Mr Yarwood!'

'Oh, I'm sorry, Maisie, I don't want to frighten you; sit down, girl, while we decide what to do,' he said.

'We must call the police, and I shall call Mr Booth.' Mrs Booth was now recovering from the shock and restoring some calm to the situation.

'Right, you do that, Ma'am, and I will put on the kettle, we could all do with a pot of tea,' said Mrs Yarwood.

'Get the cooking brandy out for Mr Yarwood. He looks as though he could do with it.' And at that, Mrs Booth went into the hall to use the telephone.

The police arrived first and spoke to Mr Yarwood. He took them into the field. They were halfway across it, and Mrs Booth watched from an upstairs window. Thank goodness Billy and Alice were at school, she thought. The police started moving round in circles through the wheat. She thought they were looking for something. At that moment, Mr Booth came running upstairs, calling her name. 'What's happened, Gladys?'

'Oh, I'm so glad you have come; it's terrible, this poor girl, dead in the field, William, it's frightening,' sobbed Gladys.

'Come here, dear,' and he put his arm round her to comfort her. 'Don't watch any more, come downstairs to the sitting room and get warm by the fire,' said William. He was so comforting and reassuring that she felt safe now he was home. They made their way downstairs and William put Gladys in the big armchair by the fire. He then went into the kitchen and told Mrs Yarwood and Maisie to go and sit with her till he came back. Mr Booth took a deep breath and walked across the lawn and into the field.

The sight he saw was worse than he expected. William

shuddered with horror. How could any human being do this to a poor defenceless girl? What person could be responsible for this terrible act and where was he now? William, at that moment, was terrified for his young children, and especially for his wife, Mrs Yarwood and young Maisie, so close was their family home to the scene of this evil. By now the police were placing the young girl's body on a stretcher and tidying up her clothes in a decent way. Then they covered her with a blanket and carried her out of the field to the road. The remaining men searched the field for anything incriminating. William suddenly realised that he and Gladys had heard the girl. It was not an animal last night, screaming, but this unfortunate girl crying out for help. William suddenly felt cold and a policeman asked him if he was all right. 'Yes thank you,' William said quietly. 'But my wife and I heard the noise last night. I wish I had come further into the field. Perhaps I could have helped her.' William was getting quite upset.

'Now then Sir, I doubt if you could have helped her. In fact you might have been in danger yourself,' replied the policeman. 'You could help us now, though. If you would be so kind as to make a statement, you and the missus, what you heard and the time, like, it would help us in our inquiry.'

'Oh, I will definitely do that. Have somebody come round now and we will do that for you,' William was so pleased to help the police any way he could. He walked slowly back across the field into his garden by the small gate. When he entered the house, Mr Yarwood was comforting the womenfolk. 'I was saying there is nowt we can do,' stated Mr Yarwood.

'Well Mrs Booth and I will have to make statements about the noise we heard last night and the time. I say it was 11 p.m., Gladys, would you?'

'Yes, dear, about 11 p.m. Oh my, that poor girl was out there all night on her own,' sobbed Mrs Booth. 'Who was she, William?'

Mr Yarwood answered, 'She was the Sewell's girl, young Norma; only sixteen years old she was.'

'You mean the baker's girl, the pretty girl who served in their shop, their daughter? Oh, no it can't be!' cried Mrs Booth. By now she was getting more and more upset.

'I think you had better go up to bed and rest, dear,' said Mr Booth. 'I will pick up the children from school today. I will not go into work again and I will stay here with you all.' They all looked mightily relieved.

Mr Booth was a good, solid citizen, someone you could rely on in bad times, and these were certainly bad times. The front door knocker went and Mr Booth left the sitting room. A moment later he arrived with a policeman.

'Just tell the constable what you heard and at what time, Gladys, please,' said Mr Booth.

As she told her story to him, the constable wrote it all down. She then signed it and Mr Booth took her upstairs. Gladys seemed to have taken this event very hard and Mr Booth was worried about her. She seemed extremely frightened and kept looking out of the bedroom window into the field. 'She was there, out there, William, being attacked and dying while we were here in our bed. It's too awful.'

'Now then, Gladys, try and get some sleep. Shall I call the doctor for you?' He looked worried about her reaction.

'No, I will try and sleep, but do bring the children home safely and don't let Mr and Mrs Yarwood and Maisie leave till you come back,' she said quickly.

'Of course not, dear. They will be downstairs all the time.' He left the room and made his way down the big stairs. 'Mr Yarwood, stay in the house and lock the doors till I get back, there's a good chap.'

'Yes, Sir. Off you go for the children.'

As the day progressed, Gladys slept fitfully. Tossing and turning in her bed, images of the girl, Norma, came into her mind, then flashes of Robert, his soft, seductive voice whispering in her ear. When Gladys woke up she was more tired and stressed than before. What was happening to her? Her mind was in turmoil. She couldn't sleep in this bedroom, overlooking that dreadful field. So she got out of bed and started moving her clothes into the Grant bedroom. 'What are you doing dear?' asked William.

'Do not stop me, William. I am moving into the other room. I can't look at that field any more,' she cried hysterically.

'Calm down, everything will be all right soon,' said William.

'No, it will not,' cried Gladys, gathering up large amounts of clothes and dragging them out of the room. 'No, it will not, William.'

He was extremely worried about her now. Should he call the doctor or should he wait till morning? He went downstairs to talk to Mrs Yarwood. She was a very sensible woman and would know what to do. The business, the men, finances, all these Mr Booth could cope with, but with female problems, he was at a loss.

Mrs Yarwood suggested that a good night's sleep for Mrs Booth in the front room might bring some sanity to the situation in the morning. Mr and Mrs Yarwood then escorted Maisie home to the little flat and to Sidney. Another day would dawn and perhaps life would return to some normality.

The police, meanwhile, worked through the night. Norma had been sexually attacked before her head had been smashed with a hard implement. When dawn broke, a dozen policemen descended on the wheat field and systematically scythed areas looking for the weapon.

Mr Booth worried that Mrs Booth would not like this new development, so he stayed at home, trying in his way to protect her from the activity in the field. He kept her in bed and Maisie brought up tempting meals to her. When she slept, he nipped out with Mr Yarwood into the field to speak to the sergeant in charge. The wheat was knee-high, so the job of scything was slow and backbreaking. 'He must be a local man to know about Norma's movement, Sir,' said the sergeant.

'What was she doing out so late?' asked William.

'Her father said she always visited her grandma up the road from your house. She lived in the cottages, you know, Whitefield cottages, Sir,' he said.

'Oh yes, I know them,' nodded William.

'Then about 10 p.m. she would walk home.'

'A bit late for a girl, I should say!' exclaimed William.

'Well, Sir, she has been doing this ever since her grandma fell ill. 'The bakery closes at 6 p.m., Norma and her family have their tea and then Norma walks to her grandma's cottage with food for the next day. You see, her mother and father start work in the bakery at 4 a.m. so it was better that Norma went later,' said the sergeant.

'Not for the better, sergeant. In hindsight it was extremely foolhardy of the family to allow their daughter to be out at that time,' announced Mr Booth. 'But we must not view our opinion for all to hear. The Sewells are suffering enough. I don't know how I would cope if it was my daughter.'

All three men stood silently and pondered the situation. It was very grave thoughts that preoccupied them. Across the field the policemen were working in lines, scything in silence, except for the methodical swish of the blades. Mr Booth looked back at his house, Shirley, and the house seemed to be watching this macabre scene. William caught a fleeting glimpse of Gladys in the back bedroom window. At that moment the sun went behind a black cloud and Shirley was plunged into a dark shadow. The house seemed to be in mourning for the dead girl. Not the cheerful abode that he had first purchased. How could an incident like this change the feeling of a house? Mr Booth shook his head; he was becoming fanciful and he did not like his thoughts.

Across the field a man shouted, 'Here, here, come over here, Sir!'

The sergeant set off across the field. 'Stay here, you two,' he commanded Mr Booth and his gardener. 'Don't come over please, Sir.'

'I wonder what they have found?' asked Mr Booth.

'God knows,' replied Mr Yarwood, then added, 'I'm sorry, Sir, to take the Lord's name in vain.'

'Do not worry, Mr Yarwood. This dreadful thing has nothing to do with the Lord.'

Mr Yarwood nodded gravely to his employer. This was not God's work but the hand of the devil. Nothing like this had happened in the village as long as he could remember. Who could have done this to poor Norma, Mr Yarwood pondered to himself. When the sergeant returned to them, he was carrying a brown paper parcel. 'I think we have the murder weapon, gentlemen,' he announced proudly. 'It has blood on it and other matter.'

'What is it, sergeant?' asked Mr Booth.

'I'm not at liberty to say, Sir,' he replied pompously. 'You will hear in due course.' And at that he marched off, carrying his parcel. Mr Booth and Mr Yarwood returned to Shirley and Mr Booth went straight up to Gladys.

She was in bed in the front room so he did not mention that he had seen her at the other window. 'What has happened, William?' said Gladys.

'Nothing at the moment, dear, just the police looking round the field. Just rest now.'

'Did you speak to the children last night? What did they say?' asked Gladys.

'Well, they were very excited and inquisitive. Children don't understand the implications of death. They are too sheltered, so they were not upset or frightened by the events.' He picked his words carefully for Gladys, not wanting to alarm her even more. She sank back into her pillows and closed her eyes. It was as though she had gone into another world, a world away from death to a world of love and tranquillity.

Chapter Six

Next day William still stayed away from the timber yard. His manager Danny Ross would cope without him. Gladys was far more important to him. Over the last few days he had been thinking how he took Gladys for granted. She was not a strong lady like the village women, but she ran his home, managed his staff and looked after his children. She never complained and was always there in the background to support him. She never put herself first, always caring for others. A real gentlewoman. But now she was not coping with this situation. It did amaze him how she had gone to pieces so quickly. The death of Norma had affected her greatly. She was genuinely frightened.

In the late afternoon the sergeant arrived at Shirley. Mr Booth took him into the sitting room and shut the door. 'Please speak quietly, then my wife will not hear,' said Mr Booth.

'Well, Sir, we have had developments since yesterday. I can tell you the weapon used on poor Norma was a lump hammer. A heavy tool, which had Norma's blood on it and, on the handle, coal dust.' Before Mr Booth could say anything, the sergeant ploughed on. 'With this evidence we have arrested one of Scragg's sons. It seemed that he was sweet on Norma but she did nothing to encourage him. They are a nasty, rough lot, the Scraggs, you would not want them near your family, Mr Booth,' announced the policeman. 'This son has a vile temper and has been in trouble before, but nothing like this. It's a wicked business. The Sewells are devastated. Their only child. What more can you say?' he said solemnly.

'Yes, it's a nasty business, sergeant, a nasty business,' replied Mr Booth. At that, he thanked the policeman for informing him and showed him out.

He went straight upstairs to Mrs Booth. 'Who came to the door, William?' cried out Mrs Booth, still very agitated.

The Booth Family

'Well, that was the nice policeman and he has some good news, dear. They have arrested one of the Scragg boys for the murder. They are sure it is him, so the episode is closed.'

'How can you say that, William?' shouted Gladys. 'It's not closed. The field still has memories of Norma's dreadful death. I still hear her screams every time I go to sleep and her family will never be the same; this house, Shirley, will never be the same,' wailed Gladys.

'Come dear, do not say that.'

'But it's true. Can't you see? Shirley has been tainted with a vicious death, life here can never be the same,' and she buried her head in the pillows and sobbed. William just stood, not knowing what to say or do. Gladys's reaction was not good and he decided to call the doctor.

But Gladys did not improve. The doctor's pills and potions did nothing to help her. The thought of bringing in the Methodist minister to talk to Gladys would not be well received. William realised that in all the years that they had lived at Shirley, Gladys had not made any new lady friends. All her old friends were in Widnes near his timber yard. He mentioned this to Mrs Yarwood and she said, 'Yes, I think that is true. She has just busied herself with us and the house and the children, Sir, but…' then she hesitated.

'Yes, Mrs Yarwood?'

'Well, Sir, she did visit the vicarage a few times because of the wedding arrangements and seemed to get on with the vicar. Perhaps he could help?' said Mrs Yarwood in all innocence.

'Did she? I did not know of these visits.' Mr Booth was not angry, just puzzled at his wife's behaviour. 'I think I will speak to him. What's his name? The Rev. Baines, I think, young chap, saw him at the wedding,' he recalled. So he solicited the help of a vicar to help his wife. He never thought he would ever do that, not in a million years. But needs must.

The next afternoon the Rev. Baines arrived at Shirley. He had been summoned by a mysterious message from Mr Booth. The Reverend was worried in case Booth had found out about him and Gladys. That would be the end of his career in the Church. Banned from the clergy and with no means of support, he was extremely worried. He arrived at Shirley, extremely nervous. To his surprise, Mr Booth seemed pleased to see him. What on earth was going on here? He was very puzzled. Mr Booth took him into the sitting room, but did not ask him to sit. Instead he started telling him about Mrs Booth.

'So you can see I am very worried about my wife. I am told she has visited your vicarage about the wedding so, as you have met her in better times, I thought you might be able to help her.' The Rev. Baines could see Mr Booth was very worried about his wife's mental state. He was a good man, a caring husband and the Rev. Baines felt weak with guilt. What had he done, what had his loneliness brought him down to, would he be forgiven in the eyes of God?

Mr Booth showed the Rev. Baines upstairs. He knocked on his wife's bedroom door. 'I have brought someone to see you, dear,' he called to her. He walked into the room followed by the Rev. Baines. Gladys looked startled as she saw Robert behind her husband. Her hand flew up to her mouth and her cheeks reddened. 'Now, dear, don't get upset, he has only come to chat to you,' whispered Mr Booth. 'I will leave you two to talk. I shall be downstairs if you need me, Baines.'

'Thank you, Sir. I will call you if needs be,' said Robert. The door closed and the two were alone. Robert thought Gladys looked beautiful, propped up in her snow-white bed surrounded by lace pillows. 'How are you, my dear?' he said softly. Gladys began to sob.

'Oh Robert, you have come for me, to take me away from this dreadful place,' cried Gladys. Robert was shocked by this statement and was temporarily lost for words.

Eventually he crossed the room and sat on the edge of the bed. He held Gladys's hands tightly and looked straight at her. 'No, my dear, I have not come to take you away, but to try and help you cope with the situation of Norma's death.' He was struggling for words.

'But if I went with you, I could leave Shirley and wouldn't have to look at the field again, would I, Robert?' Gladys looked pleadingly at him.

'No, your place is here with William and your children. They all love you dearly; William is out of his mind with worry about you. We just had a fleeting romance, no more, Gladys.' She started to speak but he put his finger on her lips. 'No, Gladys, I have no part in your life. I must find my own life again after my wife's death, not intrude into yours. You must realise that we had something magical between us, but that type of love does not last. Your husband's love is the enduring and supporting love. You must see that.'

Gladys seemed to be calming down. She was listening to Robert intently. His every word did seem to make sense. She could not lose her family. She could not build happiness on somebody else's unhappiness. But the problem with Shirley would still be there. 'I will talk to your husband, Gladys. I have a suggestion for him to think about, a possible solution to your problem. Goodbye, Gladys, I shall miss you so much. I hope I shall find a lady like you somewhere that can be my wife. Mr Booth is a lucky man to have such a wonderful wife.' He gave Gladys a kiss on her hand and left the bedroom.

Downstairs, William was pacing about. 'Well, how is she, Reverend?'

'I think calmer now, we have talked, but in the end I think it would be better, and it's only a suggestion, if you could move away from the field. Sell Shirley and find a new home for Mrs Booth. A new beginning; perhaps nearer her friends. What do you think?' Robert paused a moment, watching Mr Booth's reaction.

'Do you know, that is a good idea. It was right under my nose and I never thought of it. Yes, a new beginning for us away from Shirley and the field,' beamed Mr Booth. 'Thank you so much, Reverend,' he said, and showed Robert to the door.

As Robert walked down the drive, tears welled up in his eyes. A great sadness settled on his shoulders. He knew he had done the right thing, but walking out of Gladys's life was the hardest thing he had ever done. He walked on down the road back to his lonely existence in the vicarage, and did not notice the pale, beautiful face pressed up to the window of the house called Shirley.

The next day, William discussed his plans to move with Gladys. At first she was not enthusiastic, but she did listen and together they started planning their future. William's plan was to move back to the Widnes area nearer to his workplace and nearer to Gladys's old friends. He felt sure seeing them and being able to talk to them would help in her recovery. He started looking around the area immediately and soon found a new house in the village of Hale near Widnes.

The following weekend he took Gladys, Billy and Alice over to see the house. He wanted to include the children in the decision to move back. When Gladys and the children saw the house, they were immediately captured. It was a double-fronted detached house, close to the village square. But its best feature was its thatched roof. It was the most charming house, and William knew the builder as he had supplied the timber for it. It was like history repeating itself – he had known Shirley's builder too.

Gladys found the house instantly welcoming and friendly. It was very pretty, and with Gladys's choice in furnishing it would be a wonderful home. They walked along the road and saw that there were to be other thatched houses on either side. It was indeed a lovely place.

William took his family back to the village and he told them the history of the place. On the way he showed them the village church, called St Mary of Hale, and then showed the children the large grave of John, who grew to nine feet three inches. John was born in 1578 and died in 1623. Billy and Alice were mesmerised by the size of the grave and thought what an exciting place Hale was. As they were getting back into the car, Gladys said, 'St Mary of Hale is Church of England, dear. Do you realise this?'

'Yes, I do, Gladys, but I have decided this will be our church in the future,' said William solemnly.

Gladys was startled by his reply. 'I have been doing some thinking lately, about Maisie and Sidney, their wedding, the happiness of the village people and their friendliness towards them, their acceptance of their problem, the way the Rev. Baines handled the situation and the way he came to our house to help us in our dire time. This has given me a lot to ponder over and I have decided that we shall all go on Sunday mornings to this church and thank God for our loving family.'

Gladys gave her husband's hand a squeeze. She knew this had been a big decision for him and she admired him and how he had looked after them these last few weeks. Billy and Alice were skipping around them, laughing and chasing each other. They did not seem to mind the move, in fact, she wondered if they had felt isolated like her. Being in the village here would give them a chance to meet new friends.

As for Mr and Mrs Yarwood, they would stay on at Shirley, as good, reliable staff were hard to come by. Maisie would be leaving as her baby was due any time soon. She wanted to stay at home and look after her baby and then perhaps help in the butcher's shop with Sidney.

Shirley sold quickly, as Mr Booth didn't put a high price on it. He also decided to leave the large furniture in the house. It somehow belonged to Shirley, and would enable Gladys to choose her furniture and this would do her all the good in the world.

So, after a few weeks, the Booths packed up their personal belongings, put the hens and Napoleon into their baskets and prepared to move. Saying goodbye to the Yarwoods and Maisie was hard, but they promised to come back for the baby's christening. The removal van moved off and the Booths followed in their car.

What an eventful time it had been, Gladys pondered. She realised she had nearly lost her precious husband and family, but she felt stronger now. Perhaps the house called Shirley had done her some good in the end.

The House

I am all alone again. One minute I am full with a bustling family and their staff, the next minute I am alone. I wonder how long I will have to wait for my next owners?

The last owners arrived full of optimism. The husband so proud to have bought such a magnificent house for his wife. And I am magnificent, even though I say it myself. The children were so eager to start a new life here with me. We were so happy together, the children playing in my gardens and Mother and Father there to nurture them. And I was there all the time to protect them, but I let them down in the end. I did not protect them against the forces of evil. That night I saw the dreadful act with my large eyes overlooking the field. How I wished I could have shouted out and frightened off that devil of a man as he dragged the poor girl into the field, but I was useless to her in her moment of need. Useless, useless. What sadness fell on me through that night. I can protect my family deep inside me, but outside I have no control. The following days were terrible; my mistress distraught, my master at a loss over what to do. I knew then that my life with them was at an end; I could feel their unhappiness, which unsettled my mistress.

They would be leaving me soon, I knew it. They would not stay much longer with me. No, their time with me had been spoilt by that savage act and I could do nothing to stop it. Their decision to move had come quicker than I thought, though. Master is a man who makes decisions and he was worried about Mistress's welfare. She sobbed in my front bedroom for hours and, although I kept her away from the events in peace and quiet, she still mourned the girl's death, day and night.

So here I am once more, waiting for the next family to live in me. I am glad they have left all my furniture here as it is a part of me. I would hate these precious belongings to go to another house. I am proud of my furniture. It sits well inside me and I would not like to lose it. I would feel bare inside, each item is a comfort to me while I wait for the new family. I hope it is a family with children. I love the sound of children running through me; they keep me alive and stimulated. How miserable I would be without children!

And now I wait for my new family. I find this an exciting time and I am full of anticipation. I hope the next years will be happy years for Shirley.

The Hornby Family

Chapter One

The sturdy little dog jumped out of the car and ran up the drive into the porch. He was snow-white and his small tail wagged with excitement. Following him ran a young girl with curly blonde hair that shone in the sunlight. Her chubby legs showed from beneath her Shirley Temple dress and she was just as excited as her dog. 'Oh, Rico, what a big house this is, and look at the garden all round. Lots of places for you and me to play hide and seek.'

The little dog rubbed up against her legs and she bent down and cuddled its head in her lap. It was obvious to all that the dog Rico was her best friend and they adored each other. Her shoes were black patent leather with tiny buckles on and they were tap-dancing on the porch floor with excitement.

'Anne,' called her mother, 'for goodness sake stand still while Daddy finds the right key for the front door.' Her father produced a large bunch of keys and tried them one at a time. It was agony for Anne but she stood still. Then, suddenly, one slotted into the lock and the door swung open. Anne started to move forward but her father stopped her.

'No,' he said firmly, 'just wait, Anne!' At that he turned and lifted her mother into his arms and kissed her and said, 'Hilda, this is your new home. I am sure we shall be very happy here.'

As they mounted the big step into the big square hall, she clung to him and said, 'Joe, it is so beautiful, we shall be very happy here.' He kissed her again and popped her down in the hall. Anne and Rico followed. Hilda was a slim woman in her thirties: dark hair, very attractive and smartly dressed. Suddenly she turned round and called out to the person left in the car, 'Come along, Nana, and see your new home!' From out of the car emerged a stocky woman in her sixties. Her hair was silver and tied in a bun at the nape of her neck. Her grey coat was double-breasted, which made her look shapeless. She was clutching a big leather bag to her bosom and her blue eyes were darting around as she walked slowly up the drive.

'Well, well,' she said, 'this place will take a lot of looking after, all this wood and brass to clean, and look at the size of the windows.' Then immediately she said, 'Which bedroom am I having?'

Hilda looked at her mother and carefully said, 'Just wait a moment until we all look around downstairs, Mother.'

Joe quickly felt the unease between the mother and daughter and added breezily, 'Come along Harriet, let me show you around.' Harriet softened at Joe's words and took his arm as they started to explore the house. Hilda sighed. Her mother, Harriet, or Nana as they called her, could be difficult. Her husband had died a few years ago, before Anne was born, and there was no thought of her living on her own. She sold her house and immediately moved in with her only daughter, Hilda, and her husband Joe. She occupied the largest bedroom, so when Anne was born that only left the tiny bedroom. This was all right as a nursery, but was not suitable for a growing child.

Joseph Hornby had done extremely well in the textile world. He started as an office boy at Green, Green and Co. in Manchester. Their great mills were in Walkden. The company manufactured shirting materials and dress fabrics, and Joseph progressed through the business learning the trade until he became a salesman for them. He was a smart dresser with black, Brylcreamed hair and dark eyes, yet he had a friendly face. Joseph did extremely well as a salesman for Green and Green. His appearance helped him, as many of his customers were Jewish and thought that Joseph was Jewish as well. Joseph had a lot of respect for his customers who ran family businesses. The manufacturing trade around Manchester was dominated by the Jewish community, and Joseph liked their close family values and the way they all helped one another if anyone experienced difficult times.

Because of this, Joseph prospered well at Green, Green and Co. and became the leading salesman. Their other salesmen reported to him with their monthly turnover figures. He was a very approachable man and he ran a very happy office. Because of Joseph's advancement in the company, and Harriet's nest egg from her old home, they had been able to buy Shirley. This house was a dream home for Joseph and Hilda, and much better to house three generations.

Anne and Rico were first up the wide staircase, peeping in at all the bedrooms. But Harriet soon followed and chose the front bedroom because she thought it would be quieter over the dining room. She stood in the middle of the room, her arms clasped across her, defying anybody to move her from this room. Hilda and Joseph quietly decided to accept this and chose the big back bedroom, which overlooked the garden. This was actually the best room, as it was south facing and much warmer. Mother and Father decided that the room next to theirs would be Anne's room, as it would be sunny too. The room at the far end of the landing would be a guest room and the small room over the hall at the front would be a sewing room for Hilda.

This all settled, they all moved downstairs and waited for the furniture van to arrive. Joe had bought the big dining room table, chairs, sideboard and other pieces off Mr Booth at a nominal price. He and Mr Booth had got on well through the purchasing of the house. Mr Booth realised that Joe was stretching himself to buy Shirley, but he liked the fellow and the way he spoke of his wife Hilda and little girl Anne. So Mr Booth was extremely happy to help Joe with the purchase of the furniture from Shirley. As William Booth's business was so prosperous he could easily make this kind gesture to Joe. His wife, Gladys Booth, had accepted all the original furnishings chosen by the original builder's wife, Shirley, so it would be exciting for her to choose new furniture for their next home in the village of Hale.

Hilda wandered round the house, taking in the Chinese carpet, the suite in the lounge and making a mental note to change the curtains. She had seen some Sanderson material in a shop and she would ask Joe if he could get some at cost for her.

She was very proud of her Joe and loved him dearly. They had been married for quite some time when she fell pregnant, and were ecstatic when she delivered a baby girl in the cottage hospital.

It had been a difficult birth as the cord was wrapped around the baby's neck but the old family doctor, Dr Wyles, had helped with the birth, and she gave birth to Anne. When she saw Anne for the first time she wondered why she was so fair, but Joe said some of his family a long way back were fair-skinned.

When Hilda brought the baby home, Harriet was a great help. It filled a void in her life, after the loss of her husband; now she could help with the baby. From that week on Harriet was called Nana, not Granny or Grandma, but Nana. The baby reminded her of her happy days when Hilda was born. Hilda accepted that her mother, Nana, would come to live with them when her father died, for women of that generation didn't work and needed someone to look after them. Hilda, being an only child, had a strong feeling of responsibility to her mother, which she knew she played on from time to time. But she hoped that the larger house would ease the situation. Joe on the other hand knew how to handle his mother-in-law and they never had a cross word. Harriet thought the world of Joe, and he could do no wrong. She sided with Joe against her daughter at the slightest thing at times, but Joe was very diplomatic with the two women.

Hilda suddenly realised that she hadn't seen Anne and Rico for quite some time. Slight panic set in and she walked quickly through the kitchen and out into the garden. She called and called and the first to come was Rico, followed by Anne, cheeks flushed and running as fast as her little legs could go. She ran straight up to her mother and hugged her legs. 'Oh, Mummy, it's lovely here. Rico and I were exploring. Do come and see.' She dragged her mother across the lawn to behind a hedge where there was a summer house. 'Look,' she said, 'a fairy house for Rico and me,' her eyes shining with excitement. 'Rico and I can have this as our house and we can sleep here at night, can't we Mummy?'

'Well, we will see, let's settle in to the big house first and make your bed up there,' her mother said, smiling.

As they walked into the house the men with big brown aprons were moving the furniture into the house. One of them said to Hilda, 'My, this a grandly house, Missus. Where do you want this bed?' They were struggling with Nana's big double bed. It had an enormous cast iron frame. The head and footboards were solid oak and they laboured upstairs with each piece. Next the two wardrobes, chest of drawers and dressing table, all solid oak. A few oaths issued from the men as they trapped their hands between furniture and staircase. Once upstairs, the bedroom seemed to swallow the furniture. Nana was very pleased, and told the men where to position the furniture. Next two boys came up carrying a big striped flock mattress. Anne loved this mattress and every morning she would try and help Nana shake it up again. But the best time was to jump into it and make a little bed in its feathers. They all had more modern mattresses; none were as cosy as Nana's.

By four o'clock the men had finished and Hilda had made them a strong brew of tea for their efforts. Rico kept well out of their way; he didn't like men, only Hilda and Anne. He was really Hilda's dog. Joe had bought him in the Isle of Man. He was a Sealyham, similar to a Scottie dog, but the hair round his chin was cut into a square beard. Joe thought he would be company for Hilda when he had to travel for his work.

Rico was three when the baby was born and he knew it was his job to guard the pram in the garden, or when it was outside a shop. Woe betide anybody who wanted to look at the baby in the pram! The only problem Hilda had with Rico was going for walks. He would only go on his lead for a walk with her. Joe, Harriet and, later, Anne found he would walk to the nearest lamp-post, then sit down firmly. He would not budge an inch and you could try pulling him or pushing him but he would not budge. He never barked or snapped, he just would not move. In the end the walker would have to leave him, lead and all, and come for Hilda to take over. It was very annoying for the family but Rico was Rico. Rico's basket and brown earthenware bowl with 'DOG' on it was placed at the side of the range in the kitchen and this was to be his home.

Soon after the removal men had left, Hilda and Nana made some ham sandwiches from ham that they had cooked themselves and brought with them. They unearthed some plates and mugs from the packing cases and set it all out on the big square kitchen table. It was a huge sturdy table, which the Booths had left for them, with four wooden chairs and two rockers. Joe, Hilda,

Harriet and Anne sat around the table with Rico underneath, ever hopeful for scraps. They were all very tired but happy, as the move had gone so well and at last they were in their new home, Shirley.

Father raised his mug and gave a toast to the family and the house. They all clinked their mugs and laughed with relief that they had arrived!

Soon after, Joe scooped Anne up and carried her up the broad staircase to her new bedroom. 'This is your first night here in Shirley. Remember it as it is a very important moment in your life, Pebble.' Joe called his daughter by this affectionate name. 'We are going to be very happy here.'

Anne clung to her father and said, 'We will live here for ever and ever, Daddy.'

'Yes, my dear Pebble, for ever and ever.' Joe's eyes filled with tears of joy as he hunted around for Anne's night attire in the suitcase. Once in bed, he kissed her and said, 'God bless, Pebble.'

'Night night Daddy,' said Anne. Mother came up then and kissed Anne. She brought Rico as well and lifted him on to Anne's bed.

'There, he will look after you and we are just in the next room, so call me if you need me.'

Eventually the house went quiet, each inhabitant thinking their own thoughts about the day and their new home.

Joe was pleased that he could afford such a grand home for his family and knew this would give him extra momentum to work hard and get good orders. Hilda was a little apprehensive about running such a grand home, but her head was full of ideas about furnishing it herself. Nana was very comfortable in bed in her large room and knew that she would have the whole place polished and sparkling before the week was out. Anne was clutching her teddy and thinking about her summer house and how she could play with her dolls and animals there. Rico, well, Rico was fast asleep, snoring slightly and dreaming of bones and new smells in his new home. In a few minutes, the new owners of Shirley were sound asleep and the house gave a big sigh. The omens were good for this new family.

Chapter Two

Over the weekend, the family worked hard unpacking their belongings and positioning the furniture. Joe gave his company car a clean and drove it into the big garage. Mr Booth had left a lot of good, solid gardening tools, a few deckchairs and an old card table. Joe respected Mr Booth and, whilst locking up the car, mentally wished him and his wife well in their new home in Hale. He then hurried inside and went to his desk in the lounge.

Mr and Mrs Booth called this room the sitting room, but Joe would always call it the lounge. His desk was made of walnut and it was Joe's pride and joy. He had bought it out of his bonuses. 'Solid walnut,' the salesman had said at Waring and Gillows. The front folded down and became a writing desk. It was lined with leather and at the back were pigeon holes and a little drawer. Underneath the writing area were two long drawers, in which Joe kept all his business papers. These were very important to him and on Sunday he would plan his route to his customers and his stopovers. Sometimes he was away all week, not returning until late on Friday. But at the end of the month he spent time in his office at Green, Green and Co. going through all the travellers' orders and working out the deadlines which they had to achieve. He was very fair, but firm, and never overstretched his men, only occasionally giving them a friendly nudge if the figures were not achieved. He wasn't averse to sacking a man if he wasn't pulling his weight.

Joe worked on his figures that afternoon and then took the papers, in his briefcase, into the hall ready for Monday morning. He would travel north after a brief stop at Green, Green and Co. in Walkden to pick up his samples of cloth. He was excited at the new range of shirting materials. The quality was first class, as the mill produced fine material. The weavers worked long and hard and it was Joe's job to sell. Their livelihoods depended on Joe and his team of salesmen, and he never forgot this.

Monday morning dawned and Joe was up first. He dressed in his smart suit, collar and tie. He always insisted on a smart appearance, as they were given shirts made from their own material. Their wares were on display as soon as they entered a buyer's office.

Joe never had any trouble with his buyers; they were all like friends to him and he looked after their orders right through to the delivery day.

This week he would travel up to Leeds over Saddleworth Moor towards Huddersfield. First he stopped at Huddersfield for a few days, visiting his customers, then on to Leeds. Mr Marsden, who owned the mill at Leeds, was Joe's biggest customer. Extremely wealthy, he lived in a large mansion at Roundhay with grounds and a private drive. Joe stayed at Mr Marsden's home, as he was a lonely man. His wife had died young and left him with a daughter – Georgina. Mr Marsden enjoyed Joe's company and relished the few days that Joe stayed. Little Georgina was the apple of his eye, totally spoilt, but she also loved Joe's visits, as the house came alive again.

When Joe left Shirley on the first Monday morning the family were still in bed, but it was not long until Hilda rose and started her day. She was a little worried for this was her first day running the house. As soon as she was dressed, she made her way down the broad staircase, walking slowly, sliding her fingers along the shiny handrail. She paused in the hall to pick up a few letters and then went into the kitchen. She made a pot of tea on the gas stove and sat down at the kitchen table. How would she cope today? She was nervous but decided that her Joe had every confidence in her ability, so she would conquer her fears and get on with the tasks in hand.

Shirley was twice the size of their last home and the garden was enormous. But, with help, she would organise the tasks. One thing Hilda had was good managerial skills. She would have been a good businesswoman; perhaps one day she would be. Life had lots of twists and turns, as Hilda already knew, and she could be a match for them any day.

Just as she was daydreaming about this, there came a knock on the kitchen back door. Rico barked loudly. Hilda jumped up, smoothed her skirt down and opened the door. There stood a homely couple, Mr and Mrs Yarwood. Mr Yarwood doffed his checked cap and stuffed it in his pocket. They both wiped their feet on the large mat. Hilda shook hands with them and Rico watched them move slowly into his kitchen.

'Pleased to meet you both. I am Mrs Hornby. You have just missed Mr Hornby, my husband. He has had to go early to work. But please do come in and have a mug of tea and we can talk about your work here at Shirley. You can tell me what you have done for the Booths over the years.' Hilda suddenly stopped talking and started pouring the tea as she realised she was chattering far too fast, being so nervous. Mrs Yarwood looked very capable, used to hard work, but with a jolly disposition. She had a ready smile, quite the opposite to Mr Yarwood, who was more serious and deep in character. But when Anne came running in his face lit up and he immediately started to talk to Anne about Rico. He lowered himself to their level and spoke in a quiet but friendly way to Anne and Rico. Hilda thought this was a good omen and it relaxed all of them at once. They all sat around the table.

Mr Yarwood told Hilda about his duties, which consisted of gardening, brushing the drive, cleaning the car and general maintenance. Hilda listened intently. Mrs Yarwood said her domain was the kitchen, and the maid cleaned the house. Now, this was the first major problem for Hilda. She had to diplomatically tell Mrs Yarwood that there was to be no maid now, as they couldn't afford to keep her as well. From now on, Mrs Yarwood would help to clean the house, whilst Hilda cooked, as Mr Hornby was away so much and large meals were unnecessary.

Hilda took a deep breath, sat back in her chair and waited for Mrs Yarwood to take in this new situation. Mrs Yarwood looked across at her husband and after a long pause, turned to Hilda. With a broad smile, she said, 'Well, Mrs Hornby, I am pleased with what you have just said, as I have been getting fed up with toiling over the range and gas oven, then going home to my own kitchen and starting again. It will suit me fine, and when I have a moment

I will rustle up a pie or two for you for the weekend. How's that for you?'

'Well, Mrs Yarwood, that is wonderful as I am no great shakes with the pastry!' Hilda shook hands with Mr and Mrs Yarwood and Anne jumped up and shook their hands too. Everybody laughed and Rico barked excitedly at them. Hilda was going to look forward to living at Shirley.

A few minutes later, Nana walked into the kitchen. She was wearing a large apron wrapped round her and a stern look on her face. The conversation stopped and everybody turned to look at her. Hilda immediately leapt up and introduced her mother, Harriet, to the Yarwoods. 'This is my mother, Mrs Johnson. Mother, these good people are the Yarwoods.'

'I call her Nana,' chirped Anne.

'Be quiet, dear,' said Hilda to her daughter.

Nana never said a word of welcome to the Yarwoods, and Hilda sensed this was going to be a difficult situation. 'What do they want with us?' said Nana.

'Well, Mr Yarwood is our gardener and Mrs Yarwood will help in the house,' said Hilda cheerfully.

'Over my dead body, Hilda, I'll have no one cleaning my house for me. Do you think I'm old and past it? Never!' At that she stormed out of the kitchen and went up to her room. They all heard the bedroom door slam.

'My, Mrs Hornby, what a to-do. Perhaps Mr Yarwood and meself had better come back tomorrow.'

'No,' said Hilda. 'You will start your work. There's lots of unpacking and Mr Yarwood could leave the garden for today and help too.'

'If that's what you want, we will be glad to help out,' said the Yarwoods, and moved into the dining room, which was full of tea chests.

Anne and Rico went out into the garden to explore. 'Don't go out of the garden, stay in the back where we can see you, Anne.'

'Yes, Mummy. Come on Rico, let's go to the little house,' and off they ran across the garden.

Hilda was left in the kitchen. Well, this was it, she thought. She would have to stand her ground with her mother, or the situation would drag on for days. Harriet had always got her own way with her husband and her daughter. But now her husband was dead, she played on Hilda to get her own way. Hilda, being an only child, found the situation difficult to handle, although she was married with a child of her own. The old strings were still there, and Harriet pulled on them, manipulating situations whenever she could.

Hilda stood up, took a deep breath, and went upstairs. She knocked on her mother's door and there was no answer. She called out but again, there was no answer. This was Harriet's silent treatment of the family. Time and time again she resorted to this to get her own way. But today Hilda was in no mood to put up with it. She knew the Yarwoods were below in the dining room and would be listening.

Hilda walked into her mother's room, where Harriet was sitting on her bed, arms folded, her back to Hilda. 'Mother,' whispered Hilda, 'please come down and help with the unpacking, we need every pair of hands. And this house is very large – we need the Yarwoods to help us. You will never cope alone. Plus the garden is enormous and Mr Yarwood is needed too.' Harriet didn't say a word. She heard her daughter perfectly and knew she was right. But she didn't show it and her face did not soften. 'All right, Mother. I will leave you to think about what I have said,' and out she went.

Harriet sat on her large bed and stared out over the trees and on to the road. Would she get used to the new house and people? She loved Hilda and Joe's old semi as she had moved in with them the year her husband had died. There was no thought of her living on her own. It was automatically expected that she would live with her only child and husband for the rest of her life. So, to compensate for their kindness, she took on the cleaning and the running of the house for Hilda. Harriet loved cleaning – she found it very satisfying. She had set days for her work and never deviated from those days. Monday, washing and ironing, Tuesday, finish ironing, clean front and back porches and kitchen floor, Wednesday, upstairs and bathroom, Thursday, downstairs rooms,

Friday, brasses. Every day she cleaned the grates and laid the fires, making rolls of newspaper, wood and coal. Her windows sparkled by using a mixture of water and vinegar polished with paper. Harriet took great pride in her work and the whole house shone with her efforts. Nobody ever came into the home and found it untidy. It was an obsession with Harriet, and, from putting her pinafore on in the morning to taking it off at teatime, she never stopped.

But now what was she going to do all day? She was very upset, and suddenly felt old and unwanted. A tear trickled down her cheek as she rocked backwards and forwards on her bed. A deep sadness overwhelmed her body. She had not felt so lonely since her husband had died. How would she cope here in this grand house with its staff? Fancy, her, Mrs Johnson, who grew up in a terrace in Manchester, now living with other people who did her job, encroaching on her domain. It was frightening and unsettling. What would become of her? She would no longer be useful to Hilda and Joe. They would think of her as a hindrance and as a burden on their family. The tears streamed down her cheeks. Her arms wrapped round her bosom, she held herself tight.

Suddenly the door opened and Hilda marched in. 'Brought you a cup of tea and your breakfast is going cold. Will you come down and help with the washing? Can't cope in this huge house without you, Mother. It's Monday and things need doing as usual!' With that torrent of words, Hilda walked out.

Nana sat there, her mouth open wide. Well, that was some speech by her little Hilda! The girl had grown up and was taking responsibility for her life. What a turn up for the books! Nana sniffed loudly, got off the bed, drank her tea, put on her apron and walked out of the bedroom. She was met by Mr Yarwood, who greeted her with a 'How do!' and then Mrs Yarwood, who beamed at her and started asking her where things were to go.

So life calmed down again at Shirley and the house sighed with relief. That was a difficult moment, but the house hoped that the Hornby family would now settle and enjoy living there.

Chapter Three

Life at Shirley was wonderful for the Hornbys. Joe's workload increased week by week. He had a new air of confidence about him as the proud owner of Shirley. His finances were excellent and his future at Green, Green and Co. was secure. He could employ Mr and Mrs Yarwood as permanent help in the house for Hilda and this made him very happy too.

Hilda had at last relaxed and secretly loved the way that the shopkeepers in Ashton-on-Mersey greeted her and went out of their way to serve her and deliver goods to the house. She still went into Sale for her main provisions, to the large food store on the corner of Ashton Lane, but instead of carrying everything home, her shopping was delivered. The shopkeepers offered Hilda accounts at their shops, but she still paid for everything there and then. The old thrifty ways in which she had been brought up had not escaped her.

Nana was slowly changing her ways, but quite enjoyed the company of Mrs Yarwood as they did their chores together. Mrs Yarwood showed a lot of respect for the hardworking grandmother and also learned a few 'wrinkles' from her about cleaning.

Anne was very happy in Shirley. She loved the house and the garden. She had made friends with Mr Yarwood, who also acted as a stand-in father, as Joe was away so much. She excelled at school and soon started ballet lessons at Sale. At first she was nervous about the big class and the ballet teacher, who seemed very tall and strict. But then she started to enjoy the lessons. Quick to learn and with an ear for the music, she progressed to tap and character dancing. Hilda, who now had a sewing room in the smallest bedroom, which was once the maid's room, made wonderful ballet tutus in pale pink net with satin bodices. She made special costumes for the character dancing – Bo Peep, Elf and Hungarian outfits, lovely costumes, which were beautifully finished. Once a year, the ballet school gave dancing displays at Sale town hall. Hilda would make most of the costumes and would help to dress the girls on the night.

Because Mrs Yarwood and Nana looked after the house, and Mr Yarwood the garden and the fires, Hilda had time to herself. She secretly loathed housework and would rather run up dresses or curtains on her sewing machine. Joe was a great provider of material and under the beds there were suitcases full of wonderful cotton, wools and so on. Sometimes she would nip off to Manchester to browse the shops. Affleck and Brown was her favourite. She would make mental notes of the fashions and colours and buy a few trimmings from the shop. Then she would meet Joe and they went to the cinemas in Oxford Road. Their favourite film was *Gone with the Wind*, and they had seen it many times.

The couple could have a lot of time to themselves as Nana loved to look after Anne. Grandmother and granddaughter would play cards in the evening. They enjoyed each other's company and, sometimes, Anne would dance for her grandmother. Rico would lie by the open fire and twitch and sigh as he dreamed of large, juicy bones.

Everything seemed idyllic, but this was soon to end. As Joe, Hilda and Anne were holidaying on the Isle of Man, war was declared and they were forced to return to Shirley the next day. Men were being called up to fight and Hilda was worried as Joe had had a lot of health problems. As he travelled all week his eating habits were very erratic, resulting in the development of a duodenal ulcer. The doctors had prescribed medicine and lots of dairy products and milk to drink, but he still suffered a lot.

The house now had to have heavy black curtains at all the windows, and in the garden an Anderson shelter had been built. This was, to Anne, the best part of war. The shelter had a lid at the side which opened up and steps leading down. Inside there was electric light and a fire. Mother had made beds up and it was like a cosy igloo. Anne loved it but Rico hated it, and would not go in. So when the air raid Sirens sounded, he would run straight upstairs and jump into the bath. Nobody could coax him out and he had to be left there until the 'all clear' sounded.

Joe was called up but, to the family's relief, he was turned down because of his ulcer. Instead he joined the ARP, which patrolled the area of Ashton-on-Mersey and Carrington Moss. This large, flat area was carefully watched at night for enemy parachutists. The bigwigs at the town hall were sure that the enemy would land there. Joe left home when the air raids started, checking on the blackouts. Woe betide anybody with a chink of light showing from their windows.

During the blackouts, Nana, Anne and Hilda went down to the shelter and listened for the bombers. They could hear Manchester and Liverpool being bombed and prayed for the people in those areas. 'I wonder how Auntie Eva is tonight?' Mother said to Nana.

'Well, I think we should go tomorrow and see her, seeing as Stretford is so close to Manchester,' Nana said. Auntie Eva and her daughter, Marlene, lived on their own, as Marlene's father had died at a young age. What a tragedy for Eva, having to bring up a baby on her own! She had managed to get a job helping out at the local primary school kitchen. Hilda and Joe would sometimes look after her, as she was Joe's sister.

'Yes, we must go tomorrow and take some food for her,' Hilda said. This worried Hilda. Though she was genuinely fond of Joe's sister, Eva could be very prickly to handle. Eva had never got over her husband's death so soon after the birth of the baby, and found it difficult to cope with life. Very short of money, lonely, worn out with work and looking after a small child on her own, Eva had changed into a very quiet, sad person. Envious of Joe and his family life, she found it hard to accept help from him. But Hilda and Nana had always persevered with Eva and a visit was agreed on.

When Sunday morning arrived, they all set off to Stretford. But as they approached, their hearts sank. The road was blocked with fire engines, hosepipes and crowds of people. 'Quick Joe! Oh Joe, park up. What has happened?' cried Hilda.

'Oh God, what has happened?' Joe echoed. They got out and moved fast through the crowd. 'Hold on to Anne,' Joe shouted to Nana as she padded along behind them.

As they rounded Eva's street, they saw a huge hole in the row of tiny houses. Two houses had been hit directly and the remainder of the houses in the street had had all their windows blown out. 'Oh, this is terrible,' said Joe. In his anguish he couldn't decide which was Eva's house. He started to tremble. Hilda grabbed his hand and they walked up the street, picking their way over the pipes and through the water and rubble.

'Which one, which one?' cried Anne. Hilda held her tight.

'That's hers!' she shouted, pointing to the little terrace house two doors away from the gaping open space where the bomb had hit.

'Oh, where is she?' cried Hilda. They stood huddled together in the chaos, clutching the baskets of food. Where were Eva and her child?

From out of the chaos a policeman came to them. 'Looking for somebody, mate?' he said to Joe.

'Yes, my sister and child. They lived there,' he said, pointing to the remaining house.

'Oh, don't worry. They have been taken to the local primary school,' he said. Joe grabbed Hilda's hand and started up the street with Nana and Anne following.

As they rushed inside the hall, they stopped suddenly as they saw Eva across the room. She sat motionless, with her daughter lying against her. A shaft of light fell across them both and Eva just stared into space. As Joe approached her slowly, he called her name, but her eyes did not flicker in recognition. Joe's heart started to beat faster. 'Eva, Eva,' he whispered to her, trying to bring her back from her trance into the reality of her surroundings. But nothing happened, except her daughter lifted her head and started to cry, quietly at first, then sobbing strongly. She slipped out of her mother's arms and ran to Hilda. Hilda gathered her up and held her lightly. Eva did not react to this movement; she just continued to stare ahead.

Joe tried to talk to his sister but got no reaction. It was as if her whole body and mind had shut down completely. Joe was very frightened by this and held Eva's hands tightly. Nana took Anne and Marlene back across the room and found some books for them to look at. Joe and Hilda talked to Eva but her eyes would not focus on them. Just then, the Red Cross nurse came in, informing them that a doctor had been sent for. He would come to Eva when he had finished with the casualties in the road. Joe and Hilda sat either side of Eva, holding her. Nana got the basket of food and made a little picnic on the school hall table for Anne and Marlene. All the time, Nana kept glancing across the hall to Eva. She didn't like the look of her at all. She had seen this reaction once before after a woman who lived in her old street was told that her husband had been killed in action in the First World War. 'No good will come out of this,' muttered Nana, 'no good at all.'

Suddenly the door swung open and in came a young, harassed doctor with a Gladstone bag and two orderlies from the hospital. He stood and observed Eva for a moment, then passed his hand over her eyes. She didn't react at all. As he stepped back, he clapped his hands loudly. But Eva did not move. The doctor spoke quietly to Joe. 'You are her brother?' he asked gently.

'Yes,' answered Joe.

'Has she been like this before?'

'No, but she has suffered with depression since her husband had died.'

'But we thought she was over that now,' added Hilda quickly.

'Well, I think she is in need of care and attention in hospital right now.' The young doctor picked his words carefully. He didn't want to alarm her family, but he did not like Eva's lack of reaction. He wanted to admit her into hospital straight away. 'Will you look after her child for her?' he said to Hilda.

'Oh yes, we will look after Marlene, Doctor.'

The two orderlies helped Eva to the ambulance. She could hardly put one foot in front of the other. She looked such a sad, pathetic creature, just a stumbling shell, a terrible, tragic victim of the war.

In the next few hours, Eva was settled into the hospital. Joe and Hilda went back to her house and picked up Marlene's clothes, and they all returned to Shirley. With Marlene tucked up in her new little box room at the front of the house, the adults sat round the fire in the lounge discussing the future.

They all decided they would look after Marlene until her mother came home from hospital. In the meantime, and while Anne and Marlene were at school, Hilda and Nana had been making many journeys to Eva's house. They had noticed that the house was dirty and neglected so they set about cleaning it. Hilda also made little changes to brighten it up. She made new curtains and cushions, bought new rugs and brought the house back to life. Joe went at weekends and tidied up the garden.

Eva was eventually sent home on sedatives and Marlene returned home too. Hilda noticed that Marlene was not too keen to go back to her old life with her mother, but that was her home so back she had to go.

Chapter Four

At long last, the war ended and life returned to normal. But normal was not the word for Eva. Her behaviour was far from normal. She had long periods of depression when she was hospitalised, and Marlene returned to her box room at Shirley. Hilda noticed increasingly that this return to them caused Marlene no distress whatsoever. In fact, she loved living with them and didn't seem to miss her mother at all. By now Marlene was developing into a young woman and Hilda had to realise she was older than Anne. Eva was retreating from life, barely functioning as a mother to Marlene.

To make ends meet, Eva had decided to take in a lodger, a young Polish man who worked at the local bank. A friendship blossomed between him and Marlene. She was a young girl and, at last, she had some joy in her life. She and the young man, Peter, tried to look after Eva, but when they were out at work Eva would wander out of the house in her slippers and dressing gown, only to be brought back by a friendly neighbour. All the time she seemed to be looking for her husband and baby girl, not realising that the baby girl was now a grown woman. Life had stopped for Eva when her husband was killed in the war. Her mind was locked back in time and all the treatments, drugs and the nursing care had done nothing to help her.

Early one September morning, a police car drew up slowly outside Shirley. Two policemen entered the house and spoke to Hilda.

'There's been an accident, Madam.'

'Not my Joe. He's out travelling up to Leeds,' Hilda clung onto Nana's hand.

'No, don't get upset. It isn't your husband. It's his sister, Eva. We are very sorry to have to inform you that Eva committed suicide this morning. We need to notify her daughter, so will you come with us?' said the policeman quietly.

'Oh my goodness. Poor Eva,' cried Hilda. 'I'll come straight away. Nana, ring Joe's firm and get them to get Joe home.' Poor Eva, so weary with life, had gassed herself. She had just laid down a cushion under her head and turned on the gas. In her way she was escaping her worries and returning to her life with her beloved husband and baby.

Within a few months of Eva's death, Marlene and Peter came to tell Joe and Hilda that they had decided to emigrate to Australia. It was a great shock to Joe, but he helped his niece to fill in the forms. Later that year, Marlene and Peter left for Sydney to start a new life. For Marlene said she had lost her mother long before her suicide, long before the bombing, way back when she was a little girl. 'No good will come of this, no good at all,' Nana had said long ago, and her prophecy had come true.

While Eva's story evolved, life at Shirley moved on. Shirley became a home in which the family all enjoying living in a lovely community. Hilda had more time on her hands as Anne progressed to senior school and Nana and Mrs Yarwood enjoyed their household chores. Hilda picked up on her dressmaking and soon the ladies in the neighbourhood were wanting new outfits. Clothes rationing had finished and material was more freely available. Hilda loved to design a new dress and then find a pattern in the pattern books. She would lay the material out on the dining room floor and then, with large scissors, cut the pattern to her customer's size. She never cut on a table, always on the floor, and would then pin the material together. She would hold the pins in her mouth and could even talk at the same time!

Hilda went into a world of her own when she was sewing and the finished products always pleased her customers. She used the dining room through the week as Joe was away and her customers would come for their fittings. She also did alterations as women lost or put on weight. Sometimes she made a bridal gown. The material would come on long rolls and it was exciting to please the bride and make headdresses for the bridesmaids. This work brought her into contact with lots of ladies from the area and soon she had as much work as she could handle. Money flowed into the household purse and this stopped Hilda worrying about looking after such a large house. Though she stayed at home and did not go out to work, she felt she was contributing to the family finances. Quite a little businesswoman was our Hilda.

Harriet, on the other hand, was happy to immerse herself in household duties. Washing, ironing, cleaning and dusting were meat and drink to Harriet. Her friendship with Mrs Yarwood was good. Their mutual interest in the household filled a big gap in Harriet's life. For once since her husband died, she had found a friend she could talk to about the old days. They would clean each room together so that they could have a good 'chinwag', as they called it. Their old-fashioned ways of cleaning and polishing brought them closer as they agreed on everything.

As it was quite a feminine household during the week, Mr Yarwood would act as guardian and protector of the house. He loved the land and worked away in the garden producing wonderful vegetables and fruit from the orchard. At the beginning of the summer he bought bedding plants and set out the borders. The lawn was mown each week and the path and drives well brushed. He would cycle from the village to the house while Mrs Yarwood would walk with her basket. Going home, Mr and Mrs Yarwood would take home any vegetables and fruit that they wanted as there was always an abundance of beans, carrots, apples and potatoes.

Joe, on the other hand, worked on steadily, now that the family and the Yarwoods were happy together at Shirley. He travelled long distances in his Vauxhall 14 car, but the travelling was rewarding when he received big orders. With his bonuses one year he bought a grand piano. It was a beautiful piece of furniture as well as a good piano. The piano was a Marshall and Rose, built in 1932.

Though Joe and Hilda could not play, they thought it would be good for Anne to learn. As an only child, sometimes she was lonely and they thought the piano would occupy her time. Anne started her lessons and loved them. Playing came easily to her and she took exams and passed with flying colours. Her friends came to the house and they played duets, and often ended up under the piano, laughing and giggling together. It was like a little house underneath the piano and a very special place for Anne. Her father brought home music for her and signed the front cover, 'To Anne love Daddy', and put three kisses next to it. They were pieces he would like her to play, and at weekends he would listen to her practise.

For Hilda, Joe would bring home beautiful Doulton figures, which she would display in a bow-fronted cabinet made of walnut to match Joe's desk. He never forgot his mother-in-law and would produce a big box of Black Magic chocolates for Harriet. She loved these and Joe knew how to make her happy. Although she was more content living at Shirley, she would still give them the silent treatment if she disagreed with Hilda. It was mainly Hilda, but as Anne grew up she could get 'the treatment' as well. At the table she would ask Hilda for the salt and pepper even if it was right in front of Anne. If Anne passed them, she would say 'I asked your mother, young lady, not you!' Poor Hilda was often caught in the middle of the older woman and her daughter. But usually by Friday she had snapped out of it, as she didn't want her beloved Joe to know her darker moods.

'Joe, shall we have a holiday somewhere this year?' Hilda asked him. She and Joe were very happy together and, as Joe was away through the week, time together was precious, so they usually stayed at home and pottered in the garden and went perhaps to the local cinema. Hilda loved the cinema, watching the women's clothes and making a mental note on collars, cuffs and length of skirt for her clients.

'Now that is a good idea, love. Where shall we go?' replied Joe.

'Well,' said Hilda, her eyes shining at Joe, 'I have been thinking of Devon.'

'Oh, have you, my lady?' teased Joe. 'And how long have you been thinking of Devon?'

'Just this morning, Joe,' said Hilda, smiling away. She loved Joe so much and he could read her thoughts so easily. That was love. He was an Aries, passionate and strong. She always felt secure with Joe. He never undermined her, but gave her confidence. He thought she was a wonderful woman, very bright and talented with her dressmaking. The two of them made a formidable team. It was a pity they weren't in business together.

'I have found this thatched cottage in Cockington,' said Hilda.

'Where on earth is Cockington?' asked Joe.

'It's near Torquay,' said Hilda.

'Oh, well, get the map and let's see.'

'I have,' said Hilda, laughing. 'We could go and take two days to get there, staying at Bridgewater overnight. What do you think?'

'All right, Hilda. Book it for us. The first two weeks in August.' Then Joe said, 'What about Nana? We cannot leave her here on her own.'

'That will not be a problem. I have asked Mr and Mrs Yarwood to come and stay here. It will be like a holiday for them, a change of scenery,' replied Hilda. 'Do you think that Harriet will stand for that? You talk to her first, Joe. Say you are tired and you need a holiday. She loves you and you can twist her round your little finger.'

'Oh, I don't know about that. You are her daughter,' laughed Joe. 'All right. I'll try. I'll just have a whisky first for Dutch courage, then I'll speak to her.'

Later that evening Joe went up to Nana's room, took a deep breath and knocked on her bedroom door. 'Come in,' called Harriet. 'Oh, hello Joe. Is anything wrong?' she said, as Joe came into her room very rarely. She was sitting in her big bed with a snow-white long-sleeved nightdress on and a little lace cap in her hair. Into battle! thought Joe. So he plunged into his speech.

'I am getting rather tired, so I thought it would be nice to take Hilda and Anne on holiday for two weeks. So, instead of leaving you alone in this big house, I thought Mr and Mrs Yarwood could come here and stay. It would be a change for them and I'm sure they would enjoy the house and garden. Mr Yarwood could look after the garden for you, and you enjoy Mrs Yarwood's company, don't you?' Joe hardly stopped for breath as he spoke, weighing up Harriet's reaction to his words.

Harriet paused before speaking. 'Well, it seems as though you have all this planned out, Joe? I don't want to spoil your holiday, so I suppose I will have to do as I'm told,' said Harriet sulkily. She could never be gracious, but she could see that Joe was determined and he had looked tired of late. She loved Joe as the son she had never had, and they understood each other. Harriet would have loved to holiday with the family, but she did realise that Joe and Hilda needed some time to themselves. She had lived with them for most of their married life. She often wondered if this was why they had restricted their family to one child. The space in their first home and economics would weigh heavily on their decision. But Harriet and her husband had been satisfied with just Hilda, and she was sure they were with Anne.

When Harriet came down for tea, the first thing she said was, 'Well, we had better make up a spare bed for Mr and Mrs Yarwood.'

Hilda replied, 'No, Nana. They can have our bedroom. I will empty a drawer and some hanging space for them when we go.'

'When will it be?' said Nana.

'Next week while the weather holds, I think,' said Joe with a big beam on his face. So the holiday plan was put into action.

Chapter Five

Early Saturday morning, Joe collected Mr and Mrs Yarwood in his car and brought them home. He left money with Nana and strict instructions that Mr Yarwood was not to work in the garden, only mow the lawn and take Rico for walks. Mrs Yarwood was just to cook the meals and not do any housework – they were to enjoy their two weeks' stay, sitting in the garden, and, at night, listening to the radio and playing cards. Nana would enjoy their company and they would have lots to talk about. 'The good old days,' as Nana would say.

Departing was not too difficult for Hilda, as Harriet seemed content with the arrangements. Why did she always feel guilty when she did something for herself? It was a typical symptom of being an only child. I must make a mental note that I must never inflict this feeling on my only child, thought Hilda.

Joe, Hilda and Anne set off in the Vauxhall 14. Joe, being a skilful driver, made good headway and by late afternoon they had arrived at the Castle Hotel, Bridgewater.

They had booked one large bedroom on the first floor at the front of the hotel. It was a lovely room. There was a large double bed and small single for Anne, and a washbasin in the corner. A big bay window dominated the room, with maroon curtains to the floor. Hilda had brought all of the new dresses that she had made for herself and Anne. Joe was his usual immaculate self, with a new range of shirts, smart suits and casual trousers.

The gong sounded at 7 p.m. and they walked down the wide staircase. Joe was used to hotel life and quickly escorted his girls to the dining room. The head waiter showed them to a table in the bay window. The meal was superb and, afterwards, they moved into the lounge area for coffee. Most people were smoking, as it was very fashionable. This included Joe and Hilda. Joe smoked a lot more than Hilda with the stress of his job. To walk into a buyer's office and accept a cigarette quite often broke the ice between him and his customer. Anne sat next to her mother in her very pretty dress feeling very grown up and, for once, part of the adult world.

At about 10 p.m. they retired to their bedroom, which they realised was over the lounge. Anne was soon asleep, followed by Hilda and Joe. All three were deep in sleep when, suddenly, Joe shot up in bed and shouted, 'Hilda, Hilda wake up. I can smell smoke!'

He shook Hilda very hard and Hilda cried, 'What's the matter, Joe? What are you doing?'

'Quick, Hilda, quick. Get Anne. There's a fire!'

By then Hilda had jumped out of bed, grabbed her dressing gown and dragged Anne half asleep out of her bed. Anne was crying, but her mother shouted at her 'Stop that, Anne. Put on your dressing gown.' Hilda was very commanding when she wanted to be. Joe looked out of the window into darkness. Then a loud bell rang through the hotel. Hilda and Anne screamed out. Joe opened the bedroom door and realised for the first time that his family was in imminent danger. He saw that the main staircase was engulfed in flames and the smoke was coming along the corridor. Joe made a quick decision. As he had been in the ARP in the war, he knew about fire and how it behaved. So he wet three towels and put them round their heads. Meanwhile Hilda had thrown their belongings into the one overnight bag. Joe moved first, holding Anne's hand. He was holding it so hard it hurt, but Anne was far too frightened to speak. Mother put one hand on Anne's shoulder and carried the bag in the other. At that moment, there was a huge explosion and the building shook. The heat was getting intense and Joe knew it was now or never for his family. He felt the bedroom door panels and they were still cool so he slowly opened the door and, instead of turning right to the main staircase, he turned left, hoping and praying there would be another staircase.

Joe dragged his family, coughing and choking, along the corridor. The smoke was swirling all round them and visibility was getting poor, but there was the door to the stairs! Out they tumbled into the stairwell, gasping for breath. 'Don't stop!' shouted Joe to his family. 'Don't stop, keep going. Keep going, for God's sake, Hilda!' He was still holding Anne's hand, squeezing it for dear life. Anne stumbled along, crying, but having no option but to keep up with her daddy. Hilda followed them closely, pushing Anne along with the big bag, knowing she was knocking the girl in the back all the time. They started down the stairs and they could hear glass exploding above them. They kept moving down the staircase and the air seemed to be clearing.

Just then a voice shouted, 'Is there anybody up there?'

Joe shouted back, 'Yes, we're here.'

'Keep coming down and I'll met you,' shouted the strong voice. Round the corner came the firemen. Joe collapsed into their arms and they gently prised his hand off Anne's. One fireman picked Anne up and carried her downstairs. The others helped Joe and Hilda. Once outside, they sat in a little huddle, clinging to each other. Joe, Hilda and Anne just sobbed. It was 3 a.m. on Sunday morning. Joe whispered to Hilda, 'What a start to our holiday, love.'

'Never mind, Joe. We are all safe,' whispered Hilda, and she put her head on his shoulder.

When they looked up at the hotel, the whole place was in flames. They were quickly led away through the grounds. They were well looked after and their car had been driven to safety. By 7 a.m. they had changed clothes and had a little breakfast at another hotel. They were then ready to continue on their journey to Devon.

Joe said, 'We had a narrow escape, Hilda, and from now on, when I stay in a hotel, I will make sure I know where the fire escape or back staircase is before I ever sleep a wink.'

'Yes, please do that, Joe, or I will never sleep a wink when you are away travelling.' Anne sat in the back of the car and didn't say a word. Her father had saved their lives and she realised for the first time how precious life was. She really had grown up, and her memento of the awful night was one bruised hand and she didn't care one little bit. She was going to enjoy her holiday and nothing else could spoil her life now.

As they drove down the narrow country lane from Torquay to Cockington, the excitement mounted. They arrived in the little village and saw the forge on the left, and just along next to it was the cottage. It was a picture book classic, thatched roof, dormer windows, little porch and a beautiful country garden full of colourful flowers.

Anne's little bedroom was at the front; the roof swooped down to the dormer window and the view was perfect. Hilda and Joe were in the double room next to Anne. They unpacked all their suitcases and came down the steep stairs into the sitting room. There was a small table and Mrs Mullins had set out tea for them. She listened to Joe as he told her about the hotel fire, and she decided she would make a special effort for this brave family.

Mrs Mullins lived in the back of the cottage behind the kitchen. She rented out her home to help her income since her husband had died in the war. She did the meals if the holidaymakers needed them and she enjoyed company. She found people who came to her home liked it and were careful whilst they stayed there. She liked this family, but thought Mr Hornby looked tired after their bad experience. I will soon get the roses back in his cheeks again – plenty of good food and cream teas, that will do the trick, Mrs Mullins thought.

On Monday morning, the sun rose over Cockington village and Joe hugged Hilda in bed and gave her a morning kiss. He loved her dearly and to start the day with her was special to Joe, as he was usually away from her. Today was different and he hoped he would start feeling better and his old energy would return.

After a great breakfast they left the cottage and spent the morning exploring the village. By 11 a.m. the village was quite busy with holidaymakers. Anne loved the little shops and the village forge. It fascinated her, especially as all the houses were thatched. The whole place was magical to her. They bought postcards and sat in the grounds of the only hotel in Cockington and wrote to friends and family, not forgetting Nana, Rico and the Yarwoods. Anne loved her time with her father, and realised how she missed him through the days he was away travelling. They shared a love of swimming and would swim way out together over the waves and swell. Hilda sat on the beach with the piles of clothes and watched them until they were small dots. But as they were strong swimmers, in and under the water, she never had any worries. Anne shouted back to her father, 'Come o, Daddy, try and catch me!' Joe struggled on behind Anne. Either she was getting stronger or he was getting slower as he got older.

'I'm going back, Anne, come back now. That's far enough!' called Joe. Anne turned round and swam to his side, and they both swam slowly back. When Joe reached Hilda on the beach, he sat down quickly. 'My, that's puffed me out, Hilda.'

'You're getting older, not such a spring chicken now,' Hilda teased Joe and laughed at him. But she took a look at him and noticed how pale and out of breath he was. They would all benefit from this holiday, she thought.

The days passed by quickly. They had visits to Babbacombe, Odicombe and lots of little coves along the coast. They drove onto the moors and visited other little villages. Staying in the thatched cottage in Cockington made them feel special, as tourists came to the village to visit the forge and to walk around and admire the thatched cottages. They would look longingly at their cottage as Joe, Hilda and Anne sat in the front garden after a morning on the beach.

The time flew by and soon they were packing up ready to return home to Shirley. Their home would feel so large after this little cottage and Hilda was looking forward to telling Nana all about the holiday. Hopefully she had had a good time with the Yarwoods, and next year they would return to Cockington again.

When they reached home, Rico came out first to greet them. Anne gave him a big hug, then rushed inside to see her Nana. She had lots to tell her and the Yarwoods. They all sat and listened intently to her tale of the fire and their narrow escape. They were very shocked, but Joe reassured them that they were all right now and had had a wonderful holiday in Cockington.

He looked across at Hilda and their eyes met. Both realised that they had had a very narrow escape from the fire but were determined not to dwell on this for Anne and Nana's sake. The least Nana knew about that night the better.

At home, they soon returned to routine, Joe back to work, Hilda back to her sewing and Anne returning to school to start her 'O' level year. Anne did well at school and found exams easy, so she was looking forward to good 'O' levels and 'A' levels and then off to university. She didn't quite know what career she wanted, but something to do with biology and physics, her two favourite subjects, would be good. She still went to her music lessons and took exams every year. She loved her piano and played for Joe when she had learned a new piece. Chopin was her favourite composer and she preferred, for some reason, to play in flats, not sharps! Her teacher thought this very odd but as Anne was so good with her music she allowed her to choose new pieces.

Anne was now very much a young lady and started going out with her friends to a table tennis club, badminton and the youth club at the chapel she attended. She was lucky too as Hilda always made her new clothes. Joe would always pick her up at night and bring her home, and also her friends as their fathers didn't have cars.

Hilda and Joe were very protective of her; as she was an only child they were quite strict and Anne never got away with anything! She really didn't have any freedom, except the journey on the school bus with the Manchester Grammar School boys, Saturday mornings in Sale, wandering round the shops with her girlfriends, and swimming at the Sale Lido baths. She had some good girlfriends and found she was popular with the boys. What she didn't like was the way they whistled after her and called her 'Blondie'. As she didn't have brothers, Anne was not too skilful at handling moments like that. But she was growing up and although they treated her like a child at home still, there was no denying that Anne was blossoming into a young lady.

She brought her friends, boys and girls, back to Shirley where they would listen to records and play the piano. That Christmas they all helped with the post. This brought in extra money. Really they needed to be eighteen, but being short staffed as the winter was so severe, they lowered the age to sixteen. The Post Office assigned one girl or boy to each postman and they did the rounds twice a day. Your round was usually your home roads. This winter was very wet and cold and Anne would stop off at home for a change of clothes and hot soup before returning to the Post Office. It was hard work and Anne soon found out that some letterboxes were like metal traps, which would spring at your cold fingers. Dogs would also rush at the doors like wild animals. After five or six days of this, Anne was glad when it was Christmas Eve and the family went to the Palace, Manchester to see the panto, which they did every Christmas Eve.

The New Year dawned. What was in store for the family at Shirley? Joe's tiredness had persisted and the doctor had decided to send him for some tests and X-rays. Hilda and Joe said nothing to Nana and Anne and just waited for the results. Joe's loss of weight was very noticeable to others, however. Only Nana didn't seem to notice as she was with Joe all the time. Mr Yarwood did most of the manual work, allowing Joe to rest at weekends. He needed these days to recover from the five days spent travelling. Mr Marsden in Leeds made Joe stay with him through the week and Joe travelled around Leeds and surrounding places from his home. Mr Marsden, Joe's best customer, was now a close friend. He had sent a beautiful art deco silver clip to Hilda for Christmas, knowing that she loved clothes and jewellery. Having no wife himself, it gave him great pleasure, choosing it and sending it to Hilda. Hilda wore the piece on her dress collar. It was so beautiful.

The medical results and X-rays were not good. The specialist was brought in to assess Joe but his prognosis was grave. Hilda held on to Joe's hand as they sat and listened to the doctor. Hilda could not accept that there was nothing that they could do for Joe. 'Just go home and enjoy the time left together,' he said very quietly to them both. They walked out in a daze and sat in the car. Tears streamed quietly down Hilda's face and Joe sat at the wheel of the car in shock.

As they held hands, life at that moment stopped for them. The outside world carried on spinning but, for Hilda and Joe, life was frozen. They both held on to each other, not wanting to let go. Time stood still. Their world had stopped. Their safe, loving world came crashing down. The first to speak was Joe, and he picked his words carefully. Looking straight at Hilda, his eyes penetrating her inner being, he said, 'Now love, we are going to be strong and face this together. We will carry on our life for the sake of Nana and Anne,' Hilda tried to interrupt but Joe persisted. 'No, Hilda, we will carry on and put this behind us from today. We can't change anything but we can enjoy our time together.' These last few words reduced Hilda to tears again. In a few moments, Joe had become the stronger person and Hilda the weaker one. This was role reversal at a deep, personal level.

Joe and Hilda made their way home and started immediately to think about how they were going to cope with the limited future they both had together. From that point on they hardly ever mentioned Joe's conditions unless there was a doctor's appointment or Joe needed more medications. On the practical side, Joe traded in the Vauxhall 14, which was his pride and joy, for a small Morris Minor. It was easier for him to drive and he also taught Hilda to drive. His company allowed him to work when he could but on days when he felt tired he worked from home.

At weekends when Joe rested, Anne played the grand piano. She played the music he had bought for her over the years. His favourite was The Moonlight Sonata by Beethoven, and also the many pieces by Chopin. Anne loved playing Chopin best. She found his compositions easy to sight-read. His nocturnes were very peaceful and relaxing for Joe when he was in pain and the Nocturne in E flat would gently ease him to sleep. As he dozed, he could hear the music his daughter was playing in the background. What a wonderful touch she had and how easy she made the music sound. He was so glad he had bought her this fine instrument to play on.

While Anne played, Nana and Hilda sat by the fire in the kitchen. Nana looked at her daughter and saw distress in her eyes. 'What is it, love?' she said. Seldom did she use the word 'love' to Hilda.

Hilda looked up at her mother and replied, 'Oh Mother, I can't keep it secret any longer.'

'What are you talking about?' said Harriet sharply.

'It's Joe,' Hilda paused.

'What is it, what's wrong?' Harriet's body trembled, waiting for Hilda to reply. 'For God's sake what, Hilda?'

'Joe's not well, not well at all.'

'What's wrong with him?' Harriet stared at Hilda.

'He is very ill and he won't be getting better.'

'Good God, what do you mean Joe won't get better?' shouted Harriet. Her eyes glared at Hilda.

'Shush, Mother. Anne will hear you.'

'She won't hear. She's playing her piano. So please tell me.'

'Well,' said Hilda, slowly. 'The specialist said three months ago that Joe was not going to get better. No operation or treatment was possible. It had gone too far. It's all in his spine and it's only a matter of time.' Hilda's voice started to falter and her mother put her arms round her and rocked her. Hilda and Harriet sobbed their hearts out.

'My God, you have known all this time and kept it to yourself. You silly girl! Never mind, now that I know, there will be two of us to look after Joe. We won't let him go into hospital, we will nurse him together. Now Hilda, we won't tell Joe I know, it will be easier for him. And Anne must never know, not until nearer the time.'

Hilda couldn't believe how strong and caring her mother was. In the space of only a few minutes Harriet had changed from a jealous, sharp, moody, old woman into a thoughtful, caring human being. It was amazing! She knew her mother thought the world of Joe. He had looked after her and given her a home quite unselfishly. In Harriet's way, it seemed as if she was going to repay his kindness.

As the month went on, Hilda encouraged Anne to go out more with her friends, so Anne's social life continued. All her school exams were behind her and a great future lay ahead at college or university. As Joe was spending more time in bed, Hilda and Harriet took it in turns to sit with him through the night. In the evenings Hilda read aloud to him, which he enjoyed immensely.

By early spring, Joe was failing rapidly. Friends came to visit him, as he had always been popular at work and at home. But he was finding the visitors too much to cope with. The doctor came each day and gave him injections to lessen the pain. He did mention a hospital for the final weeks. But Hilda and Harriet were

The Hornby Family

adamant that they would look after him. 'We will cope, Doctor. We don't want Joe in hospital and he doesn't want to go,' said Harriet firmly.

The doctor knew Mrs Hornby well and he was confident that she and Harriet would cope with the situation. 'Well, I will come whenever you need me,' he reassured the two ladies. He admired their caring ways and knew Joe was in safe hands.

When Anne came in at night she would change into her pyjamas and wash her face. Then she would go in to see her dad. Joe always recognised her, as she looked like the little Pebble he remembered. When she was dressed up and wearing make-up, he didn't recognise her at all. He seemed to have missed the growing up stage of her life and only remembered her as 'his little girl Anne'.

Anne did not yet know that her father was very ill. She was not stupid and had overheard conversations between the doctor and her mother in hushed tones in the hall. But she couldn't face speaking about it to her mother. Perhaps it won't happen if I don't say anything, she thought. But she knew deep down it was going to happen. Daddy was going to die, she was going to lose him. He was so important to her, the only man in her life up to now, no brothers, nephews, or uncles, only Daddy, and now he was going out of her life gradually. It was too painful to contemplate, so she pushed it to the back of her mind and soldiered on. That's what her mother, Nana and Mr and Mrs Yarwood were doing, so she did the same. This was how they coped in Shirley for the remaining days. Spring was in full bud, but Joe would not be seeing the summer.

One Sunday afternoon Joe passed away peacefully with Hilda and Harriet on either side of his bed holding his hands. They had sent Anne to a neighbour's house for the afternoon. Harriet was more inconsolable than Hilda. She could not understand why God had let this lovely man die before her, when she was old and past her usefulness. And when the minister came to thank God for taking Joe into his care, Hilda told him to go. She at that moment did not want to thank God for anything. She felt lost, bitter and empty. Why had God taken this kind man? What right had the minister to want to thank God for Joe's death?

The Hornby Family

It had affected Hilda, Harriet and Anne in different ways but they supported each other through the coming days and weeks. Mr and Mrs Yarwood helped in the background; Mr Yarwood exercising Rico and looked after the garden, making it into a quiet oasis where Hilda could sit. Mrs Yarwood cooked meals for the family and Harriet was glad of her company while they cleaned and polished the house.

Harriet found that working in the house was good for her; at the end of the day she was tired out and managed to sleep. But Hilda stayed up late and read or wrote poetry to Joe, or about Joe. This comforted her, allowing her to fall asleep. Sometimes, in the morning, Harriet would find her daughter asleep in the sitting room and would have to persuade her to go to bed for a few hours.

Hilda was lost without her Joe about. She seemed to be in another world of her own. Not even Anne's presence could bring her back into reality. She barely functioned. The house and garden were there but Hilda was not part of them. Her mind was elsewhere, worrying about her future, Anne's future, their future. With little money left from their savings and five shillings a week widow's pension, Hilda knew they had to sell their only asset. However she looked at the situation, she could not support her daughter and mother and run the house.

She decided that it was time to discuss the matter. Gathering her family together in the sitting room, Harriet, Anne and Mr and Mrs Yarwood, Hilda began: 'Now I have been thinking seriously about our future and the only solution to our problems is to sell the house.'

'What? Sell Shirley? You can't, Mummy. It's our home,' cried Anne.

'Home is where we all live, Anne, not bricks and mortar. We can live in another house and that will be our home, as long as we are together,' said her mother firmly. 'Anyway, I have made the decision and Shirley will be sold. I have seen a small bungalow, which will be our new home.' Hilda emphasised the word 'home'.

'Then I can set up a business, dressmaking and tailoring, perhaps rent a shop. Nana can keep house and you, Anne, can carry on studying. I am afraid, Mr Yarwood, I will have to let you and Mrs Yarwood go, I can't afford to keep you on any longer,' Hilda looked sadly at the loyal couple.

'That's no problem, Mrs Hornby, we knew this would happen and we will find some other work one day. You must look after your family first,' said Mr Yarwood. Mrs Yarwood nodded her head strongly and agreed with him. It had been a tragedy, Mr Hornby's death, such a lovely man and a wonderful employer. But life moves on and they knew that such things did happen. She and Mr Yarwood would survive it. Worse things happen at sea, she thought.

So Shirley was put up for sale and Hilda spoke to the owners of the bungalow. She was a great planner and had made lists of all the furniture that she would sell from Shirley and the furniture that she would take to the bungalow. This planning kept her busy and took her mind off Joe. She noticed that Anne had started to go out again with her friends but had not played the piano. When she asked her why, Anne just said, 'I played for Daddy. He's not here any more,' and walked away. Hilda did not press her, thinking that when they moved she might play again. But Anne knew that she wouldn't play for years to come.

On the day that the estate agent, Mr Farnham, called, Hilda's heart sank. Had he found a buyer? Would they be going? If they moved, would Joe's memory come with her? This worried her. But Mr Farnham took her breath away by saying that he and his wife, Joyce, would like to buy the house themselves.

He went on to say that he would give Hilda the asking price, which was considerably higher than the valuation. But he wanted the house. He and his wife had set their heart on Shirley years ago, but they never thought the house would come on the market. Mr Farnham's company had handled a lot of large properties in the area over the years but he had always liked Shirley. As he drove around on business, he would pause in the car and gaze at Shirley. 'What a beautifully built house. So graceful and well proportioned. One day,' he had pondered, 'one day.'

Hilda had broken the news to her family, they accepted her decision without arguing. Hilda, being a good planner, listed the furniture she could sell to the new owner. She liked the idea of these pieces staying at Shirley – they belonged to the house, not with her.

The next few weeks were frantic, sorting out and packing up. But the worst moments were going through Joe's clothes and belongings. She and Nana conquered this horrible job between them and, at long last, their possessions were ready to move. Anne did little to help, a typical teenager, she floated along, still going out with her friends and only concerned that their new home was near to them.

Removal day dawned and Hilda was up early, stripping the beds for the final time. As she left her and Joe's bedroom, she looked around, 'Oh Joe, what a wonderful life we had here, I still love you so much and miss you. But I am moving to our new home and you are coming with me in my thoughts and in my heart. I know you are there all the time, it's as though you are just around every corner. I can't see you but I feel you there watching over me. There is only one man for me – my Joe – so I won't be looking for anybody else. I have had the best husband in the world and that is how I feel.' With that, Hilda walked firmly out of the bedroom, down the stairs, and into her new life.

The House

This is not an exciting day for me. I feel sad and low. Over the years, I had settled to life with the Hornbys. What a lovely family! From the day they moved in I loved them. It took a little time to love Mrs Johnson, Harriet, as I found her very difficult, but soon I understood her. Her heart was in the right place and, after a few months, I even started to like her.

She and Mrs Yarwood would scrub and polish every inch of me. My wooden panelling in the dining room and hall was a credit to them. 'Cleanliness is next to godliness,' Harriet would say as she polished the brasses and silver. I was well cared for by the family and well maintained by Mr Yarwood. It was a labour of love for him to care for my paintwork and to tend to my gardens.

I felt so full of energy over the years with little Anne, skipping and running around everywhere. She would run up and down the stairs, always jumping the last steps onto the hall rug. What a joy it was to see her change into a young lady. Her room was full of clothes and posters of film stars.

The family didn't change anything structural on my building or inside me. I was very thankful for that as the building process in the Twenties was enough for me. I found it very tiring, all that banging and knocking. I liked a peaceful life where possible because I was a mature house. I didn't want to be a modern house. Leave that to the new boxes they were building. My builder was of the old school. In fact you could call me a majestic house, solid, dependable, stately? Well no, perhaps I am getting carried away. Anyhow, my family loved me. They loved living here and it was a sad day when they left me. What a tragedy when Joe, I mean Mr Hornby, died! The heartbeat went out of me that day and it did not come back. Hilda, Harriet and Anne just survived inside me. I kept them safe for Joe until the time came for them to move on. It was sad for me when they closed my windows and my big front door for the last time. I looked down on them as they walked down my path. Hilda was the only one to look up at me and, if I could, I would have told her that she would find happiness and contentment in her life ahead.

So here I am, empty again. I suppose I can rest for a while until my new owners arrive. What will they be like? Will I like them? Will they like me? I shall have to wait a few days until they come, so I shall rest and sleep.

The Farnham Family

Chapter One

'Girls, will you all come downstairs. The removal van will be here any moment and all your things are cluttering up the hallway!' shouted Richard Farnham. He was standing in the middle of the big hall, looking up the staircase. Today was the culmination of years of hard work. He was secretly excited to be moving into Shirley, but he would not let it show. Richard Farnham always stayed cool and collected on the outside, smartly dressed in suit, collar and tie, even though it was removal day.

'Please come down *now*,' he pleaded. He could hear his blonde-haired daughters chattering upstairs and his patience was wearing thin. He went into the porch and looked out and saw the large removal van reversing into the drive of Shirley. As he went back into the house, the girls came flying down the stairs. 'Can you move all this stuff out of the way quickly,' Richard said to them.

'OK Dad,' they replied and started picking up their belongings. Fully loaded, they made their way upstairs. 'We have just been deciding on bedrooms. You and Mum can have the large bedroom at the back and we have chosen our own,' they called over their shoulders as they went upstairs.

'Oh, thank you,' he replied. He was used to his daughters. They loved him dearly but they could be a bit flippant at times. The eldest girl, Judith, was very extrovert. She was happy-go-lucky, brimming over with fun with not a serious bone in her body. She would be twenty-one later on in the year and looked forward to her party. It would be marvellous in this big house and she could invite all her friends from home and work.

She had had various jobs. Not taking work seriously had been a problem for Judith, so she had ended up working for her father and mother in the family estate agency business. Here she worked on reception, answering the phone and greeting people as they came in. Her one forte was that she was excellent with people. Her warm, friendly attitude was an asset in the office, putting clients at ease and able to find out what they were looking for instantly. People warmed to Judith; at last she had found a niche for herself in the world of work.

Her younger sister June was far more serious and wanted to be a nurse. She worked hard at school and had now become a student nurse at the nearby hospital. She loved every minute of her work there and liked to regale her family with gory stories round the dinner table in the evenings. At the moment she lived at home. Perhaps in the future she might live in the hospital, but for now she loved being with the family.

As Judith and June fled upstairs, their mother, Joyce, came down. 'Right now, Richard, calm down, we are all ready,' said Joyce quickly. 'I will get the kettle on and make the men their first brew,' she said.

'Not yet, Joyce. They haven't started,' called Richard.

'Well, if they have it now they will work faster,' she called from the kitchen. Joyce was as excited as Richard about the house. It was very grand and she knew they would be very happy here. Secretly, she knew what needed doing to the house – certain areas needed upgrading.

Joyce worked with her husband in the business and went out to the various properties to show people around. This enabled her to find inspiration from other people's homes, which she hoped to implement in Shirley. Her mind was in a whirl, plotting and planning a new kitchen, a new bathroom, redecorating – the list was endless. When she emerged from the kitchen with her tray of tea, the first packing cases were coming in through the front door.

Richard was directing the men to the different rooms and everything was going smoothly. The one thing that Joyce was good at was organisation. They had moved several times in their married life, making good profits along the way. But this house she hoped would be their last move. She hoped both daughters would marry in the lovely church in the village. Joyce had this all mapped out in her mind but today, practical things were to be done so she moved into the main part of the house to help Richard.

Joyce loved the sitting room, and the new three-piece suite, which she had ordered, was just the right colour and size for the room. She was so pleased that Richard had bought the larger pieces of furniture from Mrs Hornby. The dining room suite was extremely grand and suited the panelled room to perfection. The only thing Joyce had insisted on was that they all had new beds, and these were being delivered today. Once they had arrived, the old ones would go. But she had decided to keep all the wardrobes and dressing tables. She thought they were in keeping with the age of the house and she knew that they were of good quality.

Tomorrow she would meet up with Mr and Mrs Yarwood. They would be essential to their working life. Richard had said that they would employ help, as the size of the house and garden would be too much with the family business. She hoped she would get on with Mrs Yarwood as Mrs Hornby spoke so highly of her. The sale of Shirley had, in a way, been a sad affair – sad for Mrs Hornby and her family. But Joyce Farnham had been very sympathetic and knowing their circumstances had helped the sale along. She knew Mrs Hornby had been well pleased when Richard had decided to buy the house himself and that enabled the estate agent to stop all viewing. Joyce knew it was a very trying time for families when there had been a bereavement. As an estate agent she had an insight into people's feelings, whether it was death, divorce or just the stress of moving. She and Richard were always very sympathetic to clients and this had been their main strength, which had brought great success to the family business. All these thoughts were whirling round her head, as she busied herself with the unpacking. Move in first, meet the Yarwoods, settle in and then reorganise the house. Yes, it was all there in her head.

Joyce ran upstairs to see how the girls were settling in. Judith, though the eldest, had chosen the smaller of the two bedrooms at the back of the house. You could tell from the decor that this had been the daughter's bedroom. Judith always chose the smallest room. She liked a cosy bedroom and this enabled June, the youngest, to have the large front bedroom. June was happy with this room as it was over the dining room and at night would be quiet for studying. The spare bedroom over the hall would be kept for the occasional guest.

Joyce looked into the bathroom. What a ghastly colour that is, she thought to herself. We'll have to change that, can't live with that. They settled in that night as best they could, looking forward to their lives at Shirley.

In the morning Mr and Mrs Yarwood called round and the whole family introduced themselves to the couple. Joyce Farnham thought the Yarwoods were a lovely couple, the salt of the earth, as her father would say. She would have no problem leaving the running of the house to them. Mrs Yarwood would concentrate on tidying and cleaning the home, as she would prepare and cook the evening meal herself. As they owned the business, Joyce could leave early and do this easily. Mr Yarwood would continue with the gardening as she could see he loved working there.

'Monday to Friday, is that all right for you both?' she asked brightly.

'Yes, Mrs Farnham. We will both be pleased to carry on working here, thank you Ma'am,' Mrs Yarwood replied.

'I think we could talk of an increase in your wages, as there are four of us and we are out all days so there is no help for you,' she said to them both.

'Oh thank you. That would be grand. Thank you,' said Mr Yarwood.

'Also, if you find there is too much for you in the house, perhaps we could get a young village girl to help?' asked Mrs Farnham.

Mrs Yarwood couldn't help but think of Maisie. It was over twenty years since Maisie had left to have the baby and she and Mr Yarwood were getting on now too. But she could still cope with work. She knew Shirley inside out and she would miss the old lady, Nana as they had called her, but she didn't want to start with a new girl. She would carry on, on her own, with Mr Yarwood helping if she needed heavy furniture moved. Shirley was their life. They loved looking after the house and garden and with the family out all day they could cope on their own.

Chapter Two

The family estate agency was a thriving business. Richard Farnham was a qualified estate agent and surveyor. He had initials after his name, FRICS. He was a Fellow of the Royal Institute of Chartered Surveyors, and he was rightly proud of his achievement. His letter headings and all correspondence included his name plus the letters for all to see. He had studied hard and passed all the examinations. He could remember the day he qualified as though it were yesterday. He had built up the business through hard work and was very proud of his office. It was large and modern and was situated in the middle of the town. He had a small amount of competition from other estate agents but they were more old fashioned than him. With Joyce helping with the clients and owners, and Judith at the front desk, he had a good team. He was also very friendly with the local solicitor, Mr Wright, who he used for the conveyance of the properties. In return, Mr Wright gave him any rented properties to look after. Richard and Mr Wright worked well together and were also members of the same golf club. Golf was Richard's passion. It helped him to relax and also was good for business. Richard thought golf was the right image for him and, as his image was important to him, he strived to be a low-handicap golfer.

The right house, the right car, the right clothes, three beautiful girls – he always classed Joyce as one of his girls – he portrayed the correct image to all his contacts. He was also trying hard to get Joyce to take up golf. Then they could enjoy the social scene at the club. For now, they attended all the functions and Joyce mixed easily with the other wives. But he really wanted her to play golf and to have the other lady golfers as friends. At the moment though, Joyce's mind was far from the golf course. She was more concerned with the decor. Once Shirley was to her liking she secretly thought that she might start golf lessons to please Richard.

When he came in at night he would call, 'Where're my three Js?' for that's what he called the girls. He didn't mind living in a female household; in fact he rather enjoyed the atmosphere. There was always lots of gossip at the dinner table and his two daughters helped Joyce with serving and washing up. This enabled him to retreat into the sitting room and read his paper. He was never asked to do any household chores and this suited him. He hardly ever went into the kitchen. Washing and ironing were alien to him. He was the man in the house and they looked after him. The whole house ran smoothly. He loved this house. This was their family home from now on.

One morning, Judith and June came down for breakfast, whispering to each other. 'What's going on, you two?' said their father.

'Well, we wondered if we could join the local tennis club?' asked Judith. She was always the spokeswoman for the two. 'You see, we both played at school and it would be nice to go down and have a game. What do you think, Dad?' she continued.

'Yes, I think that could be a good idea, and it would be good for June to get some fresh air after the hospital atmosphere,' he replied.

'That means tennis outfits and racquets, you know,' said Mother.

'Well, if they meet nice people, I think it's a good idea. On the other hand, you could always join the golf club,' he beamed at them.

'Oh Daddy,' said June, 'not golf again. They are all stuffy there,' she laughed.

'All right, the tennis club then,' said Richard. 'Make enquiries, cycle down on Saturday and find out what it costs.' Joyce also thought this was a good idea for the girls. She secretly hoped they would meet two suitable young men and they would be off her hands.

Joyce threw herself into renovating Shirley. Although she loved the house, certain rooms needed attention. Through her work at the estate agent's she knew some good, reliable tradesmen, so she set to in her usual organised way. The only thing Richard had said was to install heating and get rid of the old range. So the whole of Shirley's furniture was shrouded in dust sheets, the carpets were rolled up and work began. The house bustled with workmen. Mrs Yarwood did not seem to mind the intrusion as she knew most of the young men from the village and enjoyed their company. For months she had no cleaning to do, her only job being to keep an eye on the men in case they did any unintended damage to Shirley, and brewing the tea in large mugs for them all day. When the dust and noise got too much for her, she joined her husband in the garden. The biggest job was taking out the old range. This was a massive task as it was huge and very heavy. All of the men took a hand and out it came. In its place stood a lovely new Aga.

'What on earth is this, Mrs Farnham?' inquired Mr and Mrs Yarwood. They both stood in front of the Aga, looking at it.

'Well, it's a special type of oven. In the brochure that came with it, it says that it bakes, grills, braises, boils, roasts, stews, steams, simmers, toasts and fries,' said Mrs Farnham with a smile.

'Well, I never,' said Mrs Yarwood, looking suspiciously at the monster in front of her.

'But whether I shall use it remains to be seen. Perhaps on Christmas Day for the turkey, and at weekends, but during the week I shall use the conventional cooker. Mr Yarwood, you will have to stoke it up all the time like the boiler, as it will heat the kitchen. So make sure you have adequate fuel from Scraggs,' she said. 'I think in the summer months we will let it go out though, as it will be far too hot in here.'

The plumbers tackled the heating. They installed a large solid fuel boiler in the wash house next to the kitchen and started running pipes through the house for the radiators. These were large radiators, one in each room. 'Dust gatherers', Mrs Yarwood called them, but you had to move with the times, she would say. The carpenters installed cupboards in the large kitchen, but worked around the dresser, as Joyce wanted that kept in the kitchen. She had ordered a new gas stove and a large refrigerator, which was to stand in the pantry. In the wash house next to the boiler was the new washing machine, a big, tub-shaped thing with electric rollers. This machine fascinated Mrs Yarwood and she couldn't wait to see it working. She still hand washed all their clothes in tubs and used a mangle in the backyard. All this new equipment was to be an eye-opener for Mrs Yarwood. She would have lots to talk about down in the village.

The next job for the plumbers was the bathroom. Joyce had chosen a light blue suite and blue tiles with a black border halfway up the wall. A lot of people had green, but she decided on pale blue; very modern, she thought. Downstairs 'Pink lady', as the toilet in the cloakroom was always called, was changed to pale blue. Joyce noticed that the carpets in the lounge and dining room were edged with deep blue and a lot of the floral furnishings had blues and pinks in them. As they were of such good quality, she decided to economise here and just have them cleaned. It seemed as though the house had been in a time warp – these were hardly worn.

Richard drew the line at panelling the doors out and boxing in the spindles of the staircase. 'It might be modern, dear, but Shirley is traditional and I will not have these fine doors and this magnificent staircase boxed in and that's final,' he exclaimed. Joyce knew when she was defeated, having lived and worked with her husband, and, although she could usually get her own way, sometimes he was immoveable. So the doors and staircase remained, but she did manage to wheedle out of him a new fitted carpet for the hall, stairs and landing.

After all the workmen had left, Mrs Yarwood and two female friends came and cleaned Shirley, top to bottom, ready for the decorators to move in.

After a month, Shirley's new interior was complete. Curtains and carpets were returned to their place, furniture was polished and everything shone again.

'At last,' sighed Mrs Yarwood, 'I have got the house back to normal.' She took great pride in her work, and Mrs Farnham recognised this and rewarded her and Mr Yarwood with two weeks' holiday with pay, and a little extra, as a thank you.

When Richard came home from his office he always felt proud as he entered Shirley's hall. 'This is a wonderful house,' he said to himself, 'a wonderful house.'

Judith and June just floated along while all this work was in progress. Judith was out a lot with her friends and June sometimes stayed at the hospital to escape all the upheaval. She had a lot of studying to do and needed peace and quiet. The work came easily to her and she flew through her examination. Her friends were mostly from the hospital and she enjoyed their gossip and chatter.

Judith, on the other hand, had kept most of her friends from school and met them for coffee and went to the cinema and dances with them. She did not fit in with June's friends as they were always talking about medical matters and she was quite squeamish. But they did meet down at the tennis club and developed their doubles game together. The club had social evenings and Judith and June would dance all night. They were never short of partners, but nothing serious ever came of this.

Joyce despaired of the pair of them. Perhaps June was too young to settle yet and she had her career to follow, but Judith just seemed to work hard and play hard. 'Oh, well, one day perhaps,' mused Joyce, but she never voiced her worries to the girls.

The business, meanwhile, was thriving and their reputation was excellent in the town, due to Richard's good business head and Joyce's skills in handling people. The houses that they had to sell never had similar circumstances. Some people were expanding their families and so needed a larger property, others had families who had grown up and needed smaller homes. With others there had been a death or, very rarely, a divorce, although they were handling more houses where the couple were splitting up. These latter circumstances could be very upsetting and Joyce was excellent at coping with the owners. Then there were couples moving into the area for work or family reasons, and others moving out.

It was like one giant merry-go-round, with the Farnham's Estate Agents controlling it. Most times, the sales went through and people were pleased with the handling of their property, but occasionally things went awry, sometimes due to the owners, sometimes due to the solicitors. But the bottom line was that selling or buying was most people's biggest financial investment. It was a stressful and not always happy time, and all the Farnhams could do was help the process along as best they could.

Judith took all the phone calls first and decided whether to pass them on to her father or mother. She was good at her job, calm, efficient and helpful. The number of times she had said, 'Farnham's Estate Agents. Can I help you?' she did not know, but sometimes through the night she could still hear herself saying that sentence.

'Judith,' called her father from the inner office, 'Where's your mother?'

'I think she has nipped home, to see to the delivery of the lounge suite,' called Judith.

'Oh, has she? Mrs Yarwood could have done that,' he said quickly.

'Well, you know Mummy. She will want to place it in the sitting room correctly,' laughed Judith.

'All right, well, you will have to go and meet Mr Cartwright and show him round the Victorian semi in Spring Road. Take the keys, the owners are at work. The appointment is 2 p.m. so go now. Take my car. Here are the keys. Hurry now. I think Mother has forgotten this appointment. It's not good enough,' snapped her father.

'It's all right. I'll do it. Mr Cartwright, you said? I know the house,' Judith replied.

'Have you got the house keys and details, Judith?' shouted her father again.

'Yes, yes I'm off now. Bye!' And with that, Judith went out of the back door of the house into the yard where the cars were parked. Judith drove fast to the appointment. He does go on so, she thought, I wonder if it was a good idea to work in a family business. He would not be able to shout at an employee like that; they would walk out, she considered. Poor Mummy, working hard in the office and running the home as well. It is all right for him. He has only the business to think of. Perhaps I will look for another job? She pondered this for a moment, but knew that with no qualifications she could not get the wages and the use of a car that her father gave her.

As she pulled into Spring Road she saw Mr Cartwright standing next to his car outside the house. She jumped out of her car and introduced herself. She was never nervous meeting strangers, and launched into her sales talk about the qualities of this Victorian semi, as they let themselves into the house.

She and Mr Cartwright toured downstairs first, during which time she managed to find out that he had been moved into the area by the bank he worked for. Judith was at once optimistic about this, as she knew that bank employees could get good mortgage rates and this helped the sale through. He was moving on his own and this was quite a large house. Judith guessed he was at a managerial level at the bank. Everything looked promising, so they started up the stairs. Just then, as they reached the landing, out from the front bedroom came a large Alsatian dog. They literally fell into the middle bedroom and Judith shut the door quickly behind them.

Mr Cartwright looked sternly at Judith and said, 'Well, young lady, now what do you propose to do? I do not like dogs and I have never liked dogs, so what are you going to do?'

Judith just stood. Her confidence started to drain away. 'I don't know at the minute, Mr Cartwright.'

'Well, you had better think fast, young lady,' whispered Mr Cartwright, convinced that the large and frightening dog was right on the other side of the door. Judith put her ear to the door and listened. She could hear the dog breathing. What could she do? They couldn't stay in the bedroom until the owners came home.

This was a dilemma, a huge dilemma. Mr Cartwright was getting very agitated. 'I have to get back to work, young lady,' he said.

If he calls me young lady once more I shall hit him, thought Judith. 'Be patient, Mr Cartwright. Hush, let's listen through the door,' she pleaded instead. The pair of them listened and suddenly they heard the dog padding back to the front bedroom.

'Thank God,' whispered the man. He could hardly speak.

Judith's heart was pounding. What next? she thought. 'Right, now we must move quickly,' she heard herself say, bravely. 'Out of the door, turn left down the stairs and out of the front door. Don't look back and I will be right behind you, Mr Cartwright,' she whispered.

She opened the door gingerly and peeped out to the right where the dog had come from. 'Now, move now.' She pushed him out onto the landing and they moved swiftly to the head of the stairs. They both stumbled quickly down and out through the front door. Judith shut the door firmly and looked at Mr Cartwright. He was deathly white. 'That's it, Miss Farnham. I never want to see or hear from you again. You put me in great danger. Good day to you,' and with that he marched over to his car and drove off.

Judith leaned on the front door and tried to calm herself down. That had been a very nasty situation. Wait until she got back to the office. Heads would roll.

She barged into the back door of the office and screamed at her father and mother. 'Why didn't you tell me that there was a bloody big Alsatian in that house? We nearly got attacked! He was on guard there and we went in!'

Her mother looked at her in horror. 'What? You went to Spring Road? Didn't you look in the folder, Richard? It mentions an Alsatian and not to go if the owners are at work. I know I made a special note!' demanded her mother.

'Well, I didn't know, did I? And you weren't here, and we were late for the appointment,' replied Richard bravely.

'That doesn't matter. You should have looked, not sent the girl out willy-nilly. See, here it says in red ink: "Large Alsatian dog in house on guard. Do not enter unless owners are present". I daren't tell you its name,' paused Joyce.

'Go on, Mother. What is it?' asked Judith.

'Its name is Tiger.'

At that moment there was a deathly hush, then they all burst into laughter. 'Poor Mr Cartwright! Well, we won't be selling him a house, will we?' chuckled Judith.

When they all came home at night they tried not to talk 'shop' as Joyce did not feel it was fair on June. Instead, if she was home for dinner, they would listen to her day and she could unburden her worries and sometimes her sadness with them. She was only young but had to deal with traumatic situations and death. Through the week she had been telling them about an old man she was nursing. He was very ill and had no relatives to visit him. June had got quite attached to him and he called her his 'little angel'. June knew he would not get better, but when he eventually died it shook her. She had not seen anyone die before, and although his death was peaceful, it affected her greatly. She had held his hand, right up to the end, and talked to him, as Sister had said that the last faculty to go was hearing. So June was convinced that he could hear her voice as he started on his last journey. June had been dreading this event but was amazed how peaceful his end was. She even helped to prepare him and put his photograph of his beloved wife with him as they took him away to the mortuary. Sister commended her for her caring attitude through the day but it still drained June, and she was in need of some care and loving herself when she came home.

The family listened to her in silence round the table and they all said how proud they were of her and wished they could have met 'her old man'. Joyce made sure that June got out of her system all the feelings, hoping it would help for her future in nursing. Joyce also realised for the first time that there was a lot of joy in nursing, but there was also a lot of sadness. June, being young, would have to walk this road, but today was the first step towards making her a sympathetic and efficient nurse.

That evening they retired into the sitting room and watched television. It had been quite a day for all members of the Farnham family, but for now they were all safe in Shirley.

Chapter Three

Through the months, the house was like a well-oiled machine. Mr Yarwood tended to the garden and vegetable plot and would get extra help from the village if needed. Mrs Yarwood kept the house clean and tidy. She didn't have anything to do with the meals as Mrs Farnham and the girls did these. So her day comprised dusting and polishing, which she loved. Sometimes she would think back to her days here with Nana and Maisie. She still missed them, but life changes.

Mrs Farnham kept a watchful eye on her, as she was getting older now. Both Mr and Mrs Yarwood did manual jobs and she worried that they were getting on, so she always suggested extra help if the need arose.

She knew that Shirley was the old couple's life. Having no family of their own, they seemed to adopt each family they worked for. They were loyal and adaptable to their families and Mrs Farnham would not dream of replacing them. It was up to them to decide when they would retire.

Through the summer, the family enjoyed the garden. They put up a net and had games of badminton on the lawn. They played croquet as the lawn was so smooth and flat due to Mr Yarwood's attention. The girls would cycle off to the tennis club looking very fetching in their white tennis frocks, and Richard would go to golf. It was only a nine-hole course, but Richard enjoyed playing there with his friend Frank Wright, the solicitor. Richard had worked hard on his handicap and had got it down to four. His friend was on six, so they were quite balanced in their play and had good, competitive games. When they played as a pair, they were hard to beat. Richard was very competitive and was always out to win. If he was successful he would come home in a good mood. He spent a lot on his clubs and golf clothes so as to make sure the other members knew how successful he was in business. Being a member there was very important to Richard and in the summer he would play as much as possible.

Saturday morning dawned and it promised to be a warm spring day. Richard had arranged to meet Frank at 8.30 a.m. at the club as their teeing off time was 8.50 a.m. To golfers timing was very important, so he was up early to prepare for the game. Dressed in his smart checked trousers and polo neck sweater, Richard said goodbye to his wife and daughters and set off for the golf club.

Joyce and the girls quite enjoyed the days when Richard went off to play golf as they could have a lazy day pottering around the house. Sometimes the girls would go off to the shops and meet some of their young friends, leaving Joyce to relax and read her magazines. These were precious moments for Joyce, as working with Richard plus running the house was tiring. The added responsibility of their daughters' welfare stretched her to the limits sometimes. So she was very pleased to have a few hours to herself, and the thought of hacking round a golf course filled her with horror.

As Richard arrived at the golf club and parked his car, he saw Frank unloading his clubs and clothes from the back of his car. Frank was never late. As a solicitor he was extremely punctual and precise in his manner.

'Good morning, young man,' he called to Richard. This was his usual greeting although they were of a similar age.

'Good morning, Frank. In good form this morning, I hope?' enquired Richard.

'Yes, fighting fit, old chap,' replied Frank. 'Who are we playing against today?'

'Oh a couple off ten, I think,' said Richard.

'Well, we should thrash them, so let's get going,' said Frank.

By now they had changed into their golf shoes, assembled their trolleys and started walking towards the club. They always took with them a change of clothes for after the game. The club rules were very strictly controlled by the Honorary Secretary, Colonel Braithwaite. After a game the players would have a shower, change into jacket and tie and meet for a drink in the lounge. This was always strictly adhered to – the whole club was run with military precision. All members of the club were given a book of rules when they joined. Membership was difficult as the committee controlled the club and if your face did not fit or you had not got sponsorship from other members, your application was turned down. Both Richard and Frank had entered the club's membership at the first application and were very keen to become committee members in the future.

As they walked towards the pro's hut, Frank asked Richard about his week. 'Oh, not bad Frank, sold a few and have some new properties on. It always quickens up in spring, thank goodness. You been busy this week?' he enquired.

'Yes, quite busy, old chap. The usual, house conveyance, wills, legal bits and pieces. We never have a slack time, just a steady flow of work. I'm thinking of taking on a young man to train up. What do you think?' asked Frank.

'Good idea. I was wondering the same. Joyce is fine but she has a lot to do and a young man to help with the workload may be the answer.' By now they had arrived at the pro hut and went inside to pay their ten shillings. They both liked the young pro and would often have lessons from him in the evenings to improve their game.

Today was an important day. It was the Elizabeth Cup. Both were desperate to win this cup as they would get their names on the trophy board in the clubhouse. The prizes were incidental to them but the accolade was the most important thing. They checked the list of players in the hut and moved out on to the first tee. They shook hands with the opposition. Richard whispered to Frank, 'Let battle commence', and winked at Frank.

Frank made a superb shot off the first tee, about 200 yards. Then Richard drove off and his ball went over 210 yards. They both smiled to each other as if to say to the others, 'Follow that if you can.' Although they had to give shots to their opponents, Frank and Richard had a magical round and their opponents congratulated them. 'You both stand a good chance of the cup with that score,' they conceded.

All four retired to the locker room, showered and changed. When they entered the members' lounge, Richard bought drinks for them all and they sat together and discussed the game. Richard was in his element at the golf club. He loved the company of other men, being surrounded by female company at home. He loved to escape and golf gave him the opportunity. He also knew that mixing with the other members was good for business, so he was always buying drinks for his fellow members. Most of the older members were of the old school type, running family businesses passed down through the generations, but they tolerated the new breed of businessmen; they knew that the golf club needed new blood. Although they still kept tight control of the membership, Richard and Frank were welcomed politely and courteously, but woe betide them if they infringed the rules! They would have the colonel to deal with. Richard and Frank stayed for lunch at the club and kept a wary eye on the leader board. Secretly they were getting excited as the weather had changed and was getting quite windy. The weather conditions for them had been excellent, but now it was more of a challenge. At 5 p.m. they left the club, returned to their homes, and waited anxiously for the phone call from the pro.

Just after 6 p.m., Richard received the call from the club pro to tell him that he and Frank had won the Elizabeth Cup and would they come back to receive the prize. Richard phoned Frank and he was so excited that he could hardly get his words out.

'Well done, Daddy,' called his girls and gave him a big kiss as he dashed out to his car.

Off he went to meet Frank in the car park. They shook hands and clapped each other on the back. Inside the members were waiting and gave them a standing ovation as they walked in. At that split second Richard wished Joyce could have been there to see the response from the club members.

They received the Elizabeth Cup and also six cut glass tumblers and a decanter each. A speech was in order and, for once, Richard allowed Frank to take over and he made the acceptance speech for them both. Frank was an accomplished speaker, very correct in his delivery, being a member of the legal profession. When he had finished, the club members applauded them.

'Well done, Frank, that's the first of many, old chap,' Richard whispered.

'Too true,' nodded Frank, 'the first of many, old chap.'

When Richard arrived back at Shirley, Joyce and the girls were as excited as he was. 'It's a lovely big silver cup,' he said proudly.

'Shall we have it at home?' asked Joyce.

'Oh, no, it is displayed in a trophy cabinet at the golf club. It will be engraved with my name and Frank's and the year. It's a very important trophy and this year it's ours!' he said triumphantly.

'Wonderful,' said Joyce, 'and I love this decanter and glasses. Richard, you must put in some good whisky and we will put it in the sideboard in the dining room. Well done, dear.'

'Also, Joyce, our names will go on the trophy board for winning the Elizabeth Cup. That is in the lounge, so when that is done I will take you all for lunch on a Sunday so you can see it,' said Richard proudly. He was so cock-a-hoop with himself that he never asked Joyce and the girls what they had done with their day. But that was Richard, full of himself and his world.

On Monday morning, he called Joyce and Judith into his office and informed them that he was advertising for a young man to start and train in the estate agency business. 'I've been thinking that we could do with an extra pair of hands,' he announced. He did not mention that this was also Frank's intention. 'A young man who would like to take it up as a career,' he said.

'Not too young, Richard,' said Joyce.

'No, someone out of university, about twenty-two, what do you think?'

'Yes, that's the right age. We need somebody that people will trust and take to,' said Joyce.

'Yes, Daddy, somebody good looking and dishy, I would say,' laughed Judith. The advertisement went in the local paper and they received nine replies. Joyce sorted through them and chose four to come in for interviews. She would have liked to do the interviewing but she did not stand a chance. Richard laid claim to this job and the next week the interviewees were lined up.

As they came in morning and afternoon over the next two days, Judith greeted them first. In her mind she vetted them on overall appearance, their handshake and their speaking voice and whether or not she fancied them. She made little notes from A to D and kept them in her desk drawer. C was definitely her choice. A young man, not too tall, well-built, dark, wavy hair but lovely deep eyes. She called them 'bed eyes'. Yes, he was definitely her choice, they would work well together, she was sure of that, and her own eyes sparkled. But she could hear her father's voice drone on and on about the business and each candidate would come out of his room exhausted after the interrogation. Oh, Daddy, just leave it to me, thought Judith. But Richard persisted for two days, loving to hear the sound of his own voice.

At the end of the two days, Richard still had not decided which of the four was suitable. So he invited the first and the third young men back for further talks. Joyce and Judith secretly thought that Richard was enjoying the power he had, knowing the boys were keen to be employed. After another full day of interviewing, Richard finally decided on the third one.

So he announced at the dinner table that Peter Barker would be joining the firm next Monday. 'My choice, C,' Judith whispered to June.

'What did you say?' asked Richard.

'Nothing, Daddy,' replied Judith.

'Well, as I was saying, Peter Barker will be joining us on Monday. He went to Manchester University and has a degree in the arts, but wants to get into business instead. He is intelligent and his family lives locally, so he knows the area well. He also plays golf. He is well connected as his father is a local magistrate and I think he will fit in. What do you think, dear?' asked Richard.

'Well, if I had been able to sit in on his second interview, I might be in a better position to answer that,' retorted Joyce. 'More potato, Richard?' she asked cheekily.

June was intrigued by this new man in the firm. She thought Judith lucky to be working there. Although she would hate office work and would find it boring, she secretly envied her elder sister because she could dress up and wear make-up for work. She, on the other hand, had to wear uniform, flat shoes, her blond hair tied back and no make-up. She never looked her best when a nice, dishy young doctor arrived on the ward. But her work made up for all that and she would not swap her career for Judith's job. She often thought how shallow the commercial world was against hers. Her dedication shone and she got her rewards seeing her patients recover and go home. The gratitude of the relatives and friends was enough for her. She so adored her job and nothing would stand in her way to qualify in her chosen profession.

Monday morning dawned and Judith dressed carefully. Today was the day that Peter Barker started with the firm. First impressions are important, so Judith spent longer on her blonde hair and make-up. Just a dab of Chanel No. 5 behind her ears and she was ready.

He spent his first week with Judith, watching and listening to her taking calls, making appointments and dealing with clients when they came in. He thought she was a gorgeous girl, but he had to keep his hands off her as she was the boss's daughter.

As the months progressed, the Farnhams wondered how they had managed without Peter. He was a quick learner and fitted in well with their family business. They never made him feel an outsider, just one of the family, and this pleased him. As his confidence grew he helped Mrs Farnham with the viewings, but he always left the negotiations to Mr Farnham. He found the studying easy and quickly started passing his examinations to become a qualified estate agent. He was very professional when in Mr Farnham's company, very charming and efficient in Mrs Farnham's company and a little bit flirty with Judith. Peter had all the qualities of an estate agent in the making.

Much to Judith's surprise, he joined their tennis club and at weekends played matches there. Occasionally, when Frank was otherwise occupied, Richard would invite Peter to join him in a game of golf. Peter had only been playing a few years and was impressed by his boss's handicap and play. He also noticed his name on the trophy board and engraved on a rather large cup in the display cabinet.

The girls soon found out that Peter had a large circle of friends locally, so they started to get invited to social functions and, as the winter months drew in, their social calendar started to fill up. June always tried her hardest to have the time off for these events as she had her eye on a younger member of Peter's group. Fortunately Judith and June liked quite different types of young men so they never fell out over their choices. In fact, they helped each other and these poor young men did not know what had hit them before they were snared!

Chapter Four

Life rolled on at Shirley for the Farnham family. Year by year the family business thrived. June started passing her nurse's examinations with flying colours and Joyce had more free time with the arrival of Peter. She occasionally had a day off in the week and loved spending it at home with Mr and Mrs Yarwood. She found them to be a lovely couple, who were dedicated to Shirley, and it was very nice to hear them talk about their lives over the years working at the house. She heard all about the Booths and then the Hornbys and could visualise them living in Shirley. It seemed to bring another dimension to the house, and she knew the couple would work there as long as they could. She was always quick to get village help for Mr Yarwood if it was needed in the garden for the heavier work. Likewise, at spring cleaning times, she would arrange help for Mrs Yarwood. All she wanted was for the pair to work at Shirley for as long as possible. But she knew the passage of time would catch up with them and one day they would have to retire.

After a day at home, Joyce would return to the business full of energy, ready to sell anything to anybody. She had great skill in selling. First she made friends with the clients, then quietly and slowly found out about their circumstances. After that hurdle was crossed she would endeavour to show them round properties she thought were suitable. She virtually had to sell herself to them first so as to gain their trust, and if one property did not suffice, they would go back to her to see another. But they were not to be frightened off by her, they just had to trust her and, most importantly, like her. This was a great skill and she hoped to pass it on to Peter. One day she might retire and become a lady of leisure, but not yet.

The first appointment that morning was an empty flat on the outskirts of the town. Richard and Peter had made the appointment for her. So she picked up the keys and details and set off for the flat. Joyce always arrived ten minutes before the appointment and sat outside in her car reading through the details. She knew all the properties by heart. There was nothing more embarrassing than opening up a door, announcing, 'this is the bathroom', and then walking into the cylinder cupboard!

A white car drew up behind her and in the mirror she saw a middle-aged man get out of his car. Joyce also got out of her car and greeted the man with a handshake and greeted him by his name.

'Come this way. The entrance is at the side,' Joyce said in a friendly voice. 'Looking for a flat for yourself?' she asked.

'Yes, I am. Recently on my own so I need a place to live,' replied the man. She opened the outer door to the block of flats and they made their way up to the second floor. This entailed climbing four flights of stairs, but the man never commented on the climb. Joyce had never liked blocks of flats. They seemed so unfriendly and institutionalised, even though they were privately owned.

'Here we are,' she called back to her client. 'Number Six. You get a good view of the town from the lounge and it's very quiet and private up here.'

'That's what I am looking for, some privacy,' said the client.

This sounds good, thought Joyce. Most clients were put off by now after climbing the stairs and could hardly get their breath.

They both walked into the lounge and the man surveyed the view. Next they moved into the kitchen and they had a look in the bathroom. The flat was small but adequate for one. Joyce did not like the flat but tried to muster up enthusiasm for it. She found it extremely claustrophobic and couldn't wait to get downstairs. 'How many bedrooms are there?' the man called from the bathroom.

'Oh, there are two, a double and a single,' answered Joyce. She moved into the double room and round past the bed to the window. As she did, the man came into the bedroom and shut the door.

Joyce span round and looked at him. The man slowly said, 'Well, what are you going to do now?' Joyce, by now, was getting nervous; her heart was racing and her cheeks were flushed.

'What do you mean?' she asked quickly.

Still leaning on the door, hand on the door knob, he said

quietly, 'I said, what are you going to do now? Here we are together in the bedroom and, as you said, in a very private place, so…' He looked at Joyce with a very penetrating glare. Joyce immediately changed from a friendly viewing lady to an efficient, strong businesswoman.

'Come along. We will have none of that. I am not interested in you. I am here to show you the flat and, from this moment, the viewing is terminated.' She knew then that she had to take some action. If she didn't, the situation would deteriorate rapidly. Her heart felt as though it was bursting and her legs would hardly hold her up. Everything seemed to be happening in slow motion; this was a dangerous situation.

As she spoke, she moved swiftly to the door, wrenched it open, pushed past the man and ran out of the flat and down the stairs. She could hear him coming down the stairs behind her. Her sudden movement across the bedroom had taken him by surprise and she had escaped. God knows how, but she had escaped him. Not waiting outside the flat, she rushed to her car and, still clutching the keys, she drove like a maniac to the office.

Joyce stumbled into the office by the back door and called out for Richard. She was ashen in colour and shaking from head to foot. 'Oh my God, Joyce, have you had an accident? Here, sit down. Judith, bring your mother some water,' called Richard. Peter and Judith ran into the office to see Joyce collapsed against Richard on the sofa.

'What's happened, Daddy?' cried Judith.

'I don't know. Give her time to recover.' He noticed she was still clutching the keys to the flat and he gently released them from her fingers.

'Oh Richard, I was nearly attacked by that man in the flat. It was awful. He was awful. I thought I would never get out.'

The story poured out of Joyce, and Richard, Judith and Peter listened in silence. 'He shut me in the bedroom. Oh Richard, I never thought I would get out,' she cried to him. 'I ran and ran out. He was running after me.' She was getting hysterical again.

'Don't, don't, dear. You are safe here with me,' Richard said, trying to calm her. Peter whispered to Richard that he would go back and lock up the flat in case the owners returned.

He left the office and pondered over the situation that Mrs Farnham had got into. It was extremely dangerous for a lady to take men on their own into unoccupied premises. Thank goodness it had not been Judith who had met the man. Some men were chancers and he probably thought Mrs Farnham was fair game.

When he returned, Mrs Farnham was calmer and she asked them what they had said to the man when he made the appointment. Judith suddenly remembered that she had made the appointment and when the man had asked how he would recognise Mrs Farnham, she had said, 'Oh, she is blonde, slim and attractive!' As she said this, she realised she had unwittingly sent her mother into a trap.

After this incident, the Farnhams changed the viewing rules for unoccupied premises. A male client would only be shown round by Peter or Mr Farnham. It had been a close call for Joyce, but it did not spoil her enjoyment of her job. Richard sent her home and Mrs Yarwood fussed round her with strong cups of tea and shortbread biscuits. Everybody kept saying, 'Thank goodness it wasn't Judith,' for it had been Joyce's maturity and experience which had got her through her ordeal.

Time passed, and the routine of work and play filled Judith and June's days. Their days were so different, but special in their own way. June worked hard for her examinations and on the weekends she had off she was happy to go around with Judith's friends. She soon found out that her parents gave her more leeway if she was with her elder sister. Judith's activities were harmless as her friends were all steady young people, very conservative and caring. So June was accepted into their group and they looked after her.

Judith had invited Peter to a few dances and parties and he had willingly accepted. He rather fancied Judith but she seemed always to be surrounded by male admirers. Still, he went to everything he was invited to but never mentioned it to his boss, Mr Farnham. The old adage 'business and pleasure do not mix,' he had heard him say many times, and he knew how precious Mr Farnham's daughters were to him. So he and Judith kept quiet about their friendship.

On Christmas Eve that year, her group decided to go out carol singing around the village. Armed with lanterns, they set out soon after dusk. There was a light flurry of snow falling and the evening was very still. Judith and June were dressed warmly in their thick winter coats and fur boots. Both wore fluffy bobble hats and their blonde hair fringed their faces. They all met outside the church up the road and set off. There were about twenty in the group, so first they called on all their own homes and neighbour's homes. They all sang well in the still night and carried on through the evening. The snow started to cover the ground and lightly cover the branches of the trees. In the space of a short time the whole village had become a magical winter scene. At every house they were offered hot mince pies, mulled wine or hot chocolate. The group was getting quite merry and the singing was getting stronger by the minute. Judith and Peter stood at the back of the group and soon Peter was holding Judith's gloved hand. She snuggled closer to him and he put his arm round her. They sang and sang, enjoying every minute. Snowflakes were fluttering down and one landed on Judith's nose. Peter quickly bent down and kissed the snowflake away. Judith's smile and giggle gave Peter added confidence and he bent down and kissed Judith on the lips. Judith returned his kiss and the two stood arm in arm smiling at each other. For Judith it was a wonderful moment and Peter whispered to her, 'Did you like that?'

'Oh yes Peter, I did,' replied Judith and she snuggled closer to him.

'I have been wanting to do that for ages, Judith, but I wasn't brave enough,' laughed Peter.

'I wished you had, as I will let you into a secret,' she paused.

'Go on, tell me, you tease,' Peter said.

'I fancied you the moment you walked into our office and I was so pleased you got the job,' whispered Judith.

'Well I never, you never told me, you little minx,' said Peter breathlessly.

'How could I? I was waiting for you to move first. That's the man's job,' she said cockily.

By now the group had finished the carol and started moving off down the drive to the next house. 'Stay here a minute,' Peter said to her. And he pulled her quickly off the drive and behind a big fir tree. 'Kiss me,' he demanded with a smile.

'Oh yes, Peter,' replied Judith. And they kissed each other and lost all thoughts of time.

Suddenly, they heard voices calling their names and they broke away from each other breathlessly. 'Oh, come on Peter, they have missed us,' cried Judith and she started running down the drive and up the road to the group. Peter followed her, he was in high spirits now, running alongside her through the snow.

'Where have you two been?' called somebody from the group.

'Oh, we got left behind,' answered Peter.

'Oh yes?' they jeered at them, and all started to laugh. Peter and Judith did not mind one bit and joined the group again.

At the end of the carol singing they had collected a large amount of money. They had decided to donate the money to the church funds because it was Christmas. The snow by now was lying 'crisp and even', as it said in the carols, so they decided to disperse to their various homes. Their next meeting would be at the New Year's Eve dance at the tennis club which was held every year.

They all set off home and June, Judith and Peter walked down the road together. The snow was falling heavily and they trudged along. June by now had noticed that Judith and Peter had been together through the evening, so she walked ahead of them. When she reached home she called back to them, 'Goodnight Peter. Lovely evening wasn't it?'

'Yes it was. Goodnight,' he called. June went inside the house and left Judith in the big porch of Shirley with Peter. 'Can I see you again, Judith?' Peter asked anxiously.

'Of course you can. Give me a ring on Boxing Day and we could meet up again. I would love that.' Judith looked up at Peter and hoped he was going to kiss her goodnight.

She was not disappointed. He kissed her long and deep and it made her quite giddy. She stepped back, amazed at the strength of her feeling for him. 'Goodnight, Peter. Thank you for a lovely evening. I must go in now,' she said.

'All right, I will ring you on Boxing Day. Goodnight Judith.' It was as though they did not want to separate now they had found each other, and they both hesitated.

'Bye,' said Judith as she stepped through the doorway of Shirley. 'Bye, Peter,' and she quickly closed the door.

She leaned against the big front door and swayed slightly. What an evening it had turned out to be! What an evening. She knew straight away that she loved Peter. She had never felt like this before. This was love on a starry, snowy night. Love that had kept her warm and tingling all night. She wasn't the slightest bit cold, her cheeks glowed, and when she looked in the hall mirror, her reflection was one of beauty.

When she walked into the sitting room she tried to behave normally. 'Had a good night, dear?' called her mother.

'Yes, great, thank you,' she replied, glancing across at June, who was huddled by the fire.

'Come over and warm yourself,' said her father. 'Collected quite a bit, I hear?'

'Yes, we did very well, didn't we, June?' asked Judith.

'Oh, yes. Some better than others!' exclaimed June as she smiled at her sister.

'Well, I'm off to bed,' said Judith. 'Night, night all,' she called. 'See you all Christmas morning,' and she made her way up the stairs, wanting desperately to get into her own room and dream of Peter.

Over the Christmas holiday, Judith managed to sneak off and meet Peter, with the help of June. Peter was extremely worried about these liaisons with Judith. He was terrified of Mr Farnham finding out. His boss had a reputation in the estate agency business and was not a man to cross. How he would react to Peter seeing Judith as they worked together was a difficult question to answer. Relationships between staff were frowned on, especially as one member of staff was the boss's daughter. Judith thought it was all a lot of fuss about nothing, but resigned herself to keeping the whole affair secret. The weak link in this subterfuge was Mr Farnham's golfing partner, Frank, the solicitor whose son, Frank Junior, was in the same group of friends as Peter. Peter had spoken to FJ, as he was called, and he had promised not to say anything to his father, but Peter was not at all confident about his promise. FJ was a bit of a loose cannon, the complete opposite of his father. But there was nothing Peter could do about the situation if he was to see Judith.

In the spring, they were all kept busy with new properties coming onto the market and with some of the houses which had been for sale over the winter, finally selling. It was satisfactory to the company when this happened and 'sold' signs started to appear around the area. Richard Farnham loved driving around, looking at the signs with his name on and it doubled his pleasure if they had 'sold' written on them. Good advertising for the business, he thought. Being of an extremely competitive nature, he loved to get his business to sell the houses if he knew other estate agents had been round to value them. People found him very efficient and were confident that he could sell their precious homes. He did work hard. It was all-consuming and the only relaxation for him was his golf. In a way, his family came second place to the business, although he was extremely proud of June, who would be qualifying soon as a nurse. He knew that she would have a good career as well as being respected and dedicated to her work. Judith, on the other hand, seemed to have no ambition to start a career. She was quite happy to work as a receptionist for him and to go out with her friends. Perhaps Judith would marry young like her mother and give him lots of grandchildren. He knew that he had never had time for his family when they were very young, so when he retired he would make time for the grandchildren, although the thought of retiring filled him with dread. He couldn't play golf all day. He would have to escape from the home and the family, so he would have to find another hobby. But for the time being his golf was his passion. He was currently playing the club team matches on Saturdays at other clubs, and in the summer evenings with his friend Frank.

On Saturdays, Peter met Judith at the tennis club and they would go out into the country in his car, sometimes for lunch or afternoon tea, stopping at a quaint country cafe. Afterwards Peter would pounce on Judith, trying his best to make love to her in a quiet country lane, but Judith, her head in a whirl, would refuse him. 'I can't Peter. I'm not on the pill, you know that,' she cried angrily.

'I know that, but I'll be careful,' he replied, carrying on, his urges getting stronger and stronger.

'Stop it, please!' Judith cried out again.

'Oh, hell! It's always the same with you, Judith. You tease me all afternoon then it's a no-no. What's a chap supposed to do?' He was getting very angry by now.

'I can't go on the pill. If Mother finds out, all hell will let loose. Can't you do something?' She was getting very embarrassed by now. She felt the romance was slipping away and she didn't like what was left.

'No, I won't,' Peter said. 'Hate the things. Never use them.' By now he had drawn away from her, had lit a cigarette and was staring out of the side window of the car.

'Take me home, now,' shouted Judith. She suddenly realised that her precious Peter was not so special to her after all. How many girls had he slept with? Who were they? 'Take me home, Peter!' she screamed, by now getting quite hysterical.

'OK, OK, no need to get your knickers in a twist,' he retorted and slammed the car into gear.

He drove home in silence and far too fast. He was angry with her, she was a tease, egging him on over the months. He had been patient with her but today he could wait no longer for her. In fact he lusted after her and she had rebuffed him. No girl, not even the boss's daughter, did that to Peter.

He stopped up the road from Shirley, leaned over, opened the car door and said, 'Out you get, young lady.'

'When will I see you again?' cried Judith. By now she had calmed down and was very upset. The afternoon had all gone wrong. What should have been a lovely afternoon had become a nightmare. What could she do, give in to his demands and get pregnant? Would he stand by her if that happened? What would her parents think? Her friends, her sister June? She loved Peter, he was her whole life. She dreamed and thought of him all day and night; now she had made a mess of it all. She could feel Peter's anger as he sat next to her. She tried to hold his arm but he brushed it off. 'I'm so sorry, Peter, I'm so sorry,' she cried.

'Just get out, Judith,' he said coldly. She was shocked at the tone of his voice. Was this her lovely, kind, warm Peter, or some other person sitting next to her?

'Don't let's fall out, Peter, you know I love you,' she said softly.

'Funny way of showing it, my girl,' he retorted. 'Just get out, Judith. Let's call it a day,' he replied angrily.

She stumbled out of his car, grabbed her tennis racquet and bag from the back seat and walked off down the road.

He drove off, leaving her too stunned to carry on. She found a low wall to sit on and there she sat, sobbing her heart out. After half an hour, she started to calm down, so tidied herself up and set off down the road. She was very relieved that the family were all out. She slipped upstairs to her bedroom and curled up on her bed. She felt like a wounded animal. What had happened to them in the last few hours? Why was Peter so unreasonable? What could she have done? Was she a tease? No, she didn't think so. She just loved him, dearly, he was her whole life and she thought they had a future. She had been so careful to keep their friendship a secret from her parents, for that was how Peter wanted it. Did he expect too much from her? All these thoughts raced through her head until she fell asleep, emotionally exhausted.

The next day her mother said, 'You were home early, Judith. Not many at the tennis club, dear?'

'Oh, I had a headache, Mother, so I came home early to sleep it off.'

'Gone now, has it dear?' replied her mother.

'Yes, thank you.'

'Come on, off we go to work. Your father left early. Had a meeting to go to,' called her mother.

Going into the office was going to be a nerve-wracking experience for Judith. Facing Peter after yesterday was going to be very difficult. But she dressed carefully, made her face up well to hide her puffy eyes and came down to her mother. 'You do look washed-out, Judith. Perhaps we won't be too busy today with it being Monday,' her mother said quickly.

When they arrived at the office, Peter and her father were in his office with the door shut. Judith slipped behind her desk in reception and tried to get on with opening the mail. She could hear her father and Peter laughing together in the office and at last they came out, smiling at each other. Peter walked up to Judith and said, 'Morning Judith, just out to see a new client. Hold any calls for me, I should be no longer than an hour,' and with that, he went out to his car.

He didn't look any different, no stress or strain, no sleepless night, just normal and businesslike. Her father watched Peter leave and then said, 'Fine chap. Glad we got him, or some other estate agency would have snapped him up. Been talking to him about his future when he qualifies this month. Thinking of making him a partner. I think he will be a great asset to Farnham's. What do you think, Judith?' her father asked.

'Yes Daddy, you know best.' Just then the phone rang and she went to answer it. 'Speak to you again, Daddy,' she whispered. 'Farnham's Estate Agents?' She tried to sound bright.

'Could I speak to Peter, please?' said the young voice.

'What is it in connection with?' asked Judith.

'Oh, it's a private matter,' said the young girl on the other end of the phone.

'Can I take a message?' replied Judith coldly.

'Oh, I'll leave it then. Just tell him Samantha phoned. Bye,' she called. Judith slammed the phone down.

Judith's mind went into overdrive. Who was Samantha? Why did she want to speak to Peter and what about? Was she a friend or a client? Judith sat at her desk, her thoughts in turmoil. Who was she? She wouldn't leave a message. What message would she leave? Her mind was racing so much that she didn't hear Peter enter the office from the rear. 'Penny for them,' he said cockily.

'Oh, Peter, you startled me!' she said quickly. She watched him unload some papers and details onto his desk and waited for her moment to tackle him. 'Oh, by the way Peter, there was a phone call from Samantha. She wouldn't speak to anybody else. She wanted you.' She sat still, watching his reaction to her statement.

'Ah yes,' then he paused. 'She's a client.'

'Oh, what is she interested in?' Judith asked as casually as possible.

'Those new flats,' he answered.

'I thought they had all been sold,' Judith said slowly.

'Well, it's in case one falls through,' he said.

'When did she do a viewing? I don't seem to have her in the book. What's her surname?'

'I didn't arrange a viewing,' replied Peter brusquely. 'What's with the third degree, Judith?'

'Only asking. Keep your hair on, Peter,' replied Judith. 'Do you want to use my phone?'

'No, I'll ring her later,' said Peter. There descended an uneasy silence in the office and it continued for the rest of the day. As far as Judith could ascertain, Peter did not return Samantha's phone call. Why, why did he not ring her from the office? Judith asked herself. The atmosphere in the front office was very frosty. They both got on with their individual work and hardly spoke to each other. At 5 p.m., Peter left, hardly saying a word to Judith, and drove out of the rear yard.

Judith sat quietly on her own until her father came in. 'You OK Judith? You look a bit preoccupied. Work all right today?' he asked her.

'Yes, Daddy. Everything is OK,' she replied to him. But her heart was broken. She was in despair. What had gone wrong with her and Peter? One minute they were so in love with each other, the next minute they were like strangers. She wanted to talk about Peter, but her father was not the person to confide in. She knew he would be annoyed by their secret relationship at work. Work always came first for her father. It was a religion for him. He was consumed by the business day and night. How did her mother put up with him? Judith pondered all this. She hated all men at this moment. Selfish, self-centred, egotistical, cruel men. She hated the lot of them. She hated her job; in fact she hated her life.

When she got home, her sister had just come off duty. Poor June was tired; she had had a stressful day – but her sister did not bother to ask her how her day had gone. Judith came into her bedroom and sat on June's bed. She burst into tears and the whole story flooded out. June was shocked how vicious her sister was about Peter. In a calm voice she cut through her ravings and said, 'All this because you wouldn't sleep with him? I can't believe Peter would react like that,' June said quietly.

'Well, you don't know men then,' retorted Judith.

'Who is this Samantha?' June asked.

'I don't know, but I will find out and kill her,' cried Judith.

'Oh don't be so melodramatic, Judith,' said June.

'You would be angry if this had happened to you,' replied Judith.

'Yes, I suppose so, but you can't go around killing girls just because of Peter.' This made Judith laugh and they hugged each other.

'Please don't tell Mummy and Daddy, June,' pleaded Judith.

'You know I won't,' whispered her sister. 'Now dry your eyes and put on your make-up or they will smell a rat. I'll go downstairs and you come down when you are calmer. He isn't the only man around, Judith. There are plenty more fish in the sea, so buck up! You have always been the popular one with the boys so don't let Peter get to you. When we find out who Samantha is, I'll kill her for you!' June laughed and left her sister to recover herself.

As June walked downstairs she felt very protective of her sister. Although she was the younger sister, she seemed to be more capable and sensible, and less vulnerable than her older sister, and she was very upset at how this Peter had treated Judith. It was not fair to hurt somebody as loving as Judith. Not fair at all!

As the days and weeks dragged on June found out who Samantha was. She worked for another estate agent's in town. Quite a reputation had Samantha, a good time girl, anything for a laugh, people said. She was careful what she told Judith, not wanting to upset her further. But working in the same office as Peter and seeing him every day was very difficult for Judith. Her father thought the light shone out of him and was now taking him to the golf club for lessons. Meeting FJ and his father, the four had started playing together. They were very competitive, the older men playing to their handicap, but the younger men kept going well, with youth on their side. There was lots of bragging and laughter and Richard looked at Peter as the son he had never had. Peter was very pleased with the situation, as he was ambitious and hoped that Mr Farnham would eventually offer him a partnership and his future would be set fair.

Mixing business and pleasure had been a mistake. FJ had warned Peter about it, and he hadn't listened to him. But he had learned his lesson and had scraped out of the situation without Mr and Mrs Farnham learning about him and Judith. She would get over him and this left him free to play the field again. Thank goodness, he was too young to settle down and wanted a bit of fun in his life. Judith was too heavy going and the situation between them had become claustrophobic. FJ had been right in the end.

The four had good times at the golf club. Coming in after their morning games, they would have sandwiches and drinks, then in the afternoon they played snooker. The two boys always beat the men hands down but they all enjoyed themselves. When Richard came home he was always full of the day's golf, telling his family about his game and praising Peter. 'What a good chap he is,' Richard extolled. 'Nice young man, will go far.' Joyce always agreed with him when it came to Peter. She liked him too and knew he was good for the business. He was the son she never had.

Judith and June just stayed silent. Judith clenched her hands but June's eyes warned her not to rock the boat. Her father and mother would be devastated if they knew how he had treated their daughter. So she kept quiet and suffered in silence. June immersed herself in family life when she was at home, listening to Judith, her love life in tatters, and to all the gossip from the club. From her father and mother the talk was always of the estate agency business. Though June thought the commercial world was slightly shallow compared with her world in nursing, she realised that the business was thriving and they all lived very comfortably from it. The house, the cars, the holidays were all provided by Farnham's. So she listened to their endless conversations about properties, clients, sales figures and, the bottom line, the fees.

June would hate to work in that environment. The medical world was hers. She loved her world in the hospital, the staff, the patients, even the smell of the wards. She had sailed through her exams and was waiting for the final results. Then she would be a fully qualified nurse. June had a lot of girlfriends, all nurses, and they knew how to enjoy themselves when they were let loose. She never invited Judith out with her nurse friends as they always talked shop when they were out and Judith would become bored. Judith would not fit in with her friends. Although she loved her sister, Judith's attitude to life was more superficial. June was younger than Judith, but she sometimes felt more mature. Perhaps it was the nature of her job. But she wouldn't change it, she loved her work and her life centred around the hospital. Home was a place for relaxation and comfort, which Shirley provided.

As for Farnham's, it went from strength to strength. Richard opened up another office in the next town and made Peter its manager. The whole office was fitted out in the Farnham colours and new staff were employed. Peter was an excellent manager and the move out of the main office relieved the tension between him and Judith. Although he never spoke to Judith on a personal level, he occasionally saw the sadness in her eyes. He never felt guilty about the way he finished with her. He was glad to move away to his new position. This was what he had been working for since he joined Farnham's and now he was his own boss, with a company car and a good salary. He and Richard were of the same breed, sometimes quite ruthless and cunning, always one step ahead of the other estate agents. They both loved the cut and thrust of this world and together were a formidable team.

Joyce, on the other hand, was pleased that Peter and Richard worked so well together. She was glad Richard had Peter's friendship as she always had her daughters. She floated between work and home easily. She could put on her business hat and the next day she could be helping Mrs Yarwood clean Shirley or pottering in the garden with Mr Yarwood. She kept an eye on the couple as they were getting older, but they both still seemed to enjoy their working life at Shirley.

The garden was a triumph in the summer months. The roses and bedding plants were perfection. Mr Yarwood didn't grow so many vegetables and fruit now as Joyce quite happily bought most of these from the shops. So he concentrated on the garden. Mid-morning, all three would stop and have a sandwich and a pot of tea and Joyce would hear all the gossip from the village. She still did most of her shopping in the village, supporting the local shopkeepers. The following day Joyce would go back into the office, selling properties and vetting clients for rented properties which they managed. All the time she was in the office she knew Shirley was in the safe hands of the Yarwoods. But their time there was closing in and she dreaded the day when the Yarwoods would come and say they were getting too old to work, and that they would be retiring.

As for her daughters, she still hoped they would find nice young men and settle down. Perhaps grandchildren in the future. But at present this was not to be. Judith had seemed much quieter, her sparkle had gone, and she seemed to spend more time at home. Looking back, Joyce realised it must have been over a year since they had seen the extrovert girl that her eldest daughter had been. Was she maturing or was she just bored with her job and her life? She wished Judith had taken up a career like June. Something to stretch her, not a boring desk job. But she knew Judith was just not interested in anything that involved hard work. You can't change people, children are all different, she would say to herself. She was so proud of June. She had worked hard and established a world for herself. She would be independent when she qualified and would be a very useful member of the community. The two daughters were so different. Their friends were complete opposites. But for the moment, June seemed the most satisfied of the two. Her life had more meaning for her. She had reached her goal and was reaping the rewards. Judith, on the other hand, had no goal and her life seemed to be on hold. Something needed to change, and Joyce felt unable to help her.

Chapter Five

Weekends were sacred to the Farnhams. If June was not working, she went out on a shopping spree with Judith and their mother. The three girls loved shopping and came home laden with bags, but they always bought something for Richard to soften him up in case he queried their spending.

Richard would leave early on Saturday morning for the golf club and team up with Frank and his son FJ. Peter made up the four and, come rain or shine, they were out on the course by nine o'clock. But this morning was a fine spring day. As Richard drove to the golf club, the roads were lined with nodding daffodils. On every corner and roundabout they gave a wonderful spring show. The trees were in full blossom, white and pink, and everywhere looked fresh and clean. At the start of spring the gardens were coming alive after their winter sleep. Nature was wonderful. Having been dormant for so long, life suddenly sprang from all corners. April showers and the warm sun worked their magic on the world and the upsurge of new growth gave an extra urgency to the atmosphere. Richard felt this and decided he and Frank would thrash the youngsters today. He felt it in his bones that today he would have a great round of golf.

He was the last to arrive of the four and hurried to retrieve his golf trolley and bag out of the boot of his car. He took his change of clothes into the locker room and returned to his car to put on his golf shoes. He looked smart this morning. Nothing but the best for him, from his golf clubs to his outfit. And as he walked on to the tee to join the others, he felt good in himself.

'Good morning, gentlemen. How are we today? Fighting fit?' he asked.

'Great, Richard, looking forward to the game,' replied Frank. 'And of course beating these two,' he exclaimed.

'Oh yes, Father,' sneered FJ. 'What makes you think you will today?'

'Well, I know what time you came in last night, or should I say this morning?' laughed Frank. 'And you, Peter, you were out with him too.'

'Oh, I was in bed by 10 p.m.,' said Peter with a slight grin. 'Ah, but whose bed I wonder?' asked Frank. They all laughed. This banter put them in a good mood before the start of the game.

They tossed a coin and Peter and Frank won. So Frank drove off from the first tee. The game had begun.

Richard was playing well. He out-drove the others by yards. The others were in the bunkers and the rough, but Richard kept his game together and he and Frank were really enjoying thrashing the boys. FJ and Peter were getting very frustrated. The late night was telling but they persevered. They hated getting beaten – Richard would go on about it all week. They were all so competitive that it lifted their game and they all played good shots. As they walked along they would discuss their work but the conversation would be light and superficial. Serious talk was ruled out. This was leisure time.

By now they had arrived at the fourth tee. It was a long hole, a par five. Across the fairway, a public pathway ran from right to left. It was clearly visible as it was slightly raised. To the right it came out of a densely wooded area and to the left it disappeared behind another row of trees. Richard moved on to tee and took his position. He could out-drive all three of them, so he was ready to attack the ball with gusto. Perhaps he would get a birdie today or an eagle as he was playing so well and feeling good.

'Richard,' called Frank. 'Watch out! There is a walker on the pathway.'

'OK, I'll clear him before he reaches the fairway,' called Richard. And he let fly with a terrific drive. The ball climbed high but Richard had sliced it and it flew to the right.

'Fore!' shouted the boys. But the walker didn't hear them. 'Fore!' they shouted again. The ball hit the man and dropped him like a stone.

'My God, quick!' shouted Frank. The three ran across the

fairway and down to the man. Richard remained rooted to the spot, his driver hanging in his hand.

The man lay motionless on the ground and Frank could see a mark on his temple where the ball had struck. Frank rolled him onto his side and called the boys to run to the phone in the golf hut and get an ambulance quickly. Blood was trickling out of the man's nose and mouth and he was very pale. Frank leaned over him and felt his pulse. There was nothing. He rolled him onto his back and started pressing his chest. He was getting no response. He could feel Richard standing behind him. 'Oh God. What have I done?' He will be all right Frank, won't he?' asked Richard.

'I don't know old chap. It doesn't look good. I can't find a pulse,' answered Frank slowly, not looking at his friend. It wasn't good, Frank knew, but he dared not say this out loud to Richard. They could hear the bell of the ambulance from a long way away.

'Please try harder,' Richard implored.

By now they were both kneeling alongside the man, trying to resuscitate him. Frank had taken a good look at the man. He was in his sixties, dressed for walking with heavy boots and a walking stick. Frank kept up the pumping on his chest but he knew it was in vain. He was only going through the motions for Richard's sake. The ambulance drove steadily over the fairway and the ambulance men leapt out and into action straight away.

Meanwhile, the boys ran down the fairway with the pro, behind the ambulance. They all stood in a solemn ring around the walker and watched the ambulance men work on him. Eventually they stood up and pronounced the man dead. The shock of this announcement made Richard keel over and Frank had to support his friend. 'What have I done? What have I done?' whispered Richard.

'It was an accident,' Peter stated. 'We called "fore". He just didn't heed our warning.' Frank and FJ looked at each other and didn't say anything.

'Yes, it was an accident. He shouldn't have been on the path when I was driving off, should he?' demanded Richard.

The pro ignored Richard's outburst and stepped forward. He said to the ambulance men that he needed to inform the police and then they could inform his relatives. 'Where will you take him?' he asked the ambulance men.

'To the mortuary at the hospital. We will inform the police for you when we get to the hospital,' the senior man said. 'Very unfortunate this, but he was dead before we got to him. I should say that his death was instantaneous.'

They carefully placed the man on a stretcher and lifted him into the ambulance. It made its way slowly over the fairway and out onto the road. Richard stood and watched it go out of sight. 'Come on, old chap.' Frank put his arm around Richard's shoulder. 'Come on, let's get you home.' The pro said that he would have to make a report for the police and the club, but he would leave it for the moment. Richard thanked him and stumbled up the fairway. He felt dreadful, he felt he was going to collapse at any moment. His legs were trembling and he could hardly put one foot in front of the other. Frank nodded to the boys to gather up the golf trolleys, and walked on with Richard.

He eased him into his own car and drove through the gates to take Richard home. When he arrived at Shirley he rang the bell, but nobody came to the door. He went back to the car and searched through Richard's pockets for the keys. Richard just sat. He was in deep shock. His friend found the keys and he helped Richard through the door of Shirley and into the sitting room.

He settled him in an armchair and then immediately went into the dining room and poured out two large whiskies. 'Drink this old chap. Slowly does it,' said Frank. He watched his friend try to drink from the glass but his hand was shaking too much. 'Here, let me.' He leaned over Richard, held the glass to his lips and Richard sipped the whisky. After he had had a drink, he leaned back into his chair and closed his eyes. Tears streamed down his cheeks and he started to sob. Frank held his hand for comfort. 'Now then, Richard, don't get upset. It was an accident.'

'I know, but I have killed a man. What about his wife and children?' sobbed Richard. 'What have I done? Oh God, what have I done?'

Frank was worried about the situation. He had said it was an accident, but, as a solicitor, he could see some trouble ahead for

Richard. The police and the club committee would both want an account of the events. Could it be seen as an accident or would they bring a charge against Richard? Of course there would be an inquest, which Richard would have to attend. The foreseeable future was bleak, to say the least.

All these thoughts were tumbling through Frank's mind when the door flew open. 'Hello there. Anyone at home?' shouted Joyce. 'Home early? Where's your car?' All three girls bounded into the lounge with armfuls of shopping bags. Frank stood up and shook his head.

'Wait outside, Judith and June,' he commanded.

'What's happened?' They both looked at their father huddled in the big armchair. 'Has Daddy had an accident?' asked June.

'Please will you wait outside. I need to speak to your mother.' His voice was very strong and the girls turned and went into the hall.

'Come here, Joyce, while I explain to you what has happened.' Frank whispered the events of the fateful morning. Joyce's eyes looked constantly from Frank to her husband. She slipped her arm around her husband and kissed him gently on the cheek.

'Now, Richard, I am home now and I will look after you,' she said gently.

'I have killed a man, Joyce.' He looked imploringly at her as though to say, Please make it better. Frank said he would talk to the girls and get Judith to go back with him to the club to get Richard's clothes, clubs and car.

A few minutes later, June came in and helped her mother look after Richard. 'I'll make a pot of tea. A hot drink will help.' Just then the front doorbell rang and June answered the door. Two policemen stood there asking for Richard Farnham. June showed them into the sitting room where her father and mother were.

'Good morning, Sir. Are you Richard Farnham?'

Richard stared at the two men. Joyce answered, 'Yes, this is Mr Farnham and I am Mrs Farnham.'

'Well, we don't want to disturb you too much, madam, but we do need to take a statement from your husband,' one said.

'Richard, please speak to these gentlemen, dear,' Joyce implored him.

He seemed to be in a daze but he sat more upright and shook his head. 'I don't know, I don't know,' he whispered to them.

They both looked at each other. 'Perhaps if we asked you some questions, you could answer them?'

'I'll try,' he replied weakly.

They ran through the events of the morning and Richard just answered yes or no. As they got to the end, Richard started getting agitated again. 'I think we will leave it at that, madam,' said one of the policemen.

'Well, I think I hear his friend Frank, he is a solicitor, coming back, so could you speak to him now?' enquired Joyce.

'That would be a great help to us.' Both the policemen moved out into the hall and Frank took them into the dining room. They sat round the table. Frank read through Richard's statement and then added his own.

The policemen thanked him and extended their sympathy to Mr and Mrs Farnham. 'A nasty business, this one,' said the older policeman.

'Did he have a family?' asked Frank.

'Yes, he had a wife. His children had left home. He walked across the course every day,' she said. There will be an inquest and when we get all the information, we will decide on what action, if any, we will be taking. We need to speak to the young men who were with you, so ask them to come into the station and make a statement, if you will? Well, I will say good day to you, Sir. Thank you for your help,' and with that, the two policemen walked off down the drive.

Frank looked at his watch. It was 1 p.m. In a matter of four hours, Richard's life had been turned upside down. One man had lost his life, one woman was a widow and children had lost their father. Who could have thought on that beautiful spring morning that such devastating events would unfold?

The next day, Joyce was extremely worried about Richard. He was very quiet. She couldn't get a word out of him, but she thought that if she left him alone, by Monday he would recover. If not, Joyce decided that she would call the doctor in. She also was worried. She had never had anything to do with the law and it frightened her. That poor man, just out for his usual constitutional walk, his wife at home waiting for his return; what must she be going through? When someone close to you dies, you hope that you can be there with them to talk to them, hold their hand and finally say goodbye. But this was a tragedy, his wife at home unaware of the events, his children totally unaware. Joyce's mind was working in overdrive. 'Stop it at once!' she said to herself. 'You have to keep strong for Richard.'

She called the girls down from their bedrooms, where they had been keeping out of the way all morning.

Judith and June came into the kitchen and sat down at the table with their mother. 'Now we have to be strong for Daddy. He is not coping at the moment and things could get worse,' their mother said.

'What do you mean, things could get worse?' Judith looked alarmed.

'Well, there will be an inquest, which your father will have to attend. Frank will see to the legal side, but Peter and FJ will have to give evidence.' She stopped there and looked at her daughters.

'It was an accident, wasn't it?' exclaimed June.

'We know that, but the coroner will have to decide on that too.'

'What happens if he decides it wasn't an accident and it was Daddy's fault?' said June.

'I don't want to think of that. Just let's support your father all we can and get over the next few days,' whispered Joyce to her girls. She held their hands and tried to smile reassuringly, but inside she was in turmoil.

This could be extremely serious for Richard. How he would get through this, she didn't know. In the afternoon, Frank came round and spent a long time in the sitting room with Richard. She could hear his strong voice telling Richard what was going to happen in the coming weeks. But she never heard Richard speak.

On Monday morning it was quite obvious that Richard could not go into work. She spoke to Mr and Mrs Yarwood and told them to keep out of his way. He was spending all his time in the little office upstairs. The family life went on downstairs but Richard took no part in it. His depression worsened as the days went on and he was barely functioning. The doctor prescribed some tablets and Frank kept calling round, but nothing and nobody could help him. He had taken a life, through a stupid action. He would never pick up a golf club again; he would never return to the club.

By now the police had interviewed the other three players, the golf pro and the Chairman of the Greens Committee. There was a notice at the beginning of the pathway warning walkers that they were crossing a fairway. That notice was quite large and clear. The walker must have noticed it as he walked across every day. Frank's clear statement that the man emerged from the trees too late for them to warn him of his perilous crossing, and Peter and FJ's confirmation, were reassuring. The weeks rolled on, every day more painful than the last. Richard was dreading the inquest but he had to face it; he knew this was inevitable. The coroner listened intently and tried to question Richard, but it was all too obvious that the man was having a breakdown. Joyce glanced sideways at the walker's widow and family. They were huddled together and looked very vulnerable. When the verdict was made it was accidental death. Joyce sighed with relief. Richard did not react. The coroner said it was an unfortunate accident, gave his condolences to the man's family and hoped that sometime in the future Mr Farnham would be able to come to terms with the tragedy. Joyce and Frank gathered Richard up between them and made their way down the corridor and out into the fresh air.

'Come along, my dear,' said Joyce to Richard.

'Come on, old chap, let's get you home,' said Frank.

A voice suddenly called out from the office. 'Wait please, I want a word with you, wait please!' They turned around and saw the widow of the walker coming towards them. Frank stepped in front of Richard as if to protect him. 'Please wait, Mrs Farnham, I need to speak to you,' called the woman.

'What do you want with me?' Joyce looked terrified.

'It's all right. I just want to talk to you, alone, if I may, Mrs Farnham,' the woman pleaded with Joyce.

'Come over here and we can talk,' said Joyce quietly.

The two women walked away from the relatives and sat down

on a stone bench. 'Richard is so sorry about your husband, he is so sorry,' Joyce said.

'Yes, I know that. I can see that it has affected him badly and this is what I want you to know.' The widow took a deep breath and began. 'My husband was a very ill man. He had been struggling with his illness for two years, having very nasty treatments and operations, but to no avail. He was not going to live much longer, Mrs Farnham. Do you know what I am saying? He walked the same walk every day, but was getting increasingly weak. Weeks, months, we didn't know how long he had, but I did know he was not going to recover. So you see…' the widow paused and put her hand on Joyce's hand. 'So you see, perhaps it was a merciful release for my husband. He didn't feel any more pain, he is at rest now, and that gives me peace of mind.' She smiled at Joyce. 'Tell your man not to feel guilty, but to carry on his life with you and his family.' She patted Joyce on the arm and Joyce hugged the widow and thanked her for speaking to her. She was so brave for doing this; Joyce could never thank her enough. Joyce and Frank took Richard home and sat in the sitting room with the girls.

Joyce told the family word for word what the woman had said. She was hoping it would help Richard come to terms with the death and make it easier to bear. But nothing could lift the dark cloak that had engulfed him.

In the weeks to come, Richard did get back to work. But the fire he had inside him had gone and he just went through the motions. Spring turned to summer and then on to autumn, but Richard never mentioned the golf club. Frank kept his golf clubs and trolley at his house in case his friend started playing again. He suggested that they join another club if entering their club and meeting the members again would be hard for Richard. But he had decided never to play golf again. Frank and Peter still played on Saturdays and Richard was never mentioned in the clubhouse. Nobody from the club committees came to see him to try to encourage him to come back. They seemed to close ranks and even Frank found it difficult to settle in again with the other members. He did think the president or captain would come and visit Richard at his home, or send a letter of goodwill to him, but this did not happen. Richard made the decision to resign from the club and Frank had a sneaking suspicion that the golf club was pleased.

Life at Shirley would never be the same. The accident had affected all of them so much that Judith one day said, 'Would you two mind this Christmas if I went to visit Elaine in South Africa. You know, my best friend from school? She lives in Cape Town with her husband and has asked me to visit. What do you think?'

Joyce was taken aback by this but said, 'Well, Judith, perhaps this Christmas might be a good time to go. You know we will miss you but I think Daddy and I will be having a quiet Christmas this year. And June is working over Christmas and New Year, so there won't be much fun here for you. How long will you be away, dear?' she asked.

'I was wondering if I could have three weeks off work. I haven't had a holiday this year. What do you think, Daddy?'

'It's a long way to go, Judith, but if you want to go and visit your friend, go for a month. It's expensive to fly, so make it a month. We are not busy in December and January in the office, so we will cope, won't we, dear?'

'Oh, thank you. I'll ring her now and ask her if she will have me for so long. I'm sure she will. She is dying for me to come,' called Judith. By now she was up and out of the room.

'Well, old thing, it's just you and me this Christmas,' said Richard.

'We will be fine, as long as we have each other.' They hugged each other; the accident had brought them closer together. Richard appreciated Joyce much more and Joyce admired Richard and the way he had coped in the end.

'All done and dusted,' Judith said, as she bounded into the room. Joyce looked at her daughter and for the first time she saw the old Judith, the extrovert Judith, shining through. 'I'm going two weeks before Christmas, there for Christmas and New Year and one week in January. Elaine says they barbecue their Christmas dinner and then go on the beach for the rest of the day. What fun it will be!' cried Judith.

This year had also been a bad year for Judith, and to get away from her group of friends, including Peter, would be a relief to her.

June wouldn't mind her going, as she was working through Christmas and New Year. This enabled some of the married nurses to have time off with their children. She didn't mind working over the festive period. It was good fun on the wards and the doctors and nurses had parties too.

As the holiday approached Judith busied herself getting her holiday clothes together. Her friend Elaine had written to her listing the types of clothes she would need, mostly light beach clothes and a couple of dresses for the evening. The weather would be hot so Judith was looking forward to sunbathing and coming home with a good tan.

She was looking forward to this break away from the family. Although she loved them so much, the year had been a strain for all of them, particularly their father, but just recently he had begun to look better and to take more of an interest in the business. Her mother was the one that looked tired now. She had carried the business and the family through single-handedly, and Judith was sure that she would be happy to stay quietly at home this Christmas with Daddy, just the two of them. The peace and quiet without their daughters in the house would do them both a lot of good.

Just before she left for the airport with her parents, Judith slipped into the kitchen and had a quiet word with Mr and Mrs Yarwood. She had a present for them both. 'Happy Christmas to you both. Sorry I won't be here but here's a little something for you from me. Thank you so much, Mrs Yarwood, for tidying up after me all year. I'm such a messy creature, but I do appreciate all you do.' She hugged both of them. 'Will you do me a favour? Will you look after Mummy and Daddy while I am away, please?' Judith asked.

'Of course we will,' nodded Mr Yarwood.

'Now off you go and enjoy your holiday. We will keep an eye on them for you,' said Mrs Yarwood. Judith hugged them again. They were like part of her family and very dear to her.

As Judith got into her father's car she looked up at the house and said, 'Well, Shirley, keep them safe. I'm going on a big adventure. See you soon.' And off they all went to the airport.

Chapter Six

Time passed quickly following Judith's departure. Christmas day arrived and Joyce decided to have Christmas dinner at 7 p.m. so that June would be there. She also decided to invite the Yarwoods. They were part of the family too.

They all had a wonderful evening and even managed to speak to Judith in South Africa.

So Christmas came and went. What would the New Year bring? Joyce hoped a better year for them all. Anything would be better than last year. The Christmas period was a good rest for them, Judith had been right. The house was quiet and calm and they sat together by the open fire, reading or watching television. Their life was picking up again, and Richard seemed happier than he had been for a long time, which made Joyce more content.

June, a staff nurse, was very involved with her work, working in the Premature Baby Unit. She loved looking after these new little souls and found it very rewarding when their mothers took them home. During the time they stayed in the ward, she got quite attached to the babies, talking to them as though they were little people, coaxing them to feed so they would gain weight and then be able to go home. It could be stressful at times if the baby was ill and some little ones did not make it. The grief of the parents was hard to bear, but kind words and comfort were sometimes all the staff could give. How parents coped with the loss of a baby June did not know. Sometimes the parents would thank her for her kindness in looking after their baby and sometimes they would give her a little present from their baby. But for June, this was not necessary. Just to see her babies go home with their loving parents was all the thanks she needed. So June spent most of her Christmas and New Year at the hospital, allowing her parents some time to themselves this year.

Judith's month passed quickly and soon she was on the plane

home. What a wonderful time she had had! What a wonderful country it was. Her parents and sister met her at the airport and, as she walked towards them, Joyce thought she looked radiant. What a change in her! Her holiday had obviously done her a world of good. 'Oh, come here, all of you, I missed you so much,' Judith cried out to her family. They all gathered round her.

'Had a good time, dear?' asked her father.

'Wonderful, marvellous, I'll tell you all about it when we get home,' she winked at her sister June and they all moved out of the airport to the car.

'Home soon, Judith,' said her mother.

'Can't wait,' answered Judith. She hugged her sister in the back of the car and whispered, 'Lots to tell you, June.' Judith beamed at her sister. She seemed to be bubbling over with happiness.

When they arrived back at Shirley, they all gathered in the sitting room round the fire. 'Oh, a lovely cup of tea. I've missed that. It was so hot, we only had cold drinks all the time. Lots of wine though.'

'Well, tell all, Judith,' her sister demanded.

'Elaine and her husband and children are delightful. They live in a lovely house near the beach just outside Cape Town. Would you believe, Daddy, her husband is an estate agent! He is a partner in a big group out there. They are making lots of money and they have a great life – staff in the house and a glorious swimming pool. Elaine and I spent our time lolling round the pool when the children were at school.

'What did you do at Christmas?' asked her mother.

'Oh we had a big barbecue round the pool and all Elaine's husband's family came with their children. They are a very sociable lot, they entertain at home more than going out for meals. So it was good fun. I got on with them all. They are all South African so once when I got used to the accent I was OK, but if they spoke Afrikaans I was lost.'

'Met any nice men, Judith?' her sister enquired.

'Well, yes I did, and that's what I am coming to.' She paused and looked at her parents. 'Yes, I did meet someone,' Judith said quietly.

'Well, go on, don't keep us in suspense,' her sister said.

'His name is Konrad Greeff, he is South African and he is Fritz's partner.'

'Who is Fritz?' asked her mother.

'Oh, he is Elaine's husband. They have four estate agency offices in and around Cape Town and Fritz and Konrad own them.'

'So, tell us more,' her sister pleaded.

'Well, Konrad and I really got on well, in fact, we love each other,' said Judith shyly.

'What did you say?' Joyce said quickly.

'We love each other, Mummy,' Judith said.

'What, all this happened in four weeks?' Her father looked quite startled.

Joyce laid her hand on Richard's arm. 'Just wait a minute. Let Judith talk.'

Judith looked at her family. They were all surprised at her announcement, but they were going to be even more surprised soon. She took a deep breath and said, 'I'm going back to South Africa. I love Konrad and want to spend the rest of my days with him. We will eventually marry, but just being together is all we need at the moment.' Judith stopped talking and allowed all of this to sink in.

'Oh my goodness, Judith, this has come as a big shock to us. You are going to live away in South Africa? It's miles away, girl, do you realise?' Her father had stood up as he said this. He was getting quite agitated.

'Sit down, Richard, and let's talk this through sensibly.' Joyce pulled Richard down. She didn't want him getting upset after his slow recovery. That was the last thing she needed. 'If you go, and I am only saying if, where will you live?' Joyce asked her daughter.

'Konrad already has a large house in the same complex as Elaine's. So there is no problem and you can all come out to visit us.' She was so happy – nothing was going to interfere with her plans.

All this time June sat quietly watching the reaction of her parents. She herself didn't want her only sister to live miles away in a foreign country, but the change in Judith was amazing. She had known the deep anguish Judith had suffered when Peter broke up with her. She had felt humiliated and low, the sparkle went out of her life, but now the old Judith was back with a vengeance. She was confident, glowing even, her old personality was back. It was amazing and June thought it must be due to this man, Konrad. He must be very special to get through to Judith and bring her back to the land of the living. June was pleased for her sister; the thoughts of her going and leaving the family were purely selfish. 'So you are really going back, Judith?' June asked.

'Yes, I am, I have made my mind up. Life is too short to miss this chance of happiness with Konrad, so yes, I am going. I know this is a shock to you all but there was no easy way of telling you.' Judith sat back and waited for their reaction.

Her father looked steadily at her. 'You know we will miss you, Judith, but I think you should follow your heart.'

Joyce looked sharply at her husband. 'Are you sure that's the right advice?'

'Yes, I am; what has happened to me this last year has changed my view of life, Joyce. She should take this chance of happiness – you never know what's round the corner waiting for you.' He looked sad and they could tell he was thinking of the poor walker and his family. 'Go for it, Judith, that's my advice, we won't fall apart and we will visit you regularly. We have the money to do this as the businesses are doing so well.'

'Yes, I suppose you are right, Richard. She should go, and if it doesn't work out she knows we are all here for her. He must be a very special man to sweep you off your feet, this Konrad,' said Joyce.

'Yes, he is, Mummy. It happened so quickly. We do love each other and he is waiting there for me to return. Elaine left England and married a South African man and is very happy with him and her children. They have very moral views, I should say old-fashioned views on family life, and I like that. I felt comfortable with them and Konrad. He says I could help in the estate agency, with my experience here. So it should all work out,' Judith said.

'Will you get married?' asked her sister.

'Oh, definitely, but first we will get engaged and Konrad said to wait and see if I settle out there. He will do everything in his power to make me happy and look after me, Daddy.' She looked firmly at her father. Father and mother knew at that moment that their daughter was committed to returning and nothing was going to change her decision.

'Come here, Judith, and give us a hug,' her father said. Judith got up, crossed the room, and sat down between the two.

'We are going to miss you dreadfully, darling,' Joyce said to her daughter. 'But you go with our blessing and our love.'

Judith burst into tears. 'Oh I have been so worried about this, I didn't want to upset you all. I do love you so much. In the morning, Konrad will be phoning here about 9 a.m., that's 11 a.m. there. He wants to speak to you, Daddy.'

'Well, that's fine with me, Judith, I look forward to speaking to our future son-in-law,' said Richard. 'I shall wait for his phone call. Have you got a photo of your young man, then I know who I am speaking to – it would make it easier?' her father asked.

'Yes, here you are,' said Judith. She produced the photo from her bag and they all crowded round to look. What they saw was a tall, blond man with lovely deep blue eyes. He was dressed in a city suit, collar and tie. They all said how nice he looked and Judith propped up the photograph by the phone.

The next morning, and dead at 9 a.m., the phone rang. Richard reached out for it and answered. He had insisted on being alone for his first talk with Konrad. He didn't want any distractions from the girls.

Konrad had quite a strong South African accent so he spoke slowly so Richard could understand him. Richard asked him many questions about his life there and of course his prospects. He knew this was expected of a future father-in-law. He liked the sound of Konrad, a firm but kind voice and he punctuated his replies with 'Sir'. This impressed Richard. Yes, old-fashioned values, he thought.

Konrad invited the family to come over and stay with him and Judith. It was an open house; they could come any time and stay as long as they wanted. He would show them his country and Richard could tell he was very proud of it. On the business side, they enjoyed a mutual interest and the girls could hear Richard laughing on the phone.

'Good sign,' June said to Judith.

Judith was getting more and more agitated. How long would her father be quizzing Konrad? Then suddenly her father called, 'Judith, Konrad wants to speak to you.' She rushed to the phone and Richard slipped out of the room and left her alone.

'Well, darling, what did he say?' Judith asked.

'He was great, Judith. You were right. He is a caring father. If I had a gorgeous daughter like you, I would have been much harder on this foreign man, who wants to whisk her away from him,' Konrad said.

'Ah, I love you so much, Konrad.'

'Love you loads too. When are you coming to me? I can't wait, poppet,' Konrad asked.

'Soon, darling. I need to get my papers in order and then I will fly out to you.'

'All right, but hurry and ring me all the time. Missing you loads.'

'Bye darling, missing you already,' whispered Judith.

She put the phone down and sat quietly on her own. She was going to change her life. This was the big adventure she had been waiting for. Konrad was not like any Englishman. He was quite different. It was difficult to put a finger on what was different. But his upbringing and the success in his life made him seem a more mature and a more solid person. Not as shallow as the English boys she had as friends. Konrad would look after her and protect her, she knew this. She was at the start of her new life with Konrad.

Chapter Seven

The weeks passed quickly and June helped her sister pack up her worldly possessions into big boxes. June made a list of every item in each box so that Judith would know where everything was when they arrived in South Africa. In a way it was sad for June, but she kept her feelings hidden from Judith and her parents. She went with Judith and bought new clothes, underwear and make-up. It was like buying a trousseau for a bride. Judith was getting very excited and at long last she started to say goodbye to all her friends and relatives. She even went over to their other office to see Peter. As she walked in he looked startled. 'It's OK, Peter. I have only come to say goodbye. I am going to South Africa tomorrow, so I won't see you again,' Judith said.

She looked a million dollars. She had dressed in some of her new wardrobe and her make-up was perfection. She had a lovely golden tan still from her stay in South Africa and she knew she looked absolutely gorgeous. Peter stared at her, speechless. 'Well, I had to come and see you just to thank you,' she said.

'What do you mean, thank me?' Peter asked her. He kept staring at her from behind his desk. He hadn't even stood up when she came into his office, he was so stunned by her appearance.

'It's a big thank you to you, Peter, because of you and the miserable way you treated me, I took off and found my future husband, Konrad.' She looked so proud. 'So goodbye and enjoy your life, because I am certainly going to enjoy mine.' At that, Judith turned and walked out of the office.

Peter sat still at his desk and watched her. He couldn't think of any silly remark to shout after her. She was right. He had treated her badly and through the year she had kept her silence, which enabled him to further his career at Farnham's. If Richard had found out he would have been out on his ear. He now realised he had let a wonderful girl slip through his fingertips. He would never find any girl to match up to Judith. This Konrad was a lucky man.

★

Six months later, a large photograph appeared in the local newspaper announcing the wedding of Judith, eldest daughter of Mr and Mrs Farnham living at Shirley, to Konrad Greeff in Cape Town, South Africa.

Richard Farnham gave away his daughter and June was a bridesmaid. That could have been me, thought Peter selfishly. He had lost out with Judith playing 'silly beggars' and trying to be clever. He now realised that he must have upset her a lot. How she kept on working so close to him, he would never know. It just showed what a strong character she was, just like her father. It made him feel very small and stupid.

When Judith's family returned to England, they talked about their stay in Cape Town. June loved the vibrant place, the weather and, most of all, the people. Konrad had taken her on a tour of the large private hospital near to his home, and she was very impressed. The baby unit was large and airy and the equipment was very advanced. It was set on the hillside overlooking the harbour with Table Mountain behind. The view from the unit was stunning and she thought that to work there would be wonderful.

Richard and Joyce also liked the area. Richard was very impressed with Fritz and Konrad's business. They were ahead in their outlook and very ambitious, as he had been a few years earlier.

The previous year's events had taken their toll on him. His drive had gone and he just went through the motions. He was glad Peter was his partner now and left most of the innovation to him. He was secretly tired of business now and rarely saw his old golfing partner, Frank. He had never played golf again and had sold all his clubs to Peter. He was much quieter, not so forceful, in fact easier to work and live with. Joyce, on the other hand, missed Judith immensely. She missed her at home, but mostly in the office. She could always hear her voice ringing through the office, but now with the new receptionist it all seemed so different. But she must not dwell on that because she had seen Judith's new life with Konrad and she was so happy for her. Thank goodness Judith had found a man who would look after her and adore her for the rest of her life and that, being a mother, was what Joyce wanted for her daughter.

Even the Yarwoods detected a difference. When Judith was around, Shirley seemed alive and vibrant. Her room used to be so untidy. Now Mrs Yarwood found it unnaturally tidy. No clothes strewn around, no make-up littering her dressing table; it was as though Judith had never existed. Would June be the next to leave Shirley? Mrs Yarwood wondered. The family would be dwindling and soon there would only be Mr and Mrs Farnham. She and Mr Yarwood had been talking about retiring soon. Mr Yarwood's arthritis was playing him up and she was getting more tired. They both had their pensions now and, with what they had saved, they knew that they could live comfortably. They were not used to having a lot of money and as they got older they seemed to need less. So they would be all right in their old age. But they had not discussed this with Mr and Mrs Farnham. They thought they would wait a while; perhaps nearer the wintertime would be a good time for them to retire.

Mr Yarwood did not think he could work through another winter. His old body was slowing down and every morning it was getting harder to get going in the garden. He dreaded a severe winter and he thought Mrs Yarwood was right; they should give up soon. He and his wife had worked for so many families living in Shirley and had shared all the traumas of the family lives.

As they had not had any children, Shirley had been their whole life. It would be hard saying goodbye, but it was long overdue. Only through the kindness of the Farnhams had they been able to carry on in the last few years. So Mr and Mrs Yarwood had stayed on and continued with their valued work at Shirley.

The next few months passed swiftly. Time seemed to be non-existent. June worked on at the hospital and played hard in her leisure. She phoned Judith regularly and listened to her sister's life in Cape Town. She could visualise all the places Judith mentioned and also her new circle of friends. Judith seemed to have blossomed again due to new life there with Konrad. She did miss her sister and looked forward to her next visit to Cape Town. Richard and Joyce continued to work in the estate agency business. Both offices were extremely busy. Their reputation was excellent in the estate agents' world. Richard was shrewd and calm these days, not so volatile, and Joyce excelled with the personal touch. This still brought in a lot of business. People trusted them with the biggest transaction of their lives – a time fraught with stress and emotion – but in the Farnhams' capable hands, their professionalism lessened the problem.

Richard had been unusually preoccupied of late and Joyce wondered if he was slipping into a depression again. She called in at Peter's office and had a talk with him. 'How are you, Peter? Everything all right in the office?' she asked.

'Oh, certainly, Mrs Farnham, the business is flowing in and the sales are good. You and Mr Farnham have seen the figures?' he asked Joyce.

'Yes, I have. We were only discussing them last night. You are doing an excellent job, Peter. No, what I came to see you about was Richard. He seems so... well, I don't know how to say it.' She faltered a little.

'Preoccupied, do you mean?' Peter asked.

'Yes, that's the word. What do you think? He isn't slipping into a depression, is he?' she enquired.

'Oh, I hope not, but I know he has been calling into Frank's office recently. FJ mentioned it. But of course he wouldn't say. Confidentiality and all that, you know,' Peter paused.

'I wonder what he is up to?' Joyce said.

'Perhaps he may be thinking of opening another office. The time is right, so perhaps he is discussing that. Mrs Farnham, I certainly don't think he is ill again. Rest assured he seems quite happy again. Why don't you ask him?'

'Yes, I might do that, though most decisions I leave to him. Well, thank you, Peter. By the way, you have heard Judith is married now and living in South Africa? She is very happy and making a new life for herself there. We all miss her dreadfully but as long as she is happy that is all that we want for her. I always thought that you and she might make a go of it. I know Richard hoped that, but it wasn't to be, was it? Bye, Peter. I'll speak to Richard.' Joyce smiled at Peter and left the office. Peter stood still for a moment. What a lovely family they were; what a fool he had been. He had ruined what could have been a great future together. I hope you are very happy Judith, you deserve it, Peter thought.

That night after dinner Joyce poured Richard a drink. They were together in the sitting room. June was at the hospital, so Joyce decided to speak to Richard. 'Richard, dear, is anything troubling you? You seem far away at times. Are you all right?' Joyce asked softly.

'Yes, Joyce, I am fine. I was going to talk to you. Something has cropped up to do with the business. We need to discuss it,' He looked very serious.

'What on earth is it?' She looked alarmed.

'It's all right, Joyce. In fact, it's a nice surprise,' Richard smiled.

'Well, don't keep me in suspense, Richard,' Joyce said quickly.

'You know the big estate agency Barrat and Brown?'

'Yes of course I know them. They are the biggest firm going,' Joyce said.

'Barrat and Brown have contacted me. It seems our success has been noted and they have made the first move to take us over.'

'What, take us, Farnham's?' She was shocked.

'Yes, that's what I said. Take us over, lock, stock and barrel,' Richard stated. 'The buildings, the businesses, the staff and not forgetting our goodwill.'

'My goodness, when did this happen?' Joyce asked.

'Last week, and I have been discussing the implications with Frank before I discussed it with you.' Richard paused.

Joyce was staggered by Richard's words. She had not expected this at all. 'So, what did Frank say?' she asked.

'He said we both should go to meet Barrat and Brown and see what they are offering.'

'You and Frank?'

'No, us two; you are a partner in our firm, Joyce, so we both would go with Frank and see what they have in mind.'

'Where would we go?' Joyce asked.

'I would think their representatives would come up from London and meet us in a hotel. We would not want them to come to our offices in case our staff caught wind of this. We have to listen carefully and then discuss the offer with Frank and our accountant, then make a decision.'

'I can't believe this, Richard,' Joyce said.

'You see, Barrat and Brown want a toehold in the north and, as we are so successful in this area, we are their first target.' She could see Richard was proud of this and she was too.

Richard was proud and excited, but he was also apprehensive. He was in unknown territory; lawyers, accountants, these people were not in his world. 'We will tread carefully, Joyce, and if we don't like what they are offering, we won't sell,' Richard announced.

'All right, Richard, but let's be careful. Our offices are our life's work so we must be sure of all the facts.'

'Oh, we will be, Joyce, we will be sure,' Richard said.

Next morning Richard spoke to Barrat and Brown and arranged a meeting. Richard contacted Frank and his accountant, and with Joyce they drove to a quiet hotel in the country. The discussions went on all day with a break for lunch, for which Barrat and Brown footed the bill.

The meeting was quite amicable. The partner from Barrat and Brown was a very pleasant and courteous man. Richard got on with him surprisingly well. The rest of his team talked to Frank and his accountant. Joyce just sat in on the discussions, listening intently but silently watching the group. After lunch they retired to a room on their own. Frank, as Richard's solicitor, said he was happy with the contract, Richard's accountant was more than happy with the amount offered for Farnhams. Richard and Joyce were stunned by the offer. They had no idea their business was worth so much. It was obvious that Barrat and Brown were desperate to start up in the north. They had already covered the south and part of the Midlands. All four decided there and then to accept the offer.

The Farnham Family

'You are quite sure that this is what we both want?' Richard asked Joyce.

'Yes, I am sure, and are you, dear?'

'Yes, I have been getting tired of the business lately and I think we both could benefit from this,' Richard replied.

'I should say so,' said Frank, beaming at them both. 'Do you realise this will set you up for life. If you invest this money, you will be very comfortable, old chap.' Frank patted Richard on the back and hugged Joyce. 'You both deserve this. You have worked long and hard to get to this point. Congratulations. So come along, let's go back in and you can give them your answer,' Frank said. The Farnhams' accountant was also very pleased with the offer and he agreed with Frank.

They all walked back into the meeting and Richard announced to Barrat and Brown's that they would accept their offer for the businesses. But one clause he wanted adding in the contract was a clause that they keep on the existing staff, including Peter. That was agreed. Until the papers had all been signed and the finances were in place, nobody would say a word to anybody.

When they got home, Richard and Joyce were exhausted. They sat on the sofa together, holding hands, and could hardly believe what had happened.

'Joyce, you realise we are made for life?'

'Oh yes, I do realise that. You won't miss the office, Richard, will you? You won't miss going in every day, dear?' she asked.

'No, I won't. I think my heart went out of the business a few years ago when I had my breakdown. But now I see this as a fresh start, just us together again, more time for us.' He smiled at Joyce. He loved her so much. He had never looked at another woman. She was the only woman he wanted for the rest of his life. He kissed her and looked into her eyes. 'I love you, Joyce. I love you so much.' His eyes filled with tears.

'Now then, dear. I love you too. Hold me tight.' Joyce snuggled up to him and they sat on the sofa like two little lovebirds.

'What's all this, you two canoodling on the sofa?' a voice said. They both sprang apart. 'Oh, June, you gave us such a shock. When did you come in?' Joyce asked her daughter.

'Just now. Finished my shift, so I thought I might have a sleep for a few hours. You two OK?' June asked.

'Yes we are. We finished early today so we have just got in,' her father said. Richard and Joyce looked at each other.

'Everything all right? You look very secretive,' June asked them both.

'No dear, everything is fine. Go and have a rest. I will call you when dinner is ready,' her mother said.

June left the room and Joyce said, 'I suppose we will have to keep it a secret even from June?' she asked her husband.

'Yes, we better had, just in case,' he answered.

'Oh, Richard, isn't it marvellous?' Joyce sighed.

'Yes, dear. It is marvellous,' Richard agreed.

Through the following weeks papers, documents and contracts flowed backwards and forwards from Richard's solicitor and accountant to Barrat and Brown's. Eventually everybody was happy with the negotiations and the final contract was signed. It was left to Richard and Joyce to inform their staff, although their jobs were secure with the new owners. Peter was the most shocked, but Richard was sure his future was secure with Barrat and Brown and there was more chance of promotion in a large company.

June was told at last and was staggered at the large amount her parents had been paid for Farnham's. She had no idea that their businesses were worth so much. The only thing that saddened Richard was the fact that the name Farnham's would be lost in favour of Barrat and Brown. He had always liked to see his family name around the area on the 'For Sale' boards.

Life settled down again and Richard and Joyce took to retirement extremely well. They visited Judith again in South Africa and on the way back Richard sprang another surprise. 'How would you like to live in Cape Town, old dear?'

'What did you say?' She was shocked.

'You heard. Cape Town with Judith and Konrad,' Richard said.

'Oh, I don't know,' Joyce said. 'What about June?'

'June will come with us. We could get Konrad to find us a nice house by the coast outside Cape Town and June could work in that hospital she visited. How about it? There's nothing keeping us here. We have no elderly parents to look after now, so now's the time. Judith had an adventure, so it's our time, old girl, to have an adventure, and we would all be together again, think of that.' He paused and looked at her.

After a time she said, 'Yes, Richard, let's do it. A new start, a new life for us all. It would be lovely to be with Judith again. I know June has missed her sister like we have. Let's talk to her when we get back.' Joyce was getting excited now.

When June came off duty, they couldn't wait to talk to her. Her reaction was as they had expected. She was all in favour of the move to South Africa. She had nobody special in her life and what she had seen of Konrad's friends was what she wanted in a man. 'Oh yes! It's a brilliant idea. When would we go?' she asked.

'Wait a minute,' said her father. 'First things first. We will have to sell Shirley. I wouldn't want to go and leave the house empty. And Konrad will have to find us another house.'

'No, I think we would be better staying with Judith and looking for our home ourselves. I would rather do that,' Joyce said.

'Yes, you are right. We will sell Shirley and then go and stay with Judith,' Richard agreed.

'You have both forgotten one thing,' June butted into their conversation. 'You haven't told Judith of your plans yet,' she added.

'Oh no, we haven't! Get on the phone, Richard, now. It will only be 8 p.m. there. Ring her now,' Joyce replied. Richard made the phone call and they could all hear Judith squeal down the phone. She was so excited about their news. To have all her family with her again would be wonderful. She loved her life with Konrad, but to have them with her would be the icing on the cake.

Plans were put in motion. June gave in her notice at once and Richard called in Mr and Mrs Yarwood. He told them of their plan to move to South Africa and the old couple were very pleased for the Farnhams. This also meant that they could retire gracefully themselves. Richard had already discussed with Joyce a lump sum to be placed in the Yarwoods' savings account, which would secure their old age. Mrs Yarwood burst into tears when she heard and thanked the Farnhams from the bottom of her heart. The couple agreed to keep on working until a buyer had been found. Shirley had to look its best for the sale.

Within a few weeks, a buyer had been found. Barrat and Brown did a good job in finding a purchaser for Shirley. Richard and Joyce decided that Shirley should be sold with all its furniture, as they would not want to ship it out – it would be too costly. The Yarwoods retired and Richard, Joyce and June packed up their personal possessions. They had a little drinks party for friends before they left. Richard found it hard to say goodbye to his friend Frank. They had been pals for a long time and had been through some good and bad times too.

When the guests had all left, Richard and Joyce sat in the sitting room, exhausted from the long day. They had just started to relax when June called down from upstairs. 'Daddy, come and look. Come quickly.'

Richard ran upstairs and found June in the back bedroom. 'What is it, June?' he called.

'Look, look out there. I was just putting Mummy's handbag in her bedroom. See there, who's that?' she whispered. Richard looked out from their bedroom across the back garden over the fence into the field, and there stood a man. He seemed to be staring at the house. He was very dishevelled and looked menacing.

Richard watched the man from the window but the man never moved. He just stood still in the middle of the field and stared. 'What's he doing, Daddy?'

'I don't know, June,' said her father.

'I don't like the look of him. He is quite frightening,' June whispered to her father.

'Come away from the window now,' her father ordered. 'Don't watch him any more, June. Tell Mother to stay in the house and I will keep an eye on him,' her father said.

June raced downstairs and Richard moved to the side of the window behind the curtain. To him the man looked either down on his luck or completely lost. He didn't seem threatening to Richard. In fact he just looked like a lost soul in clothes.

Hour upon hour the man just stood in the field and, as dusk was falling, Richard started to get worried. He thought by now the man would have gone, but he hadn't, nor had he moved. Richard was getting unnerved by his presence. Should he go out and speak to him, or should he ignore him? It was getting quite dark and the man was now a silhouette against the night sky. This made him look more menacing, so Richard decided to call the police.

They came round quickly and Richard escorted them up to the bedroom window. They looked at the man and the older policeman suddenly said, 'Stay where you are. Keep your family inside. Leave this to us, Sir.' The policemen made their way through the gate at the bottom of the garden and, in a matter of moments, Richard could see them on either side of the man.

He seemed to crumple to the ground and the men helped him to his feet. He watched them walk him slowly to the large gate leading on to the road. Next minute the older policeman was back at the house. Richard let him in. 'Who is he?' Richard asked the policeman.

'I need to speak to you alone, Sir, if I may?' he said politely.

'In here then,' Richard showed the policeman into the dining room. 'Sit down, will you,' Richard asked.

'It's all right. I will stand if you don't mind, Sir.' He cleared his throat and said, 'That man lived in the village years ago. He was one of the coal merchant's sons. A bit simple that one, always in trouble with the girls. Well, he attacked a young girl and killed her, in the field there. Didn't you know, Sir?' he asked Richard.

'No, I never knew, nor my family,' Richard was shocked.

'Yes, it was a nasty business, but because he was, well, a simple soul, he got manslaughter and was then in a mental home for a long time. He had just been released. We were notified at the station, but we didn't think he would return here. None of his family have kept in contact with him, you see, so there was no reason for him to come back here.'

'Well, he obviously thought he had a reason, Sergeant,' Richard exclaimed. 'We should have been warned. I have a young daughter and a wife here. You should have warned us.' Richard was getting angry.

'We are not allowed to do that, Sir. I am sorry this has happened.' The policeman looked uneasy.

'What are you going to do now?' demanded Richard.

'We will keep him at the police station tonight.'

'Then what?' demanded Richard again.

'I think judging from his appearance and his behaviour he will be put back into a mental home. He is a broken man. He can't look after himself. He is institutionalised now and needs protective care,' said the sergeant.

'I should think so. I shall come to the station tomorrow and demand to know what is to be done with him. I won't leave this alone. He is not safe to be left to roam around on his own. It's disgraceful.' Richard was getting very worked up.

'Yes Sir. Call in tomorrow and I will ask my superior to speak to you. I am very sorry this has happened, Sir.' At that the policemen left and Richard joined the girls in the sitting room.

None of them had ever heard of the man or the poor girl. Not even the Yarwoods had mentioned the murder. Perhaps they thought that nobody would even want to buy Shirley if they knew. 'I hope this doesn't get into the papers or we might lose our sale of Shirley,' Richard said quietly to the two girls.

They had had a narrow escape. Goodness knows what would have happened if June or Joyce had approached the man. The thought made Richard shudder.

Next day, Richard presented himself at the police station.

★

A few months elapsed and the sale of Shirley was complete. The Farnhams had booked their flight tickets to South Africa and their new life was to begin. They were looking forward to seeing Judith and her husband, Konrad, and settling into Cape Town. Konrad had lined up some wonderful houses overlooking the ocean that he felt sure his in-laws would like. He was so pleased they were coming to live with them – he knew they would make wonderful grandparents in the near future. Judith and June would be together again and life would have come full circle. What more could they ask for?

The Farnham Family

On the day they left Shirley, the Yarwoods came up from the village. Once again they helped the family to leave and told the Farnhams they would clean through the house for the last time, ready for the new owners. They would not be working for the new owners, following their retirement, but wanted to do this for the Farnhams. Mr Yarwood mowed the lawn for the last time and Mrs Yarwood tidied up the house. By 6 p.m. the house and garden were shipshape. The Yarwoods left the key under the mat in the big porch, and set off home.

The House

'Do not go and leave me, do not go!' I call out, but they don't hear me. The man and woman put my front door key under the mat and walk away from me. Who will look after me now? The woman has cleaned and polished me for years and the man has tended to my garden and orchard. What is to become of me? They have always been with me. All my families have come and gone, but they have stayed with me. I see them walking down the lane to the village. I try and call to them, but they do not hear. If only they would turn and look up at me, they might return to me. But they do not. They walk slowly into the distance until I can see them no longer.

I am all alone again. One minute I am full of life, the next empty, silent. Sometimes when this happens I like the peace and serenity and enjoy the solitude. But today I feel lonely and neglected. I feel sorry for myself. My life is the family that lives inside of me. I have learned this over the years. I used to be glad when the families had gone, but now, as I get older myself, I get lonely. Old age is hard to bear.

Although a lot of my rooms are different now – they call it 'more modern' – I still feel old. They can do lots of things to my inside, but my structure makes me feel old. I liked this family a lot. They were caring with me. They took a pride in living in me, I could tell that. I meant something to them and I did think they would grow old with me. But they are not doing that. Off again to pastures new, leaving me here. I am the solid foundation, which doesn't move. Let them all move around, I don't care as long as I am strong. I can accept a new family graciously. I shall welcome them and try and give them a secure life inside me. What happens in the world does not interest me at all. My world is deep inside me and my gardens are like a moat around me.

So here I am again, shining and gleaming as the sun goes down, waiting for the next family to come and live their lives in me. I wonder who it will be, and I hope again that there will be children, not too many, to run and play in my garden. A happy, loving couple to breathe life into me again. I will sleep now and rest. Perhaps tomorrow will be a new beginning for me.

The Baxter Family

Chapter One

Dr Jonathan Baxter was exhausted when he turned on to Shirley's driveway. The journey from Beaconsfield had been a long and tedious one. The family had made frequent stops along the way to enable his two sons to stretch their legs and let off steam. The boys, Paul, aged nine, and Mathew, aged seven, squabbled in the back of the car constantly and this made concentrating on driving more difficult for him. Margaret just sat in the front, oblivious to the mayhem in the rear of the car and gazed out on to the countryside. As they approached the North, Margaret started to think how gloomy and grey everything looked. Even the sun had hidden behind large, foreboding clouds. She had not been to see their new home and had left the viewing to her husband. Margaret worked as a nurse in a local care home and would not take time off for house hunting. It was her way of conveying to her husband that she did not want to move north. She couldn't broach the subject with him seeing as he was so excited about his promotion to Senior Consultant Radiologist at this large hospital.

Jonathan was overwhelmed at landing this prestigious position and looked forward to his career enhancement at the hospital. He couldn't wait to start his new job and had found the estate agents Barrat and Brown in Beaconsfield most helpful. They had just acquired two new offices in the area where he was looking for a house. This was a marvellous coincidence and Jonathan thought it a good omen for his future in that area. Barrat and Brown had shown him the details of Shirley and he liked the house immediately. They said it was only half an hour to his new hospital, so Jonathan travelled up to see the house alone. He took photographs of its interior to show Margaret and he was sure she would love the house. There was no chain in the sale, as the owners were moving to South Africa. Their own house sold quickly; there was no delay in either completion. The house had a wonderful garden and orchard, which he knew Paul and Mathew would find a good use for. He toyed with the idea of changing the orchard into a tennis court, but that could be decided later.

'Settle down, boys, while I open the house up, please,' Jonathan said, turning to the two in the rear of the car. 'Shan't be a minute.' He leapt out, took out a bunch of keys and proceeded to open the large front door. 'OK, come on in all of you,' he called to his family. He hoped they liked the house as much as he did.

The first thing Margaret said was, 'We shall have to change the name. Fancy calling a house Shirley!'

'It's a daft name,' said Paul.

'Daft, daft, daft,' mimicked his brother.

'Now just hang on, you lot. This house was named after the builder's wife, who tragically died before they could live in it. He built the house for her and she never managed to live in it so he called it Shirley after his wife. I think that was a lovely thing to do. So the name stays.' Jonathan looked at his wife.

'All right, I suppose,' she said begrudgingly.

'Have a look around the house.' Jonathan was feeling weary and fed up trying to appease his family. The boys ran up the stairs and they were soon claiming a bedroom each. Margaret walked around the house, trying to show Jonathan enthusiasm for their new home. It was the first time she had seen the house and she was surprised at the quality of the panelling and the wonderful fireplaces in each room. The house was surprisingly light and very spacious. She particularly liked the sitting room with the French door opening on to the garden. She also noticed that the furniture left by the previous owner was good quality. It was in perfect condition. The dining table did not have one scratch on it. She did think that the furniture would be shabby and need replacing, but this was not the case.

Margaret started to warm to the house as she wandered round the rooms. She particularly liked the large kitchen, which had been modernised, and the large utility room, which was useful for muddy boots and sports clothes.

She went upstairs and along the landing. The main bedroom

was at the back, overlooking a large field. They were bringing their own beds so the existing beds would be taken down and away by the removal firm.

'Margaret, quick, they are here,' Jonathan called out from the hall.

She ran downstairs in time to see the large removal van reverse up the drive. She called the boys and said, 'When your belongings come into the hall, carry them up to your rooms and out of the way, do you hear me, you two?'

'Yes, we will do that, Mother,' said Paul.

'Mat, did you hear what I said?' she called to Mathew.

'Yes I did. I'm coming.' Mat came downstairs two at a time.

'Right, boys, let's get started. Mother, find the kettle in the kitchen boxes when they come in. I'm very thirsty and the men need a brew too,' called Jonathan.

The day flew by, and, surprisingly, everybody worked well. The new beds were in place and Margaret had made them up ready for sleep. 'I could just crawl into bed now,' she moaned.

'Keep going, the van is nearly empty,' Jonathan said encouragingly. He was amazed how the boys buckled down and helped the men unload. The removal men were a very jolly lot and, plied with lots of tea, sandwiches and cake, they laughed and joked all day.

When they left at 6 p.m., the house was reasonably straight. Margaret was pleased with the progress made, as a disorganised environment was the one thing worrying her about moving. But the day had been a success. Jonathan set off to the village, brought back fish and chips, and they all sat round the kitchen table for their first meal in Shirley. 'Not been too bad a day, Margaret?' asked Jonathan.

'No, it all went well, didn't it?'

'You haven't said yet what you think of Shirley,' he asked her.

'I am surprised. From the photos you took it looked too large and foreboding. But it's not. It's a real family home. It has a good feel to it. I noticed this when I walked in. I think there have been some happy times here. The atmosphere is good. Yes, I like Shirley and we will keep the name.' She beamed at her husband.

'In time we will change a few things, make it ours, but just for the time being we will live in it, get the boys settled in their new school and I will start my new job,' Jonathan said.

'Yes, I think you are right. We need to settle, find our feet and then later in the year if we need to change anything, that will be the time,' said Margaret.

That night, their first night, they all fell asleep quickly, exhausted from the day's activities and emotional upheaval. Jonathan and Margaret were in the main bedroom overlooking the field, Paul was in the front bedroom overlooking the garden and Mat in the smaller bedroom at the rear. Silence and peace descended on Shirley. Tomorrow would be a new start to their lives.

The next few days passed quickly for Jonathan and Margaret. Their first priority was to settle Paul and Mat in their primary school. They had made enquiries at the estate agents before purchasing Shirley as to the standard of the local schools and, as luck would have it, the closest school to them was the best. Paul was extremely clever, like his father, and always excelled academically. He found lessons easy and sailed through exams with hardly any revision. If his parents pressured him about homework, he would say, 'I've done it,' and he had, quickly and accurately. In a year's time they would have to think of senior schools. Jonathan wanted his eldest to go to his old boarding school in Wales. He had loved it there and he thought Paul would do well there. Mat, on the other hand, was less academic and more practical. He could hold his own in class but had to do more revision to get good results. He was more outgoing than Paul and excelled at sport. He left the clever stuff to his brother. Moving school was no problem to him. He would soon make friends. He was extrovert while Paul was more reserved and slower with friendships.

Margaret did not mollycoddle the boys. She soon packed them off to their new school. They would quickly find their feet, and anyway, there was no other option. They were here now and they would have to settle in. She made no fuss about it. Her view was to just get on with life. She was practical and firm with her sons and this attitude stood them in good stead.

Dr Jonathan Baxter took up his new position at the large city hospital. He was given a large, fully staffed office, which had been vacated by the previous senior consultant. There were three departments which he controlled: Outpatients' X-Rays, which dealt with accidents, fractures and chest X-rays, Main X-Rays, which dealt with more clinical X-rays like barium meals, IVP and so on, and Neuro X-Rays, where they dealt with neurological X-rays. Jonathan had a team of radiologists, who in turn worked in the different departments. These departments were run by radiographers, who did the X-ray work and developed the films, which were then reported on by the doctor radiologist. The more invasive X-rays were carried out by these doctors, who were assisted by the radiographers. Each department also had an office with clerical staff, who made appointments and watched over the comings and goings of patients. As this was a huge teaching hospital coupled with a very large accident and emergency department, the workload in the X-ray department was enormous. Jonathan's position was head of this domain and he was looking forward to the challenge. It would be a couple of months, though, before he felt relaxed and could find his way round. It also took time to learn the names of his colleagues, but his secretary helped him a lot and soon he felt at home in his new position. His rewards were a much larger salary and longer holidays. This was his life's work and he did feel well rewarded.

As for Margaret, she had no need to work now. Her job as a carer in a private nursing home had been quite exhausting but, as she wasn't qualified in anything, the wages had been a little extra for her and the boys. With extra time on her hands, she decided that her first priority was to sort out the house and the garden.

When Jonathan and the boys went off, she worked long and hard sorting out the removal boxes and rearranging Shirley's furniture. She was a natural homemaker and organiser and could tackle anything in the house. Each room, starting with the sitting room, received her personal touches. Changing only the cushions and lamps, and displaying her own ornaments around, made the room look totally different.

At the centre of the dining room table, a huge bowl of freshly cut roses filled the air with their heady scent. Again, table lamps and standard lamps were placed around the room to give it an intimate feel. Shirley's hall had a new Chinese rug at the foot of the stairs and, on the hall table, Margaret placed another bowl of flowers. Upstairs Margaret changed all the curtains and bed covers to more modern ones and bought new bathmats for the bathroom. A long Chinese runner was placed along the landing and matching lamps were placed on either side of the long hall table.

When it came to the kitchen, she redecorated the walls in a pale yellow and put up yellow curtains which had patterns of herbs on them. She made a couple of tablecloths to match and painted the kitchen table yellow again. The wooden units blended in with the new colour scheme and the whole effect was bright and cheerful. Perhaps next year she might persuade Jonathan to refit the kitchen.

But Margaret was happy with Shirley for now, and she was not one to push for new things. She was quite content and knew that money was limited, even though her husband had a good salary. The house looked like her home now and she was very pleased with the changes; even though they were small, the difference in the house was quite dramatic. She had a real talent for this and enjoyed the process.

At weekends, they both set about the garden, weeding, pruning and mowing. The garden, front and back, was large. They hadn't realised just how large at first. So Jonathan thought it was time to visit the Yarwoods in the village. He had been left their address in case they had any questions about Shirley.

Jonathan called on them one morning. 'Good day, Mr Yarwood. I am Dr Baxter, the new owner of Shirley,' he said.

'Oh, come in, pleased to meet you, Sir,' said Mr Yarwood. He was shown into their home. It was small but it shone from top to bottom.

Mrs Yarwood rose as he came in. 'Good morning, Dr Baxter,' she said.

'Well, I just thought I would come and introduce myself to you, as the Farnhams spoke so highly of you both.' Jonathan beamed at them.

'Sit yourself down, Doctor,' said Mr Yarwood. 'Would you like a cup of tea?' asked Mrs Yarwood.

'I would love one, if it's not too much trouble,' he replied. Mrs Yarwood bustled out to her small kitchen.

'Mr Yarwood, I know you are not working any more, but Shirley's garden is beyond us. We wondered if you knew of anybody who would give us, let's say, two days a week?' Jonathan asked.

'I'll ask around; somebody reliable, somebody I know, that's what you need,' replied Mr Yarwood.

'Yes, that's exactly what I need,' laughed Jonathan.

'Here you are, Doctor, a nice cup of tea.' Mrs Yarwood came into the room carrying a tray with her best china on it and some homemade biscuits.

'This is lovely. Thank you, Mrs Yarwood,' Jonathan felt at ease with the couple. No wonder they had worked so long at Shirley for so many families, he thought. He would have loved to have them around his children. They would have been like an extended family. But he could see that they needed their retirement, and to enjoy the rest of their lives together.

Jonathan stayed with them for a long time, asking them about their life at Shirley. They were extremely interesting to talk to and he promised to bring his family to meet them. They in turn were interested in the Baxters, and the time flew by.

Eventually, Jonathan left the couple, shaking their hands warmly. On his way home he thought, What a shame that his parents and Margaret's had died so young and that Paul and Mathew had no grandparents to talk to! He made a mental note to take Margaret and the boys to visit the Yarwoods, or perhaps ask them up to Shirley for tea. Yes, that would be nice, he thought. When Mr Yarwood contacted him about the gardener, he would do just that. Talking about the old days at Shirley would be fascinating for his family.

'How did you get on?' Margaret called from the garden.

Jonathan went out to her. 'They are a lovely old couple. You would love them. Their home is so clean and tidy and Mr Yarwood's little back garden is a picture and he has an allotment too,' he added.

'Can they find someone for us, dear?' she asked.

'Yes, he will ask around and find somebody he knows who is reliable,' Jonathan answered. 'But I still think I will change that large orchard into a tennis court. I can't see you bottling away all that fruit each year, can you?' he laughed at Margaret.

'No way, I draw the line at that. But won't it be expensive?' she asked.

'Well, if we put the kitchen on hold until next year, I see no reason why we shouldn't go ahead. The boys would love it and they could bring friends to play. I'll get some estimates and then we will take it from there,' Jonathan added.

The orchard was a perfect site for the court, as high hedges bordered three sides. The side next to their garden had a pergola full of climbing roses, which divided the main garden from the orchard. Jonathan was a little worried about telling Mr Yarwood his plan but, when he spoke next to the old man, he immediately said it was a good idea, with them having two boys. The orchard was labour-intensive, he added, and if you weren't going to use the fruit it was a wasted area.

Mr Yarwood introduced a new gardener to them that very week. Alan, who was a neighbour, was in his thirties and came two days a week and was able to get on with the job. Mr Yarwood had talked to him about the work, so there was no problem with him.

The tennis court company descended on the orchard and, after a month, the new court was laid. The family stood around watching the men mark out the new court, measuring and drawing the white lines. A new net was wound up and, at last, the court was ready to play on. It was very exciting and the whole family rushed out to play. Every evening and at weekends they had tennis matches. The family got quite competitive. As Jonathan had rightly predicted, the tennis court was a big draw for the boys' school friends.

Margaret was for ever carrying trays of orange squash and biscuits to the court for all these would-be tennis aces to devour. At weekends the front door knocker would go and a stream of boys would descend onto the garden for a game. Paul and Mat were so popular that they never noticed the move from south to north. The tennis court was a huge success.

Once a week Margaret would shop in the village and she always called at the Yarwoods. They in turn came up to Shirley regularly. She realised that, though they were retired, they missed their life at Shirley. Not having any family of their own, they had adopted all the families that they had worked for. So they still wanted to keep Shirley in their lives. Margaret liked the couple and Jonathan was right – their visits were good for the boys, and enabled them to meet and speak to another generation. Mrs Yarwood always brought homemade cake and biscuits with her. These were much appreciated by the family.

When Christmas came, Margaret invited the Yarwoods to share Christmas Day with them. It was a natural progression, she didn't need to ask for Jonathan's agreement as she knew he would be very pleased to include them. Mrs Yarwood provided a wonderful rich Christmas cake, beautifully iced and decorated with candles and snowmen. She also cooked a ham, which again was decorated with cloves and glazed in a diamond pattern. Jonathan had insisted that the Yarwoods brought no presents, so this was her contribution to Christmas Day.

After a wonderful dinner, Mr Yarwood introduced the boys to lots of parlour games, which he had remembered over the years. Paul and Mat really enjoyed these and they all joined in. It was their first Christmas at Shirley. The Christmas tree stood in the corner of the sitting room laden with decorations. The boys had put up streamers round the room and, with the open fire roaring up the chimney, it was a very festive scene. The only thing missing was snow; for this year at least, the two new sledges would remain in the garage.

Chapter Two

Once the festivities were over, the decorations came down and all that remained of Christmas was a lingering smell of pine needles. The start of the new year meant back to work for Jonathan and back to school for the boys. Margaret sighed with relief. It was a busy time for her over the Christmas period. The house was much larger than their previous house and it took a lot more looking after. But now she had some breathing space, until next half term at least, so she decided to do some extra work on the house. She had the small bedroom at the front of the house made into a games room and study for the boys.

Mrs Yarwood had said that years ago, this room had been the maid's room. She was a young girl called Maisie, who lived in. I wonder what happened to Maisie? I must ask Mrs Yarwood next time I see her, thought Margaret. I bet she lay in her bed in this little room and dreamed of meeting a prince, who would whisk her away on a snowy white horse and she would live happily ever after, thought Margaret. I wonder what did happen to her?

Life passed merrily at Shirley. The whole family came to love the house. It was as though they had been there for years. Jonathan couldn't wait to come home; but he was also happy in his new position at the hospital. He was well liked by his staff. He seemed to have the knack of organising everybody and every department without upsetting anyone. This was a great skill, and the X-ray departments were the envy of the other less well-organised departments. He made sure that his departments had the latest equipment and that it was in full working order; in particular that appointment times were strictly adhered to. No patient was left waiting and they were always handled in a caring way. He would move around his departments talking to both staff and patients, finding out if there was any need to improve standards.

He tried to not bring his work home, leaving time for his

family. He was a very caring man and would have made an excellent general practitioner, but had veered to the diagnostic side of medicine instead. The technique of radiography intrigued him and he hoped that in his lifetime new machines would be invented that could make diagnosis of disease deep in the body more accurate. He hoped this would happen in his working life.

Back at home, Margaret was beavering away as usual. She had made a few friends through the boys' school. Mothers who congregated at the school gate chatted to her and she soon found she was invited to coffee mornings and Tupperware parties. Her little social circle started to widen and Margaret felt comfortable in the area. She invited friends back to Shirley and she showed them what she had done with the rooms. They were soon asking her advice about colour schemes and materials to enhance their own homes. Margaret loved giving advice – she had a natural talent and flair to change the most ordinary, boring room into a fantastic area. 'That's just marvellous,' they would say. 'How did you think of that? I would never dream of that colour or doing that in this room,' they would chorus together.

'I don't know. I just seem to pick on something and work round it,' said Margaret, not wanting to sound too confident. 'You could all do it, I am sure,' she said to her friends. 'Pigs might fly,' one of them said, and they all fell about laughing.

One day Margaret heard the postman drop the letters through the letterbox. She ran downstairs and scooped them up. There were a few bills, which she put on one side, a postcard from one of her new friends, who had gone to London to see her mother, and a thick envelope with a foreign stamp on it. What's that stamp? thought Margaret, as she took a closer look. New Zealand? Who do we know in New Zealand? She pondered a while and nearly opened the envelope. Although it was addressed to Dr Jonathan Baxter, she would always open up his mail. But this time she didn't. She propped up the large envelope with the colourful stamps against the vase on the hall table. And there it sat until Jonathan came home.

'What's in this envelope, Mummy?' called the boys, later that day.

'I don't know, don't touch, leave it for Daddy,' she called from the kitchen.

'Who lives in New Zealand?' Paul asked.

'Nobody I know, dear,' his mother replied. 'We will have to wait until your father comes home.' But every time she walked through the hall, the letter caught her attention. Come on Jonathan, come home, she kept thinking to herself. She was impatient to know its contents, but she still wouldn't open it. Something kept stopping her. Would it be bad news? she thought. Oh, that's for telegrams. This is a letter. She comforted herself with this thought.

For once Jonathan was late. A brain operation needed extra X-rays in theatre and it took longer than usual. He waited in Neuro until the operation was complete and told the surgeon he would be on call if further work was necessary.

As he arrived in, Margaret and the boys were at the front door. 'What's going on, you lot? A welcoming committee.' He kissed Margaret and hugged his two sons.

'Look, a letter from New Zealand in a large envelope. What is it?' said Paul.

'Hey, wait till I get in,' said his father. He put his briefcase down and picked up the letter. 'Yes, you are right. It is from New Zealand.'

'Who do you know there, dear?' asked Margaret.

'Nobody, my dear. Absolutely nobody.'

'Open it up, Daddy!' The boys were getting impatient.

He held the envelope up over his head. 'Hang on you two, let's go into the sitting room, shall we?' Jonathan shouted. They all sat up close to Jonathan on the big sofa. He slit open the envelope with his letter opener and pulled out numerous pieces of paper. He sat quietly reading the first page.

'What does it say, dear?' Margaret asked him.

'Well, it is from New Zealand, from a firm of solicitors in fact. It seems that an Arthur Baxter has died at the age of ninety-six and I am his only relative.' Jonathan was shocked at this information.

'Arthur Baxter. Did you know of him?' his wife asked.

'No, I didn't. I knew my father had one brother but I didn't know what happened to him. My father never talked about him. I gather he left home after a bad argument with their father and never returned. From that day his name was never mentioned. If I asked my father he wouldn't answer, so I stopped asking him.' Jonathan started to read the letter again. 'They want me to contact the solicitors by letter or phone. What do you think I should do?' he asked.

'Well, if you write it will take ages. That letter has taken three weeks to get here,' Margaret said. 'I think you had better ring them. It will be expensive but it'll be better to do that, rather than worrying about it.'

'I will ring tomorrow. Their number is on the letter. There is also a form here which they want me to fill in, and also send some identification and a letter from a solicitor here that I shall need to send to confirm it. What on earth is it all about?' he said.

'Perhaps he has left you a gold mine, Daddy,' said Paul.

'They don't have gold mines in New Zealand. They are in America, silly,' said Mat.

'Well, you never know,' said Paul, he and gave his brother a dig in the ribs.

'Ouch, stop that. That hurts,' called Mat.

'Hey, calm down you two, don't get too excited. It's probably just a few meagre possessions that Arthur Baxter left and they will just parcel them up and send them to me in a shoe box, no doubt.' Jonathan laughed but secretly he was intrigued. Arthur Baxter must have left home in his early teens. What his father and he had rowed over would never be known, but it must have been serious. To think a son would leave and never return was too dreadful to think of. If Paul or Mat did that he would never get over it, and nor would Margaret.

The following day, very early in the morning, Jonathan put a phone call through to the New Zealand solicitors. He and Margaret listened to the phone ring. At last a female voice answered. 'Blackshaw and Jones, can I help you?'

'Well yes, I am Dr Jonathan Baxter, speaking from England. I have received a letter from Mr Blackshaw regarding my relative Arthur Baxter.'

'Oh, just wait one moment. I will connect you with Mr Blackshaw,' she answered.

'Hello, Mr Blackshaw speaking. Is that Jonathan Baxter?' he asked.

'Yes, it is. I have received your letter. What is it all about?' Jonathan enquired.

'I sent the letter some time ago. Have you just received it?' Mr Blackshaw asked in a strong New Zealand accent.

'We have just moved house and it went to my old address first,' Jonathan answered quickly, wondering how much the phone call was costing him.

'I am your uncle's executor. We dealt with his estate and his will, so if you will forward the information I asked for, we will speak again,' Mr Blackshaw said firmly.

'Yes, but what's this all about?' Jonathan asked again.

'I am sorry. I am not at liberty to say until I have proof of your identity.'

Jonathan realised he would get nowhere with this Mr Blackshaw. A typical solicitor, he would not give anything away. 'All right, Mr Blackshaw. I shall get on to it right away and send it by recorded delivery. Is that all right?' Jonathan asked.

'Yes, that's fine. Please send the information as quickly as possible. Goodbye, Dr Baxter,' he replied.

'Goodbye, Mr Blackshaw.' Jonathan hung up and then sank into his chair.

'Phew, that was difficult. He wouldn't answer my question at all, just kept saying send the information first,' Jonathan said to his wife.

'What a fuss. I wonder what old Arthur got up to in New Zealand. Did you know he lived there, dear?' asked Margaret.

'No, I didn't. As I said to you and the boys, he was never spoken of in the family. It was a taboo subject.' Jonathan paused. 'It's all very intriguing though, so I had better get on to our solicitors for them to draft a letter confirming who I am. I'll do that this afternoon – make an appointment with that solicitor. Mr Farnham put his name on that list he left us.'

'Yes, I'll do that and ring you at work with the time,' Margaret answered.

The Baxter Family

'Bye now, must go or I'll be late.' Jonathan kissed his wife and went off to work.

Throughout the day his mind kept wandering. What had Uncle Arthur Baxter got up to in New Zealand? Had he married? Had he any family? They would be his age if there were any. They would be his cousins. He might have a large new family out there. It would be nice to have relatives. Perhaps one day they might all meet in New Zealand? But wait – the solicitor had said that Jonathan was the only relative, so there couldn't be any family... In the late afternoon, Jonathan made his way to the solicitors.

'Call me Frank. I was a good friend of Mr Farnham, whose house you bought. We played a lot of golf. Do you play?' Frank beamed at his new client.

'No, I don't. I have two young sons who keep me busy at weekends, not much time for myself yet,' smiled Jonathan.

'Well, if you ever want to join, just let me know and I will sponsor you,' said Frank.

'That's exceedingly kind of you.'

'Well, Doctor, what can I do for you?' Frank asked.

'I have this letter and form. Perhaps you could read it and advise me, Frank? Please call me Jonathan.' He warmed to Frank. He seemed a very likeable man.

Frank sat quietly and read the letter from Mr Blackshaw. 'This is very intriguing, isn't it?' Frank said. 'Let's fill in the form and then you sign it and I will countersign it, that should do it. But I think I will send a covering letter to confirm that the man here in front of me is the genuine Dr Jonathan Baxter of Shirley. That should be fine,' smiled Frank. They worked away at the form and signatures. Frank dictated a letter to his secretary, who typed it up immediately. 'Get that in the post, Jonathan, and let's see what happens,' said Frank.

The following day Margaret took the letter to the post office. It was weighed and registered and off it went on its journey to New Zealand. Life got back to normal, but they couldn't help rushing to the hall whenever they heard the letters drop through the door.

Chapter Three

The summer was a glorious one and Margaret took the boys to the park for picnics. They loved playing football and Margaret would lie on the rug sunbathing while they were occupied. She also took them to the local baths as she loved swimming. At holiday times it got very crowded but just being in the water was great fun.

They had decided not to have a holiday this year. The cost of the move and refurbishing Shirley had been quite high, and there was the cost of the new tennis court to consider. Jonathan said he would take odd days off work and they would go out to the countryside or perhaps the seaside instead. The whole area, including Wales, was new to them, so there was lots to explore.

One day Jonathan came home tired and said to Margaret, 'Let's go away for the weekend, dear. I feel I could do with a break, what do you think?'

'That would be great, Jonathan. Actually, I saw an advert in the local paper for a cottage in Wales, a place called Abersoch. I put it in the kitchen somewhere. There is a telephone number. Shall I ring them?' She sounded excited.

'Yes, do that. I'll go and play football with the boys in the garden,' Jonathan went into the garden through the French door. Margaret found the scrap of paper in the kitchen and went into the hall.

'Hello, is that Mrs Roberts in Abersoch?' she asked.

'Yes, it is Mrs Roberts,' her voice sang out.

'My name is Mrs Baxter and I am answering your advert about a cottage. Could we take it for a weekend?'

'Of course dear. This weekend suit you?' she asked.

'Oh, that would be marvellous. There would be my husband and my two sons, Paul and Mathew. If we came on Friday and stayed Friday and Saturday night, would that be all right?' Margaret asked.

'That would be fine, Mrs Baxter. If you like I can do breakfast and an evening meal. Mr Roberts and I live at the back of the cottage, so I could do that for you, at a little extra charge,' she said.

'That would be perfect. Dr Baxter and I would very pleased for you to do that. The boys will eat anything. They are not fussy eaters,' Margaret said proudly.

'So your husband is a doctor? Very nice, I must say. I look forward to you coming. The address is on the advert. We are near the harbour. If you come over the bridge, you have come too far. We are on a little road opposite the harbour near the boatyard. See you on Friday,' she added.

'Thank you, Mrs Roberts, and goodbye.' Margaret put the phone down and went outside. 'I have phoned her and we go on Friday.'

'How much is the cottage?' Jonathan asked.

'Oh, I didn't ask. Shall I ring her back?'

'No, don't worry. It won't be much. Bring the cheque book and we will take some cash in case the bank is shut. Well, boys, we are off on Friday. I will come home at lunchtime.' He beamed at his sons.

'Where are we going, Daddy?' asked Paul.

'To the seaside,' he answered.

'Yippee!' shouted the boys and they started racing round the garden shouting, 'We are going to the seaside! We are going to the seaside!'

They set off on Friday lunchtime, with a full boot and a good map. They had no idea where they were going but Margaret took control of the map reading. 'Head for Chester then out on the A49. We will go through the country seeing as we have never been to Wales. It will be a nice drive.' She settled in to the front seat and Jonathan set off on their journey to Wales.

They had frequent stops along the way as Mathew was not a good traveller. But eventually they arrived at Portmadoc and paid at the toll bridge, which fascinated the boys. Soon they were through the town, heading for Pwllheli. 'What a funny name and spelling, but that's our last town before Abersoch. So look out for the sea. First to see it gets sixpence,' called their father.

Through the small town of Pwllheli, they travelled past the railway station and off again through the lanes. 'Not far now, boys,' said their mother.

Soon they were dropping into the village of Abersoch and both boys called out at once. 'Sea, sea, I saw it first!'

'All right, sixpence each,' said their father to avoid a squabble.

'Go slowly, Jonathan, there's the lane, on the right before the boatyard.' He pulled across the road and down the lane. 'There's the cottage. It's not a cottage, it's a house,' said Margaret.

They pulled into the drive and, at the same time, out stepped Mrs Roberts, wearing a big white apron. 'Glad you got here safely. Come on in, I've got the kettle on,' she added.

Mrs Roberts showed them round the house. It was spotless. She had laid out tea in the front room. It was more like a parlour with its old-fashioned furniture. 'Mr Roberts and myself, we live round the back, so you have the whole of the house to yourselves,' she said. 'I will come in only to do breakfast and an evening meal about 6 p.m., if that suits you, Doctor?'

'That will be fine, Mrs Roberts, thank you. I am sure we will be very comfortable,' he said.

'You can walk to the beaches and shops from here, no need to use the car, Doctor,' she said. She was very proud of the fact that a doctor and his family were staying at her home and she had told all her friends in the village. She was well pleased with them. They looked a very respectable family and the boys looked well behaved too.

She left them alone and they unpacked quickly, before setting off to explore Abersoch. 'This is a lovely place, Jonathan, the beach at the harbour is so clean and the water looks so safe.'

'Yes, I have been thinking that too,' he added. They walked over the bridge, where swans were swimming in the narrow river below, and on into the village where they saw a sign for another beach. They walked down a narrow lane and reached the large beach. Little beach huts surrounded one end and a few yachts were bobbing in the bay.

The boys raced down the sand to the water's edge, flung off their socks and shoes, and were soon paddling in the warm water. 'This is great,' they cried.

Their mother and father sat on the warm sand and watched their sons. The sand dunes behind seemed to curve round and protect them. 'This is a lovely spot, Margaret. I think if the weather holds we will have a good few days.'

'Yes, I like it here and Mrs Roberts is a nice woman. I wonder what she will cook for us tonight. Nice to have a few days out of the kitchen,' Margaret said.

As they sat together, the boys started wading out deeper and deeper into the water. 'Paul, Mathew, come here and change into your trunks, then you can swim. Not too far out though,' called Margaret. They were soon out and changed, and back in the water. Lots of splashing and shouting followed.

The family spent all afternoon on the beach until around 5 p.m., when they started to walk back to the cottage across the bridge. 'Look at the boats in the harbour, Daddy,' said Mathew.

'Well, after tea we could come back and walk round the harbour if you like. I think the tide is coming in so we could do that,' said Jonathan to his son.

Mrs Roberts had laid out a tasty meal for the family and, after washing up, they set off again. Over the bridge, round the corner and on to the harbour they went. Along the sea wall quite a few people were dangling lines into the water. 'What are they doing, Daddy?' asked Paul.

'They are crabbing.'

'Can we do it?' asked the boys in unison.

'We could, but we need the lines and hooks. Tomorrow, if the weather holds, I'll buy you both a set. Then tomorrow night we can come and join in. We'll get some bacon for the bait. They like that.' Jonathan was quite knowledgeable as he and his father had done this years ago.

'We'll need a big bucket too,' piped up Mathew.

The boys couldn't wait for the next day and as soon as their heads hit the pillow that night, they were asleep.

'Wonderful day, Jonathan,' said Margaret, as they sat down together. 'I think I am going to love this place,' she added.

Next day, the sun was cracking the slates, as her mother would have said. Mrs Roberts had told them about another bay, back along the road where the beach was surrounded by sand dunes and a few caravans and chalets were dotted along it. They piled into the car and turned left up the hill and soon arrived at the new beach. This was even more spectacular than the one they had visited yesterday. The sand was perfect, the whole area was so clean, and only a handful of people were on the beach.

They left their car in the little car park and walked through a gap in the sand dune. There was a little cafe on the right, which sold ice cream and beach equipment. 'Look, Daddy. They sell crab stuff. Can we get ours now?' asked Paul.

'Let's get it when we leave, shall we?' The boys started running to the sea, across the perfect beach. The sand was lovely and warm to their bare feet and they plunged into the water quickly.

The parents set out their rug and picnic basket and called out to them. 'Now, not out of your depth, boys!' commanded their father.

He and Margaret lay down side by side holding hands. 'Love you Margaret.' He smiled at her.

'Love you so much, Jonathan. We are so lucky to have each other,' Margaret sighed.

'Yes, we need these little breaks to appreciate the boys and each other.'

'Yes, we are very lucky.'

In the late afternoon the crab lines and hooks were purchased on the way back to the car, together with a large bucket. They were all set for an evening of crabbing.

After tea Paul shouted to his father, 'We've forgotten the bacon, Daddy.'

'Oh yes,' said Jonathan, kicking himself for forgetting. 'Ask Mrs Roberts if she has a couple of rashers spare.'

'I'll go without tomorrow. Just a boiled egg will do me. I'm eating too much anyway,' said Margaret.

High tide was at 7 p.m. and by then the family had arrived at the sea wall. They perched on top of it, surrounded by other families, and lowered their two lines into the water. By the end of the evening, they had caught two large crabs and lots of baby crabs. All the time the boys kept looking into the bucket, watching the crabs.

'What are you going to do with them?' asked mother.

'Take them home,' said Mathew proudly.

'All right, but tomorrow you must return them to the sea. That is their natural home and it would be cruel to leave them in the bucket. They will die if they are not in the sea, as they need to live there to feed,' said father.

'Oh, all right then. Tomorrow we will bring them back, I suppose.' He looked disappointed and trundled off carrying the bucket. They all walked slowly back to the cottage, the boys exhausted from their long day, but what a day!

'That was a great day, Margaret, loved every minute of it, did you?'

'Oh, I did, Jonathan, and I know the boys did too. Look at them, they can hardly put one foot in front of the other.' Margaret laughed and held on to Jonathan. She leaned her head on his shoulder; she felt so happy.

Night fell on the cottage and soon all the Baxter family were asleep, Paul and Mathew dreaming of giant crabs and Margaret and Jonathan dreaming of golden sands and clear blue seas.

They all slept so heavily that Mrs Roberts had to call them down for their breakfast. Today was their last day and the boys started to plead with their parents to stay longer. 'Look, it's no good you whining to me, I have got to get back to work tomorrow, to earn more pennies for you two, to buy more ice cream and more bacon!' he laughed at the boys. 'But before we head home, we could go back down to the big beach which has all the sand dunes, how about that?'

'Great, come on let's go!' Paul called.

'Hang on, we have to pack and see Mrs Roberts first. You two play outside while we sort everything out.'

Jonathan and Margaret quickly packed up their belongings and paid Mrs Roberts. They both thanked her and vowed to come back. Then they climbed into the car and set off for the beach.

Margaret and Jonathan walked along the edge of the sea watching the boys playing. 'Look at those little houses in the sand dunes. Wouldn't it be lovely to own one of those? The boys could play all day on the beach and you could keep an eye on them.'

'Yes, it is a safe place for children. The area is off the main road and there is no traffic. Quite an idyllic place,' agreed Jonathan. 'But, come on, stop day dreaming. It would cost a lot of money to buy one of those chalets and we have only just bought Shirley,' he said, looking longingly at the row of little houses nestling in the dunes.

On the way home, the boys kept saying, 'Can we go again, Daddy? We loved it there.'

'Yes, maybe we could manage another weekend in the summer at Mrs Roberts'.' Jonathan agreed with them that Abersoch had been a lovely, magical place.

On arriving home, Jonathan sifted through the mail. His eye was drawn to a large envelope with foreign stamps on it. His heart started to race. What was this? What were its contents? Probably more forms and documents to read. Jonathan took the envelope into the sitting room and proceeded to open it up. He sat quietly reading the documents and the concentration was apparent on his face. It was a letter from Mr Blackshaw, the solicitor in New Zealand, confirming that Arthur Baxter was indeed his long-lost uncle. Arthur had died at his farm some six months earlier and had left a will lodged with Mr Blackshaw. Arthur had instructed the solicitor to sell off the land and sheep farm, and his home and its contents. He had apparently talked to Mr Blackshaw about leaving his family home in England after a big argument with his father. He had made his way to London and vowed that he would never set eyes on his father again. What the row was over, nobody knew.

He worked his passage over to Australia and then on to New Zealand, where he went to work for a couple who owned a sheep farm, and stayed with them and looked after them when they were old. In fact, to Arthur, they reminded him of his own mother and father, whom he sorely missed. In return, they rewarded Arthur for his love and care by leaving all of their estate to him.

They had had no children, but Arthur had become a son to them over the years. He often wondered about his family and, as he grew older, wondered if his father and mother were alive and particularly what had become of his brother. Some days, when he was alone on the farm, Arthur told Mr Blackshaw that he thought of contacting his brother, but then he had never tried to contact him in New Zealand. The family probably thought he was still in England somewhere, and by now, his parents would be dead and his brother would not want anything to do with him. All this information was in Mr Blackshaw's letter. Jonathan read the letter again and tears ran down his cheeks. What a waste, to think he had an uncle in New Zealand longing to hear from him and he had done nothing about it. What a waste, Jonathan thought to himself.

'I should have tried to contact him, but I was so brainwashed by my father. I pretended he didn't exist,' he told Margaret later on in the evening.

'You weren't to blame, Jonathan. You were very young when Arthur left and to try and find him later would have upset your parents, you know that.'

'Well, it's too late now, isn't it?' said Jonathan bitterly.

'Read on. What else does Mr Blackshaw say?'

'He says he is in the process of winding up the estate. He has found a buyer for the land and the farm and he will be in touch when this is complete. I think I will ring him early tomorrow morning and confirm that I have received the letter.'

'Do you think you will have to go over and see him, Jonathan?' she asked.

'I don't know. I don't want to, as it's a long way and expensive to fly to New Zealand, but I will wait and see. If Arthur trusted Mr Blackshaw, I am sure he is all right. Arthur seemed a steady, kind man to look after the old couple, so I am sure his judgement on the solicitor is sound. Yes, I trust him with Uncle's affairs.'

When they went to bed, Jonathan's head was spinning. New Zealand, sheep, farm, house, land; what had his uncle's life been like? Had he been happy there, did he ever regret leaving England? Well, he would never know now. It was too late to find out.

Next day he phoned the solicitor, Mr Blackshaw. He was extremely friendly this time and said everything was going smoothly with the sale. He asked for the name and address of Jonathan's bank, his account number and the name of his bank manager. When Jonathan came off the phone his hand was shaking. Mr Blackshaw never mentioned money to Jonathan and

Jonathan didn't dare ask him. 'I think, Margaret, we could get a couple of thousand. The farm was probably a small, run-down one. I have been told that there are thousands of farms in New Zealand, like smallholdings. Anyway that amount of money would be lovely. We could put it away for the boys' education. A nice legacy from Arthur, my uncle; what do you think?'

'Yes, that would be lovely, dear,' Margaret agreed.

Chapter Four

Days rolled into weeks, weeks rolled into months, and not a word from New Zealand. Both Jonathan and Margaret got on with their lives. The initial excitement of Mr Blackshaw's letters faded into the background.

The workload of Jonathan's position at the hospital was monumental. He came home extremely tired and Margaret worried about him. They seemed to have more free time where they had previously lived, and she often worried that the promotion had not been a good idea for Jonathan.

As for herself, she had settled down and she knew the two boys were happy living at Shirley. They loved the house and tennis court. They had lots of friends and she also had a lot of lady friends. The main concern was Jonathan. He was a conscientious doctor, very thorough in his work, who treated his patients more like customers who deserved the best he could offer.

One night he came home late again. An awful incident had happened in one of his departments.

An elderly man had come into the main X-ray department for a barium meal. A student radiographer had placed him in a cubicle and told him to undress and put on the green towelling robe. She put his card in her pocket instead of handing it in at the office. The list of patients' names were called out every hour and by the end of the day, all the X-rays had been processed in the darkroom ready for the radiologist to report on the following day. That evening, just as Jonathan was leaving his office, a face popped out from one of the cubicles. 'Can I have a drink? I am very thirsty,' said the old man.

Jonathan was startled to see someone there, as he was always the last to leave. Usually the department was deserted. 'What are you doing here?' he asked the old man.

'What did you say?' said the man.

'I said, why are you still here?' he shouted to the man.

'I'm waiting for my X-ray and I am fed up and thirsty,' the old man moaned.

'What time was your appointment, Sir?' said Jonathan.

'Ten o'clock, Doctor, and I am still waiting,' he said.

Jonathan was shocked. The poor old man had been waiting in the cubicle all day, having had nothing to eat or drink since the previous night. It was obvious that the old man was stone deaf and would not have heard his name called out and the staff had gone on to the next patient. Nobody had opened up the cubicle doors and checked before going home. 'Come, this way, Sir. I am the doctor in charge. There has been a terrible mistake, but I will X-ray you myself and get an ambulance to take you home.'

With that he ushered the man into the main screening room. He put on his protective apron, turned down the lights and gave the man the barium drink. Jonathan took his time screening the old man, being very thorough, then he took a series of X-rays. Jonathan helped the patient back to the cubicle and told him to get dressed and wait. He phoned for an ambulance from the accident department and was told that one would be available in half an hour. So he went into the kitchen and made a nice cup of tea, found some biscuits and went back to the cubicle. By then the old man was dressed. 'Come and sit in the waiting room and have your tea and biscuits. I will sit with you until the ambulance comes,' he said, his voice raised.

Jonathan looked at the frail, old man. This was somebody's husband, father or brother, and here he was all on his own. Somebody's head would roll in his X-ray department tomorrow. How could he have been left all day? Typical of his generation, he had not complained at sitting there all day, thirsty and hungry. No, he had just sat and waited his turn.

Half an hour later the porter came to collect him. 'Working late, Dr Baxter?' the porter asked.

'Don't ask. Just don't ask,' sighed Jonathan. The old man thanked Jonathan for his kindness and Jonathan felt very humble. When he got home, he told Margaret all about it.

'Well, you have to laugh. The poor old fellow could have been sitting there all night if I hadn't seen his head pop out at that moment.' By that point, Jonathan could see the funny side of the incident and both he and Margaret roared with laughter.

The school holiday dragged on and Margaret tried hard to occupy her two energetic sons. Fortunately Paul and Mathew were popular boys, so a steady procession of friends came to the house to play tennis. While this occupied them, Margaret found she was in charge of four to six boys instead of just two. Drinks, biscuits and ice cream were in demand and there was a steady trundle of children in and out of the kitchen across the hall to the toilet. If they were not playing tennis, they were making dens in the garden from old sheets and clothes maidens. Sometimes an odd game of cricket or rounders on the lawn kept them busy. Margaret wondered what the other mothers were doing while their offspring were at Shirley. They were probably out shopping or sunbathing in their back gardens. It seemed to Margaret as though Shirley and its gardens were a big draw for all their school friends. It was like a youth club during school holidays. Perhaps in the winter holidays Paul and Mathew might be invited to their friends' homes and she could get some well-earned peace! But, all considered, she was pleased that Paul and Mathew had so many friends, or else they would be squabbling between each other and feeling extremely bored.

One day, while Margaret was making up another tray of goodies for the boys, the phone rang. Margaret answered it. 'Hello, Mrs Baxter speaking,' she said.

'Good morning, Mrs Baxter. This is Mr Ashworth, your bank manager,' he replied. Margaret's heart missed a beat. Were they overdrawn again after the holiday? Surely not.

'Are you there, Mrs Baxter?' enquired Mr Ashworth.

'Oh yes, Mr Ashworth, what is the matter? My husband is at work,' she said quickly. Margaret did not deal with money matters. She left that to Jonathan.

'Ah well, it is Dr Baxter who I would like to speak to, Mrs Baxter, if that can be arranged?' he asked rather pompously.

'Yes, Mr Ashworth. He could come in tomorrow. It is his day off as he worked the weekend,' she rambled on nervously.

Margaret didn't like banks or bank managers. They intimidated her.

'Tomorrow would be convenient. Shall we say eleven?' Mr Ashworth asked.

'I am sure that will be convenient. I shall tell my husband when he comes in tonight,' she said.

'Thank you, Mrs Baxter. A pleasure to speak to you. Goodbye.'

She put the receiver down and wondered if she should phone Jonathan, but she decided not to worry him at work. She would tell him tonight.

All day Margaret couldn't concentrate. Mr Ashworth seemed very officious to her. They must have gone over their overdraft limit and she wondered what he would say. Surely Jonathan must have known this, but last night he seemed happy and not worried about anything, only the old man in the cubicle. She really should take more interest in their finances, but she had always thought that as Jonathan earned the money, he should be the one to decide how much they spent. He gave her housekeeping every month and she always managed on that. She never asked for more money, as Jonathan was very generous. But as for household bills, he saw to all of them. They came through the post and she left them unopened for her husband. Once a month he sat at his desk in the small room upstairs and sorted out their finances. She always said he was in his 'counting house,' and that was how they ran their lives. Perhaps he had been worrying and had not wanted to tell her.

By the time Jonathan came home Margaret was in an agitated state. 'Jonathan,' she called out to him as soon as the front door opened. 'Jonathan, the bank manager has been on the phone and wants to see you tomorrow at 11 a.m. It sounded urgent to me.'

'Mr Ashworth, do you mean?' he replied.

'Yes, that's him. He wants to see you. What can it be, Jonathan?'

'I don't know, I am sure we are well within our budget, even after our holiday.'

'Well, it didn't cost much, did it?' said Margaret.

'No, you're right. Mrs Roberts' bill was very reasonable.' Then Jonathan paused. 'I wonder if he has heard from Mr Blackshaw in New Zealand about Uncle's will?'

'Oh, I hope it's that and not anything else. I don't like him. He is so pompous,' said Margaret.

'All bank managers are. They can wield a lot of power, you know. Get on the wrong side of them and you are in trouble, but he was quite good with us over the loan for the tennis court, you know,' mused Jonathan.

'Yes, I suppose so, but he still worries me when he phones here,' Margaret said.

'Now don't worry, Margaret, until I see him tomorrow. Would you like to come with me and meet him? Perhaps if you met him, he would be less of a dragon for you?'

'Oh no, I don't want to come to the bank. I don't like them at all. I find them quite intimidating,' she wailed. 'No, you go, you are braver than me,' she added.

He put his arm round her shoulder and hugged her. Yes, she was a lovely wife. The home was immaculate, his sons were healthy and happy and he was so lucky to have her. So the matter of the bank manager would be shouldered by him.

That night, as Margaret slept peacefully beside him, Jonathan mentally went through his accounts. They were not well off, but certainly comfortable. Buying Shirley and refurbishing parts of it had been costly, but he had a good salary and his career was secure in the medical world. As he thought this over, he felt sure that it was to do with Arthur, but still there was a niggle in the back of his mind about his finances, or the lack of them.

★

Mr Ashworth's office was rather splendid, panelled throughout and with a large desk covered with what looked like important documents. 'Pleased to meet you again, Dr Baxter. Keeping well, I hope?' asked Mr Ashworth. They shook hands and Mr Ashworth showed Jonathan to a leather chair opposite him.

'Very well, thank you, Mr Ashworth,' Jonathan answered.

'I suppose you are wondering why I want to see you?' Mr Ashworth peered over his spectacles.

'The thought had crossed my mind,' answered Jonathan.

'Well, Doctor, I have had some correspondence from a Mr Blackshaw, a solicitor in New Zealand, appertaining to your uncle's estate,' Mr Ashworth hesitated, pulled out a folder and placed it on his desk. Opening it up, he started sifting through the papers. 'It seems you are the sole heir to an Arthur Baxter, your uncle. He was a sheep farmer, I gather.' Mr Ashworth peered again over his glasses. At that moment Jonathan wished his uncle had been a brain surgeon, any other profession than a sheep farmer. Mr Ashworth seemed a little disdainful of this profession! 'It would seem you are the only living relative he had and in his will, of which Mr Blackshaw has sent me a copy, he, Mr Baxter, has left his estate to you. You know about this matter?' he asked.

'Yes, I do. My uncle left England when he was a young man, never to return. I gather he never married and so does not have any children. Mr Blackshaw says I am his only living relative. I have spoken a few times to Mr Blackshaw and have found him extremely professional. So I have left all my uncle's business with him to sort out,' Jonathan said.

'Very trusting of you, but in the circumstances, except for going out there, I suppose that is all you could do.'

'Well, I discussed it with my wife and we both decided to leave it with Mr Blackshaw. He spoke very highly of my uncle and had been his close friend for many years. He also saw to his funeral, so I thought it fitting to leave my uncle's affairs with him.'

'As I say, very trusting of you,' Mr Ashworth commented. 'Would you like some tea, Dr Baxter? I can get some brought in.'

'No thank you, Mr Ashworth.' Jonathan's stomach by now was in knots, the tension was getting to him and tea was the last thing he wanted.

'Well, then, let's get down to business,' Mr Ashworth said. 'This is a banker's draft from New Zealand via Mr Blackshaw. This is the complete estate of the late Arthur Baxter. Mr Blackshaw has deducted his fee from the estate, which, looking at the amount, is an extremely reasonable fee. So I have no trouble with that. So I have pleasure in handing over the banker's draft to you, Dr Baxter.' Mr Ashworth beamed at Jonathan and handed him the bit of paper. Jonathan looked at it. He had never seen a banker's draft before. It was for the amount of two thousand five hundred pounds.

'That is wonderful, Mr Ashworth. That will secure my sons' education. That is a wonderful amount and I am very grateful to my Uncle Arthur. Two thousand five hundred pounds! My only regret is that I cannot thank him,' added Jonathan sadly.

'Please, Dr Baxter, please, will you read the banker's draft again?' Mr Ashworth was quite agitated. 'Please, Dr Baxter.' Jonathan felt startled by his bank manager's behaviour. He took the draft in his hand again and looked carefully at it. 'Dr Baxter, it's not two thousand five hundred pounds, it's two hundred and fifty *thousand* pounds.'

'*What!*' exclaimed Jonathan.

'It's two hundred and fifty thousand pounds.'

'Oh my God, it can't be. It was only an old rundown smallholding. It can't be right,' mumbled Jonathan, his head spinning.

'No, you are wrong. His farm was thriving. He also had many acres of prime land. When he was ill he gave all his sheep stock to his trusty farm workers, and also he bequeathed money to his staff and housekeeper. So his estate was much larger than two hundred and fifty thousand pounds. Your uncle, Arthur Baxter, had done extremely well in New Zealand but he never forgot his friends and staff. They were well looked after at his death. He also never forgot his family in England, hence your inheritance. Congratulations, Dr Baxter, now I think we need a proper drink to celebrate.' He rang a bell on his desk and in came his clerk bearing a tray with drinks and glasses. The clerk shook Jonathan's hand and said, 'Congratulations, Sir. I hope it brings you and your family great happiness.'

Jonathan sat in the big leather chair, dumbfounded. It was like a dream. He could hear Mr Ashworth and his clerk talking to him, but it was not registering. They were talking about accounts and investments, but this was all far too much for Jonathan to take in.

Just then there was another knock at Mr Ashworth's office door. In came a young girl from the bank carrying a large bouquet of flowers. 'These are from the bank and my staff for Mrs Baxter, if I may be so bold,' said Mr Ashworth. Jonathan came to his senses quickly and thanked the girl. There he sat in Mr Ashworth's office, with a bouquet of flowers across his knee and a drink in his hand. What an amazing morning this had been! 'Now, Dr Baxter, I am sure you will want to go home and tell your wife your good news. We will put the money into your current account for the time being and then when you have had time to digest the amount we can have a further discussion. This can be arranged at your convenience; no need to be hasty in these circumstances, Dr Baxter.' Mr Ashworth stood up and shook Jonathan's hand firmly.

'Thank you, Mr Ashworth, thank you for the flowers. Mrs Baxter will love them. I shall speak to you soon.' As Jonathan walked out through the bank, all eyes followed him to the door. As he slid into his car, his legs felt weak and his heart was pounding.

'Two hundred and fifty thousand pounds. I can't believe it,' He looked up at the sky. 'Thank you, Uncle, wherever you are, thank you so much. We will use the money wisely. I wish I could have known you and you could have got to know us,' Jonathan said out loud. 'Thank you so much.' After a moment's thought, he put the car in gear and drove home steadily to Shirley.

Jonathan arrived on the drive of the big house and looked up at Shirley. He loved this house. It was a real home. He felt as though he had lived there for years. He knew Margaret and his sons were happy here, so he made his first decision not to move to an even bigger house. This was the family home and here they would stay. He sat still in the car for a moment gathering his thoughts. In less than an hour his life had changed, thanks to Uncle Arthur. Last night's sleepless hours were a thing of the past. The family was now secure. Margaret and the boys were secure if anything should happen to him. It had always worried him being the sole breadwinner, especially since in his work he was surrounded by illness and death; he knew how vulnerable a man was. But now his wife and sons were secure. Careful management of the money would ensure peace of mind.

He got out of his car and let himself him. Margaret was standing at the head of the stairs. She had heard him arrive on the drive and had been waiting for him to come in. He seemed to take ages to come into the hall, but there he stood, her beloved Jonathan, with a big bouquet of flowers and a smile on his face. She ran downstairs and stared at him. 'What has happened, Jonathan?' she cried.

'Look, these are for you, Margaret.'

'Oh, you shouldn't have,' she answered.

'I didn't buy them. The bank did.' He beamed at her.

'The bank!'

'Yes, the bank. They are from the manager and his staff,' Jonathan said.

'You are joking, aren't you?' said Margaret.

'No. I am not. They are from the bank, not me.' He was amused at her shocked expression. 'Come into the sitting room, dear. Come and sit down while I tell you what's happened.' He took her hand and led her into the sitting room.

They sat side by side on the sofa. 'Now, Margaret, Uncle Arthur's estate has come through from New Zealand,' he started.

'What does it say?'

'It's not what it says, it's what it is,' said Jonathan. 'Let me explain to you slowly. I will tell you what has happened to me this morning.' And he started to tell her of his meeting with the bank manager. Then he slowly explained his mistake in reading the banker's draft. 'So you see, Margaret, we now have in our current account, thanks to Uncle Arthur and a sheep farm in New Zealand, two hundred and fifty thousand pounds.' As he finished speaking, he sat back and waited for a reaction from Margaret.

'Say that again, Jonathan,' Margaret asked.

'Two hundred and fifty thousand pounds, it's a quarter of a million pounds and every day that figure will rise with the interest it makes,' Jonathan looked at her.

'Oh, my goodness. That is a lot of money, and we thought we only had a little rundown smallholding. Jonathan, he must have had a big farm. He must have been a good farmer.'

'Yes, he was and also a very caring man. Before we got our inheritance, he had already given his sheep to his helpers and money to his staff and housekeeper at the farm. He did this when he was very ill so that they would be looked after. No wonder Mr Blackshaw thought highly of him. It seems it was a big funeral. A lot of friends and staff attended. I wish I had known, I would have loved to have been there. In fact I wish I had known him. In all those years he must have thought he would not be welcome in England. What a shame, to think he died thinking that.' Jonathan was very saddened by this and Margaret moved over and hugged him tightly.

'Well, we have a chance to put his money to good use. It will secure a good education for the boys – perhaps it will fund a university education for them. And we will keep his memory alive. We will have a headstone erected next to your parents' grave where we can go with the boys and put flowers there for him.'

'Yes, that would be nice. We will get a nice memorial stone for him. He sounded a great chap, Uncle Arthur, didn't he?' Jonathan said. 'One thing I want to do if you are in agreement, Margaret, is to give some money to the Yarwoods,' Jonathan paused.

'Go on, I'm listening,' Margaret prompted him.

'Well, I thought ten thousand pounds would be a nice sum for them, to help them in their old age. They still have to pay their rent and live. What do you think, dear?'

'That's a brilliant idea, Jonathan. So like your Uncle Arthur, wanting to share your good fortune,' beamed Margaret.

'*Our* good fortune, don't forget that,' said Jonathan firmly. '*Our* good fortune.'

And so, in the next few days, Jonathan drew out ten thousand pounds for the Yarwoods and both went round to see them.

Jonathan explained to them their inheritance from Arthur and asked them to share their good fortune. At first they refused, but after some gentle persuasion from Jonathan, they accepted the money. Both the Yarwoods loved the doctor and knew this offer was a result of his kind, caring ways.

Jonathan and Margaret came home happy that they had made the Yarwoods more secure.

They both sat on the sofa for a long time thinking and talking about Arthur's life in New Zealand. Jonathan even mentioned that one day the family might visit New Zealand and see the farm and land for themselves. That would be a big adventure. Perhaps over Christmas they might fly out and make it a special event, he suggested.

'That would be lovely, Jonathan. It would help you come to terms with all that has happened and also help the boys to understand where the money has come from.'

So they made a decision to go to New Zealand in the Christmas holidays. They had to tell the Yarwoods because they always came to Shirley for Christmas. But Mr and Mrs Yarwood were so pleased at the family's good fortune, they did not mind one bit.

'One Christmas does not matter, after all the lovely Christmases we have had at Shirley. Good luck to you all and have a wonderful holiday exploring New Zealand. We will come in from time to time and look after Shirley for you,' said Mrs Yarwood. Everything was settled – they should go for two weeks to New Zealand.

Chapter Five

In the coming weeks, the Baxters spent a lot of time at the bank with Mr Ashworth. He turned out to be a very astute businessman and helped them with their investments. Even Margaret accompanied Jonathan now and listened to all the sound advice. Money was put aside for the boys and the rest was invested in Margaret and Jonathan's name. Mr Ashworth asked politely if they had any ideas about spending some of the money. The only thing planned was the trip to New Zealand, but Jonathan did mention at one of the meetings that he had been thinking of buying a holiday home in Abersoch for the family. Margaret was very surprised at this as he had not mentioned it to her. But she kept quiet as secretly she thought it was a lovely idea, and Mr Ashworth agreed. 'Bricks and mortar are always a good investment. As you have paid off your mortgage on your home here, a second property would be a very good investment. But buy wisely. Nothing too dilapidated or too near the sea,' he added.

When they got outside, Margaret grabbed his arm. 'Hang on, what's all this about a holiday home?' she asked.

'I have been thinking; we loved Abersoch so much, why not? We could have our holidays there and you could stay with the boys,' Jonathan said.

'You do come up with surprises, Jonathan, but yes, it's a lovely idea.'

'This weekend we will go and stay with Mrs Roberts – if she can put us up – and I will take off Monday and Tuesday too. If we can get down by Friday afternoon, we can hit the estate agent in the village first thing.'

'Good idea. The boys will be so excited. What did you think of those wooden chalets on that lovely beach?'

'I liked them. Good and safe for Paul and Mathew, but they are

The Baxter Family

not bricks and mortar; perhaps not a good investment like old Mr Ashworth advised,' Jonathan replied.

'Well, we could go and see them. There is an office on the site there. We could just find out about them on the Sunday, perhaps.'

'Yes, we will do that as well. Then the boys can use the beach again.'

'It's so exciting, Jonathan. I can't believe our good luck. What a pity our parents aren't alive to share our good fortune,' she said sadly.

As the week went on the boys got more and more excited. 'We are going to Abersoch,' she could hear them singing round the garden. The place in Wales had been a great hit with them and she was also looking forward to returning.

Through the week she started packing and making up a food box, which would be useful down there. If they bought a holiday home, she would have to get used to packing up on Fridays and unpacking on Sunday night and having the boys' uniforms ready for school the next day. But that was a small price to pay. She already cooked all weekend, and swapping one kitchen for another was no hardship, not if Paul and Mathew were happy.

They arrived at Mrs Roberts in Abersoch on Friday afternoon and went straight to the estate agent's. They had already decided on a figure they would pay for a holiday home and, after a discussion with the agent, came away armed with lots of brochures.

The evening was spent crabbing on the harbour wall and, when the boys were asleep, Jonathan and Margaret started to look at the brochures. Some houses and cottages were too far away from the beaches. 'What's the point of a holiday place if you have to get in a car to go to the beach. A short walk is the distance we want,' said Jonathan.

'And we don't want it to be too big. I don't want to be doing housework all the time. Three bedrooms in case the boys want their friends to stay. No more. We could look at a bungalow. We don't need a garage and certainly not a large garden,' said Margaret.

'You can say that again,' said Jonathan. 'Let's narrow it down to say four, then go and look tomorrow from the outside first, shall we?'

'Yes, that's a good idea. Then if we like any we can view on Monday.'

On Saturday morning they set off to look at the properties. They seemed to be able to afford most of the houses up for sale, but some were just too big and the upkeep would be enormous. Along the harbour one house was for sale, which overlooked the crabbing area. The boys loved this, but Margaret felt the area by the harbour was too busy. Too many cars and people, not quite safe enough for the family.

Up through the village and on the left was a bungalow for sale, the gardens of which ran down to the sand dunes on the main beach. Again the boys loved the garden and how it joined the dunes, but Jonathan was against it this time, for the garden was very big with large borders and would need a full-time gardener. Shirley's garden was quite enough for Jonathan and his part-time gardener. He didn't want to take on another.

On the way back to where they were staying, they looked at a bungalow on the beach opposite the boatyard, across the road from Mrs Roberts. This had a small garden and steps down onto the beach. The bungalow looked sound and well cared for. In the brochure, it had three bedrooms, a lounge, a large kitchen and bathroom. Its windows were painted blue and the outside walls were whitewashed. It was very pretty and Margaret fell for it straight away. 'You haven't been in it, yet,' stated Jonathan.

'I know, but I love it,' she said.

'So do we,' echoed the boys.

'Well, we can't view until Monday now,' said Jonathan.

But Mrs Roberts knew the owner as she was a neighbour. That evening, at 6 p.m., they walked across the road to view the bungalow. Once inside, Margaret was enthralled. The kitchen and lounge were on the beach side of the house, so the view was of the beach and the sea. A veranda ran along the side of the house, and the bedrooms, though small, were on the road side. There was a drive big enough for two cars and an outhouse full of boating equipment. The owner was a friend of Mrs Roberts, but since her husband had died, she had decided to move back to Pwllheli to be near her sister.

Paul and Mathew played on the beach while the adults talked. The owner could move out quickly, as her sister was ready for her to move in. It all seemed to be happening too quickly for Jonathan. Margaret was already planning where they would sleep. Taking over the house, including the furniture, would make it an easy buy. They could replace curtains and carpets at a later date. She had had experience of this at Shirley, and this bungalow would be easy for her to organise in comparison.

'We need a survey done. Remember what Mr Ashworth said. Invest carefully,' Jonathan warned.

'Oh, be blowed to Mr Ashworth! We might miss out,' cried Margaret.

'No, at the minute nobody is interested in it, the owner has said, so let's get it done properly, Margaret.' Jonathan sounded serious. Margaret gave in and hoped they could get the survey done quickly or they would be having their first serious row.

The next day they went to the big beach, dotted with caravans and chalets in the sand dunes. It was a beautiful beach, very natural, with the buildings nestled in the sand hills. Little roads ran in between the sand dunes and petered out into sandy tracks. A small office stood near the entrance and Jonathan, Margaret and the boys went in. A short, fat man sat behind the desk and Jonathan asked about the chalets. 'Well, as it happens, one chalet has come up for sale. The occupants are divorcing, so they are selling it. The rule is that they have to sell it back to us and we sell it on. It's not new but it is fully furnished. I'll give you the key and you and the boys can use it for the day if you like,' he said.

'Yes, that would be marvellous. My name is Doctor Baxter and I'll write my address down for you,' said Jonathan.

'No need for that. I trust you. Just bring the key back before 6 p.m., all right?' he said in a sing-song voice. 'Down the road and take the third turning on the right, up the sand hill and it's sitting on the top, front side this one. It's got green curtains and that's the number on the key ring. Well, off you go and have a good day there.'

The family drove carefully along up the sandy track and arrived at the chalet. It was as the man had said, right at the front overlooking the beach. The boys tumbled out of the car and ran down the side path and off on to the beach. Jonathan and Margaret opened up the chalet. It was spotless inside. Somebody had looked after it well. What a shame that they had to sell it! It had a large lounge with a kitchen opening onto it, pine furniture, a double bedroom, two single rooms with bunk beds and a small bathroom.

They opened up the French doors onto a concrete path with a little wall, and the sand sloped down onto the beach. On either side large sand dunes protected the chalet from the winds. 'What do you think of this?' Jonathan asked.

'It's very cosy, not much housework here. I could cook and see the boys on the beach at the same time,' said Margaret.

'Yes, I think they would be safer here. We are a long way from the road and they could play in the sand hills as well. I would think at holiday times there would be lots of children. They could make good holiday friends here,' he added.

'Yes, you are right, but what about your bricks and mortar now?'

'At this price it doesn't matter, as long as we have good holidays. Later on,' he said, 'if we wanted, we could sell it for a larger, more modern one.'

'I think you are talking yourself into this,' laughed Margaret.

'Yes, I think I am. You have to pay a ground rent, but that's not much, and you can't come in the winter months, but I don't think we would come to Abersoch then anyway. What do you think?' he asked her.

'All right, Jonathan. I think it seems more like a holiday place, right on the beach, handy for the children and less work for me!' she laughed.

'So not the bungalow, we will buy the chalet then?' he asked.

'Yes, you go down and speak to the estate agent and tell him that's what we're going to do,' Margaret said.

'All right. I will be back soon.'

Jonathan drove back down to the office and spoke to the manager. He agreed to send the money when he got home if he would keep the chalet under offer for five days.

The manager agreed and they shook hands. 'By the way, Doctor, do me a favour and tell your neighbours you have been on the list for years for a front site.'

'Why?'

'Well, they don't come up for sale often and people at the back always want to move to the front. The problem is who to choose without upsetting the others. You have come along and I can see you are a nice family with two well-behaved boys, so I would rather it went to you than be causing trouble choosing off my list,' the manager sighed.

'Well, that is exceedingly good of you. I can assure you we will be good owners,' Jonathan added gravely and the two men shook hands.

When Jonathan got back to the chalet, he said the manager had agreed and they could keep the key and Jonathan would send the money. 'Margaret, I think I will take another day off and personally drive down with the money to be sure.'

'No survey this time,' she laughed.

'No, you don't even get any deeds, just a receipt and a set of keys,' laughed Jonathan. 'And I don't care either,' he added. 'Look down there. Those sons of ours have already made friends. They are having the time of their lives, thanks to good old Uncle Arthur,' he said, pointing up to the sky.

The next week Jonathan returned to Abersoch with his payment for the chalet and drove back home late in the afternoon. He was very tired when he arrived back at Shirley, but the reception from his sons and the excitement on their faces was well worth all the driving. 'Now we are the proud owners of a holiday home, and here is the paper to prove it,' Jonathan held up a scrap of paper triumphantly.

'Is that it?' enquired Margaret.

'Yes, this is the receipt and the so-called deeds all rolled into one,' Jonathan laughed.

'My goodness, not like when you buy a house,' she said.

'You can say that again,' Jonathan agreed. 'We need to buy bedding and kitchen stuff, Margaret.'

'Yes, I will go out tomorrow while the boys are at school and buy all we need. There aren't any shops to buy that kind of thing in Abersoch but perhaps Pwllheli may have a few.'

'We'll go down this weekend with a few clothes and fill the boot with it all,' said Jonathan.

'What shall we call our new home?'

'I don't know. What do you think, boys?' he asked his sons. 'Make a list of names and then we will pick one. It's all so exciting.'

The boys ran off to make their list and in the evening they sat round and voted on the names. The name with the most votes was *Seashell*. 'Right, that's it. I will get a plaque down in the village and then we can christen the chalet,' said Margaret.

That weekend they went to Abersoch and set up home in their chalet. Jonathan and Margaret worked most of the weekend and Paul and Mathew played all day on the beach with their new friends. At night the sea was so calm and the moon hung in the sky, casting a beam of light across the sea. The only sound was the waves, which would ripple along the edge of the water from one end of the bay to the other. This little ripple was very soothing and lulled the family off to sleep. They all slept soundly and woke late. The chalet was so peaceful, nestled between the sand dunes. It was an idyllic place and Jonathan knew he had chosen the right home for his little family. It would make a huge difference to him, somewhere quiet and peaceful to retreat to after the pressure of hospital life. He was so pleased with *Seashell* and couldn't wait for his fortnight's holiday there.

★

The summer holiday was all that they had expected and more. Jonathan and Margaret had more time together, sitting on the front reading or just talking. They hardly saw the boys except when they came home to be fed or to ask for money for ice creams. The only extra chore was brushing up sand, which occasionally drifted onto the concrete patio or was carried into the chalet in the boys' sandals.

Paul made lots of friends and Mathew, being younger, joined in the group cycling round the sandy lanes on their choppers. The boys got to know the man who ran the ice cream shop on the beach and the youngsters would congregate on the steps outside the Sundae Bar, as they called it. Paul and Mathew played and swam all day and their parents could watch them from up on the patio. They commanded a full view of the whole of the beach so they could keep an eye on them. It was parental supervision in low key surveillance mode. Paul and Mathew thought they were free and this added to the excitement of Abersoch.

Through the years the Baxter family had long holidays there. Every free moment was spent at Abersoch. They could not wait for the holiday times to roll round year after year.

Chapter Six

For the first time the family closed up *Seashell* for the winter, but they knew that they had their big adventure to New Zealand. Margaret had taken out library books on the two islands and had been reading up on the country. She pinpointed Uncle Arthur's area, which was in the South Island, so she decided they would fly into Auckland and hire a car. She also wrote to Mr Blackshaw and told him of their intended trip. He was extremely pleased and said he would personally escort the family around Arthur's land and introduce them to the new owners. The farm had been turned into a bed and breakfast so he had booked the Baxters in there for a few days. He also arranged a gathering of all Arthur's friends and staff in the local hotel so the family could meet them and learn about their uncle's life. Jonathan was very pleased about this and was looking forward to meeting everybody.

The day of their departure arrived, and the Baxter family flew out to New Zealand, leaving Shirley in the capable hands of Mr and Mrs Yarwood.

The two weeks spent in New Zealand were the most memorable Jonathan and Margaret could imagine. It far outshone buying Shirley and even buying *Seashell*. What a wonderful country! No wonder Uncle Arthur did not come back to England. His farm and land were beautiful. Acre upon acre rolled out as far as the eye could see. The fields were dotted with sheep and the farm buildings nestled amongst them. A lake shone in one field with trees bending over the water. Yes, it was a magical place, a world apart from the North of England.

Friends and loyal staff congregated in the hotel to greet the Baxters, warmly shaking their hands, all eager to meet relatives of Arthur Baxter. Jonathan could tell he had been well respected as a person and also a farmer. They spent all evening talking about him. Lovely stories and anecdotes came spilling out and they were all eager to tell their tales. By the end of the evening Jonathan and Margaret were reeling from hearing about the life of Arthur. It had been well worth coming to meet and see them all. They thanked everyone and said they might return in the future, but Jonathan knew that this journey was a one-off. He had come to his uncle's home, he had seen for himself his country. He had even met his friends, but not one could shed any light on why Arthur had left home at such a young age, never to return. It seems his uncle never discussed his life in England and although they knew there had been a serious rift, they were none the wiser.

Jonathan was a little saddened as the last piece of the jigsaw was lost for ever. He would never understand and perhaps it was wiser for him not to know. It could spoil the illusion of Uncle Arthur, beloved benefactor of so many people.

The last year had been an eventful one, buying Shirley, their dream home, Uncle Arthur's bequest, which enabled them to buy *Seashell*, and then their journey to New Zealand. It had been quite a year and Jonathan hoped the next few years would be peaceful.

★

And so it was Paul and Mathew matured into young men. Still holidaying down at Abersoch and driving their speed boat – which Jonathan had been pressured into buying – a Blue Glastron with a fifty horsepower engine on the back. This gave the boys hours of pleasure, Father driving and the boys skiing behind. Hour upon hour they spent honing their skill on the skis, first two then on to mono ski, showing off to the girls who sat on the beach and occasionally allowing a special girl to sit in the boat and watch them whiz across the water.

All this activity cost Jonathan a fortune in petrol and the maintenance of the boat, which was always breaking down, but he loved every minute of it. He thought that, in a way, it kept the family together. Paul and Mathew couldn't wait to get down to Abersoch and the boat, so they all still holidayed as a family. A lot of young people were holidaying abroad, but not these two and their friends. Abersoch always called at the beginning of the year. The Baxters even changed the old chalet for a newer, larger one and later replaced the boat with a bigger one with an inboard engine. Gone were the days of the pull-start temperamental engine.

Paul studied hard at school and eventually secured a place studying medicine at Manchester University. This was the career he wanted, to become a doctor. He loved to hear his father talk about the hospital, whereas Mathew was quite squeamish and had no intention of following his brother. His interest lay in farming. Ever since the visit to New Zealand, when he saw the working farms there, he knew that was what he wanted to do. So he eventually gained the qualifications to enter Agricultural College.

Jonathan and Margaret were very proud of their sons and the boys would return to Shirley whenever they could. To them, Shirley was a solid base in their lives; Abersoch, university or college were transient places. Shirley was home and they returned frequently to see their mother and father.

With the help of Mr Ashworth, over the years Jonathan's investments had increased dramatically. When the time came, he was able to help Paul join a general practice in a local town nearby. A few years on, he would also be able to help Mathew buy a smallholding in Cheshire with an option to buy more land in the future. Again, Uncle Arthur's money helped the family to secure the boys' futures.

Margaret on the other hand was helping to look after the Yarwoods. They were both in their nineties and not in good health. She had persuaded them both to move into the Cottage Hospital Home for the Elderly. Mr Yarwood was bent over with arthritis and Mrs Yarwood had serious heart problems. Margaret visited them every day. She never failed. She looked on them as the grandparents of the family. They were a lovely old couple and would still sit in their room at the home holding hands. They looked forward to her visits and she would tell them her news of Paul and Mathew. Their eyes would shine with pride as though the boys were their own flesh and blood. On some weekends, Paul and Mathew would visit them, but Paul was extremely worried about Mrs Yarwood. Her health was deteriorating fast and her breathing was quite laboured. She was bedridden now and Mr Yarwood would sit by her side, holding her hand. To Margaret and the family it was a very sad scene and they just hoped and prayed that they would pass away in their sleep, and not suffer any pain.

One day the phone rang and it was the call Margaret dreaded. The staff said to come quickly. Mrs Yarwood was fading fast. Margaret went immediately and, once at her bedside, could tell by her shallow breathing that the end was near. Mr Yarwood just sat, never taking his eyes off her. The nurses kept coming in to check on her, but mostly left Margaret and Mr Yarwood alone with her in her final moments.

'Mr Yarwood, I think she has passed over now,' Margaret said quietly, looking steadily at Mr Yarwood. Tears ran down the old man's face and Margaret moved round the bed and cradled him in her arms. They sat for a long time until Margaret managed to take him outside so that the nurses could come in and see to her.

Margaret stayed with Mr Yarwood all afternoon and the nurses put him in another bedroom for the night. Tucked up in bed, he looked a lost soul. He and Mrs Yarwood had been together all their lives, marrying so young and working together at Shirley, and then retiring together.

He looked so weak and vulnerable, Margaret asked the nurses to make a special effort to look after him. They said that they would – everyone was fond of the old couple.

Early next morning, Jonathan and Margaret got another phone call. Mr Yarwood had passed away in his sleep. Some might say that he died of a broken heart or that God decided that they should not be parted. Either way, the Baxters took charge of their funeral and the service was held at the village church and was attended by most of the village people.

They were buried in the churchyard together. Jonathan had a black marble tombstone erected and they all laid flowers on the grave. It was a very sad day, an end of an era, Margaret felt.

When she returned to Shirley, she sat in the garden Mr Yarwood had created, breathing in the fresh air and the scent of the flowers. She then wandered around the rooms, fingering the highly polished panelling, and as she climbed the stairs her hand ran up the balustrade which Mrs Yarwood had polished for so many years. She entered her bedroom and sat on the edge of her bed. Slowly and quietly she started to cry. The loss of both Mr and Mrs Yarwood was hard to bear. Margaret felt bereft. It was like the passing of her own mother and father years ago. Memories flooded over her and time stood still for a moment. She only hoped that Jonathan and herself would have time in the future to grow old together and remain in love like the Yarwoods until the last second of their lives.

In the coming months the death of Mr and Mrs Yarwood seemed to affect them both deeply. Margaret was getting increasingly worried about Jonathan. He seemed preoccupied and quiet when at home, not his usual happy self. Margaret decided to tackle him about this, so after dinner one day she asked, 'Jonathan, are you all right? These days you seem very quiet. In fact you hardly speak unless the boys are here. Is anything wrong?' She looked worried.

'No, I'm fine,' he said.

'No, you're not. You are not ill or anything, you are not hiding something from me, are you?' She was frightened now.

'No, dear. I am perfectly well, but I am thinking more about our future,' he said.

'What do you mean?' she answered.

'Well, I have been thinking about retiring,' he said.

'Retiring? But you have years to go before you are sixty-five,' she snapped.

'That's it. I know I have, but the death of the Yarwoods affected me as much as you and I have been wondering if we need to do something else with our lives…' He hesitated.

'What do you mean?' She looked shocked.

'I have been speaking to our accountant, you know, the one who looks after our finances since Mr Ashworth retired. Well, he says our investments have nearly doubled. So if I took early retirement on a reduced pension, we would still live comfortably on our investments.'

'Yes, that is good, but what do you want to do?' she asked.

'I thought we could sell Shirley and buy bricks and mortar in Abersoch. How do you feel about retiring there?' he asked.

Margaret was stunned, but said, 'You have been doing a lot of thinking, Jonathan. No wonder you have been quiet. Well, if you think it's a good idea, I'm all for it. I would love to live by the sea,' Margaret smiled.

'I have also spoken to the head of radiology at Bangor Hospital and I could do locum work for them. You know, if somebody is on holiday or sick, I could be on call. It would keep my hand in if I get bored or you get fed up with me at home all day,' Jonathan teased her.

'Oh, it will be lovely to have you at home, now the boys have left. I get quite lonely on my own.'

'Do you, dear? I shall remind you of that when I retire,' and he hugged her close to him.

He thought how beautiful she was, how loving towards him. His attraction to her had never diminished as they had got older. He could see them making love still in their old age, perhaps not as passionately as now, but still as lovingly.

They discussed their plans with Paul and Mathew when they came home one day. 'What, sell Shirley? You can't do that. This is our home,' stated Paul.

'Don't be so selfish, Paul. It's their decision what they do with their lives. We have our own lives now,' snapped Mathew.

'Oh, I'm sorry, you two. It was a bit of a shock,' added Paul.

'Yes, I know, but I have to think of Mother and myself now, and Abersoch is where we want to live out our days,' said his father.

'Yes, I understand Father. I am sorry,' said Paul.

'I should think so,' whispered Mathew. 'Right, how far have you two got with your plans?'

'We will look for a property perhaps overlooking the harbour. Then in our dotage we can watch all the activity on the water,' Jonathan smiled. 'And, as for *Seashell*, we will keep it for you two. Eventually we may have grandchildren and it would be sad to lose it. What do you think?' Jonathan paused.

'That would be marvellous, Father. So if we come down, just

the two of us, we could stay with you, but if we bring friends down we could use *Seashell*.'

'That's the general idea, and we will get a local woman to come in when you have used it, to clean up. I don't want your mother skivvying after your untidy friends,' Jonathan laughed. 'So that's decided. Mother and I will start looking and will put Shirley on the market. Agreed?' They all nodded and the plans were set in motion.

In the coming weeks Jonathan and Margaret travelled backwards and forwards to Abersoch. They stayed in *Seashell* and hounded the estate agents. Nothing was available that was suitable. Margaret was getting very despondent. She didn't have the patience of Jonathan and wanted things to happen quickly.

One day they got a phone call at home. The estate agent had a property which was coming on the market. Would they like to see it? 'Would we just!' said Margaret. So on a Friday evening they set off again. They knew the road to Abersoch like the back of their hands. Over the hills, along the side of the reservoir, dropping down to Portmadoc, over the toll bridge and on to Criccieth and then Pwllheli. Soon they were at Abersoch where they spent the night at *Seashell*.

Next morning the estate agent took them to a property which overlooked the harbour from the side and caught all the sun. There were only a few built on this side backing onto the main road down into the village. The other harbour properties were over across the water, but they were in deep shade in the afternoon. They were perched on the rocks and had difficult access. Margaret was ecstatic that this property was on the right side. It was a good omen. The bungalow was lovely, perched on the cliffs, but with lawn surrounding it. A good big drive enabled you to park off the main road and high hedges screened the bungalow from the street. Inside the bungalow had a very large lounge with low windows, and the view was incredible. Jonathan and Margaret just stood and looked out. The view sold the property. It was wonderful.

Jonathan said to the estate agent, 'We'll take it.'

'Hang on, Jonathan. We haven't seen the bedrooms or kitchen

yet,' laughed Margaret. As the bungalow was a dormer one, all the bedrooms were upstairs overlooking the sea. The bathrooms were at either end. Although small, they were adequate. The kitchen needed refitting, as it was the original one, but the size was big enough for a table.

'I have saved the best till last,' said the estate agent and he started out across the lawn to a small gate. Steps led down over the rocks and there at the bottom was a sandy little cove. 'This goes with the bungalow. It covers at high tide but you can use it when the tide is out,' he added.

'Well, that's it. We *will* take it. It's a cash sale, so speak to the owners and find out when they are going to leave. We are in no hurry as long as the property is secure for us,' Jonathan spoke firmly.

'Oh, I will ring them when I get back to the office, Dr Baxter. They will be very pleased with the quick sale. Thank you,' he said, then added, 'Call in at the office later in the day and we will do the paperwork. Could I have the name of your solicitor?' he asked.

Jonathan wrote down his name and telephone number. 'Just ring him and he will verify that we are in a position to buy.'

Margaret was very impressed by her husband. He had made his decision quickly and decisively. By the end of their stay in Abersoch, the owners had accepted the asking price on the bungalow and Margaret and Jonathan returned to Shirley.

In the meantime their own estate agent had been busy showing people round Shirley. After a few weeks, he brought a family to view the house. They came up the drive and Margaret opened the front door. She was amazed to see parents and their four children standing there. The estate agent ushered them into the large hall. Margaret left him to show them round and she went and sat in the garden. She could hear them moving about and then trooping upstairs.

They seemed a lovely family with well-behaved children, and nicely dressed. Just then the father of the family, a youngish man, came out to see Margaret in the garden. 'Mrs Baxter, may I introduce myself? My name is Mark Booth and I am the grandson of William Booth, who was the first person to live in Shirley.'

'Oh, how do you do, Mr Booth? That is interesting,' she said, quite startled by this revelation.

'Yes, my grandfather bought Shirley in 1925 from the builder when, unfortunately, the builder's wife died suddenly. They were friends through business, my grandfather being in the timber trade.'

'Oh, yes I see. So you have family connections with Shirley?' she asked.

'Yes, that's right, and the moment I found out it was for sale, my wife and I decided to view it. You see, I have always wanted to live here and now I am in a position to purchase it. With my four children it is the ideal home.'

'Yes, you are right,' agreed Margaret. 'Shirley is a family home. It needs children running through it. That's why we are selling and moving to Wales, now ours have grown up. It would be very fitting if a Booth came back to live at Shirley.' Margaret loved this idea. She would not be sad leaving Shirley to them, knowing that they already loved the old house.

Within a few weeks, Mark Booth had bought Shirley and the Baxters prepared to move to Abersoch. It was an exciting time for all of them – the Booths looking forward to living in their grandfather's old home and the Baxters starting a new adventure by the sea.

There is an old saying; 'What goes around, comes around', and in this instance the ownership of Shirley had come full circle. Happy days lay ahead for the Booths in Shirley, happy days.

The House

I am alone again, but I am used to this now. One minute full of life, the next empty.

But from the past I know it will not be long before my next owners come. I wonder if other houses feel the same way as me? Perhaps they do. As I peer down from a great height, I wonder who will come up my drive next. It is quite exciting now that I am getting used to families coming and going. I know I will not be lonely for long.

Since I was built by that fine builder for his wife, Shirley, so much has happened deep inside me. Much laughter has echoed throughout my walls, and much sadness. Many tears have flowed, which I have shared with my owners who arrived here so full of optimism. I myself have changed from old to new, always showing the same face from the outside, but inside I am more modern and up to date, as they say. Fortunately my structure is sound and will stand all the changes deep inside my walls. I suppose I have no option but to move with the times. Some previous owners seemed to want to make their mark on me, regardless of whether or not it was necessary. But that is me talking as an old-fashioned house, not one of those modern boxes you find on estates. I am glad I am detached from all that and can stand alone.

I have caught a glimpse of my next owners. The young man and his wife look very excited by me. They also have children, so I have got my wish. There seems something familiar about the young man. Is it his face or is it the way he walks? I have seen him twice now, walking around my gardens and something is definitely familiar about him. I must find out – I do not like secrets. There are no secrets in my house. I know everything. I know what is discussed at the dining table and what is gossiped about in the sitting room. I know what goes on in my bedrooms at night. I hear talking, teasing, shouting and arguing – every part of their lives here. Nothing escapes me. Sometimes the whole atmosphere of my inner being is light and happy, as if filled with air. Then, at other times, a darkness descends, despair and sadness, and this affects me greatly.

But here I am on the crest of a new beginning. My new owners will be here soon and I shall welcome them with all the love and protection I can muster. I am still the same Shirley that I was years ago. I have not changed one iota. Only the people inside me change.

The Last Family

The Booths' Grandson, Mark

The whole porch of Shirley was filled with the Booth family. Mark Booth was struggling to find the right key to open up the large front door, while their mother, Katherine, was clinging on to their two fair-haired children.

'Stand still, you two,' she shouted at the twins. 'Will you stand still. Linda, Angela, do you hear me?' The twins were getting more and more excited. The other two children, Marcus and Kay, were crowding in from the rear into the porch.

'At last,' said Father as the big door swung open. The family burst into the hall and Shirley's peace was shattered for ever.

The two eldest children raced upstairs to grab their bedrooms and the little ones followed. 'I want this sweet little room,' wailed Kay.

'All right. That one is for you,' said her mother.

'You can have the other back room, Marcus, and the twins can have the large front bedroom, so that leaves Daddy and me with the large back room.'

'But I wanted…' started Marcus.

'No, I have decided. That's your room. No arguments,' and with that, their mother went downstairs. 'Phew, that's that,' she said to Mark.

'All decided, dear,' he said.

'Definitely.' She smiled at him.

'This is a marvellous family house,' beamed Katherine.

'Yes, I told you so. I have always wanted the family to come and live here and now it has happened.' He sounded so content and happy. He just couldn't stop smiling.

'Lets have a look round the garden before the removal van arrives,' she said to him.

They unlocked the back door and walked outside. 'To think my father and grandfather were here where we are standing, it's fantastic,' said Mark. She held on to his arm, and rested her head on his shoulder.

'I am so pleased for you, Mark,' she said.

'No, Katherine. This is for both of us. We will be happy here, I am sure of that. I tell you what, I will get that favourite rosebush you have brought out of your car, and we will have a planting ceremony.'

'Oh, what a good idea, Mark,' she said.

He went off to her car and retrieved the rosebush from the boot. She had even put in a small spade. What was she if not wife-like? he thought to himself. Her father had given her this rosebush just before he had died, so it was ceremoniously moved from house to house. He walked through the house, rosebush in one hand, spade in the other. 'Now, where do you want it?' he called.

'Over here. There seems to be a space under this tree. I will be able to see it from the kitchen window,' Katherine added.

'OK, I'll plant it here, then give it a good water tonight.'

He started to dig down, but he had not got very far when he heard the big removal van reversing up the drive. The children all called out from the house. 'They are here, Mummy. They are here!'

'I will go and see to them. I know where everything is going,' called Katherine, running over the lawn.

'Don't forget a brew for them,' called Mark. Mark returned to his digging, but suddenly his spade struck something hard. 'What on earth!' he exclaimed. He knelt down and started to remove handfuls of soil and there, nestled in the earth, was a small tin box. He managed to free the box and dusted it down. It was extremely rusty but the lid lifted quite easily. His imagination ran riot.

Was it a burial place for a small pet, or perhaps some buried treasure? But inside was a neat bundle of letters. They were all addressed to his grandmother. Curiosity got the better of him and he started to read the letters. They were love letters, beautifully written to his grandmother Gladys, from an admirer called Robert. They were so intimate and tender that Mark felt overwhelmed with emotion. This man Robert had loved his grandmother with all his heart and soul, but from what he knew of their family history, she had stayed with William, her husband. Mark wondered why, and what had happened to Robert, his grandmother's admirer. Did Gladys return his love. And where were her letters to him now?

He knew William and Gladys Booth had moved back to Hale near Widnes. He knew they had lived there happily for the rest of their lives. Mark stood up and looked at the small bundle of letters until he heard his wife call him. He quickly made a decision and placed the letters back in the tin box. He put the box back down into the hole and covered it with soil, and bedded the rose bush in firmly.

Her secret would be safe with him. Mark Booth stepped back, turned slowly, and looked up at the house. 'I wonder how many other secrets you hold, Shirley? If only you could talk. What wonderful tales you could tell me.'

Printed in the United Kingdom
by Lightning Source UK Ltd.
107464UKS00002B/17